THE BROKEN SHARDS CHRONICLES

Episode I: The Birth of the Eye

THE BROKEN SHARDS CHRONICLES
Episode I: The Birth of the Eye

Cover And Spine Art Design by Robin Vuchnich

ISBN 978-1-7353267-0-2 (Hardback)
ISBN 978-1-7353267-1-9 (Paperback)

THE BROKEN SHARD CHRONICLES

Episode I: Birth of the Eye

August Van Corbin

Table of Contents

Prologue

"The wind is picking up, I can feel it..." Gauvain yelled with a whiny matter-of-factly tone. Lucius' brown eyes opened from a deep slumber as he was rising from the cot. It took only a moment for Lucius to gather his bearings. Lucius squinted in anger when he realized why Gauvain was rambling.

Gauvain continued to pace as his dark, brown, well-groomed hair, started to hang over his stressed and pale face. He walked from one side of the room to the other and Lucius saw that Gauvain wasn't alone.

Before Gauvain could continue ranting, Maria interrupted, "You're raising your voice again... Lucius is resting," Maria explained as her eyes strayed from Gauvain to Lucius as she continued with a sigh, "Was trying to anyway."

Gauvain did a double-take at Lucius, who's now standing beside him. Gauvain becoming regretful of his easy forgetfulness waking Lucius. Lucius rubbed his eyes and asked in a groggy voice, "What time is it?"

"Almost afternoon from the looks of it," Gauvain peered out of the ship's window behind him. "I didn't mean to wake you. But since your awake, I have a hunch that a storm is coming..." Gauvain took a long breath, ready to give his spiel from the top; like it was some sort of sermon he's perfected.

Maria laid her hand on Gauvain's shoulder, gaining his attention. Softly shaking her head at him to save Lucius the lecture. "Gauvain, don't. He only now woke up."

1

"Neither of you want to hear me fuss but this is a big deal and everyone has to know what's going on around us. It'll only be a matter of time before we're hit by some sort of invisible storm."

"Sporadic, heavy winds on occasion don't mean anything," Maria reassured, "and even if these winds did throw us off course, we will have plenty of food to last us a few weeks longer than our expected arrival."

"This isn't about an irrational wind for one. It's everything leading to it. The closer we are to our destination, the stranger things are becoming. Earlier it was the birds hitting our ship because they were flying so low. Care to explain?"

"That doesn't happen because of high winds," Gauvain aggressively argued, pointing at Maria, almost poking her. "You saw it happen too and you don't think something is going on... If it's not a storm," he paused a moment, "We'll be lucky to make it a couple of days before this ship gives way from the pressure of some sea serpent, taking us in its grasp. To the bottom of the ocean we go." Gauvain waited for Lucius' input.

The only response Gauvain got was a confused eyebrow raise.

"You're working yourself up. Besides, sea serpents are only a myth." Maria said, crossing her arms.

"I guess I'll wait for my pending doom since neither of you can comprehend my warning; like I'm some kind of freak!" Gauvain summarized, stomping out of the cabin. He was holding onto the railing outside while watching the waves with caution.

Maria rolled her eyes in frustration with an emphasizing breath, "Gauvain beginning his paranoid streak again. He'll come back to his senses." Maria explained, pulling her blonde hair back behind her ears, showcasing her one of a kind, lime eyes.

Ernaldus happened to see Maria and Lucius through the window as Gauvain bumped into him, now knowing Gauvain was in a hurry. He entered the room with Maria and Lucius, pointing behind him, "What's going on with the insomniac, He knows I can beat him into a pulp right?"

"With that frustration, I wouldn't count on it." Maria admitted with a scoff. "He thinks a crazy storm is coming. He'll be himself again, once he's convinced there isn't one on the way." Maria said with frustration.

"Only one way to find out," Ernaldus chuckled. "Gauvain's the least of our worries at this moment. I need someone to help out Aelienor with this damn map in the captain's cabin. I tried to explain it to her," he rolled his eyes, "but I make it complicated."

"I'll go." Lucius admitted passing Ernaldus. "Thanks, Lucius." Ernaldus let him pass.

Lucius overheard Ernaldus speaking to Maria as he was leaving.

"As much as I want to say Gauvain is wrong, he does make a valid point. We should've done more research before we hopped onto your father's ship and took off." Ernaldus admitted, hiding his frustration as his ginger, curly, fringes of hair; which more often than not fell into his gray eyes. He blew it away before it could block his sight.

"I'll help your sister out instead but don't take your annoyances out on me." Maria spoke out in protest.

"How much gold did you give your father your life savings?" Ernaldus joked stopping her dead in her tracks.

Lucius turned around, letting go of the bronze doorknob before he could turn it. "Let her be, Ernaldus."

"Yeah, I will, after she answers. I wanted to know how much we owe the old man when we go back. Must be a fortune... He wouldn't let her get this so easily."

"About that..." Maria said hesitantly.

"You stole it..." Ernaldus announced. "Must be a full moon Lucius." Ernaldus joked elbowing Lucius in the chest.

"I hope the All-Seeing Eye is there." Lucius admitted.

"I did steal it, are you happy?" Maria admitted.

"I wanted to be wrong, so we better come back successful," Ernaldus said with a sternness in his voice.

"For Silas' sake, I hope so too." Maria commented with a faint cheer in her voice.

"You forget, the All-Seeing Eye has been folk-lore, a myth. Like the sea serpent Gauvain keeps talking about. The likelihood of the treasure map taking us to the All-Seeing Eye Aelienor bought could've been raided if the treasure ever existed." Ernaldus admitted.

"I have a feeling it's there." Lucius assured, causing Ernaldus to be speechless for a moment.

"Your feelings, Lucius, will lead us into trouble. Like Maria stealing her father's ship because she listened to you. If it weren't for my sister, Aelienor, being so eager to join, I wouldn't have boarded in the first place."

"I thought we were all friends here," Maria said bewildered.

"We'll see how this trip turns out and I'll get back to you. This won't be a simple retrieval of a rare artifact, possibly worth the world in coin. NO, it'll be a fight! We won't be the only ones looking for this, you understand? Will you be ready to accept the fact when the time comes to make those sacrifices?" As Ernaldus made himself clear, the ship started to shake violently, knocking the nearby candle lights, books, and all sorts of jars to fall.

Maria was knocked off her feet. "What's going on out there?" Maria asked as the shaking stopped just as quickly as it had begun. She helped herself to her feet with the aid of a nearby table.

"It was nothing. A few unexpected waves." Lucius admitted realizing there was a sudden change in the skies from the window. "I think Gauvain was right."

Maria and Ernaldus huddled behind Lucius as they saw lightning strike the water, spraying the ship like a mist. Each of the three flinched, hoping the glass would hold. They could hear a slight delay in the thunder, roaring in the distance. Lucius had started counting the seconds between the thunder and lightning to determine how close the storm was.

"I'll check on Aelienor." Ernaldus said rushing to the door.

"Watch out." Lucius yelled before the next wave of thunder came.

The succeeding lightning strike flashed, disorienting the crew. Regaining their senses they realize a massive wave form. The ship became dark from the shadow of the waves, revealing the waves' true form; twice the size of the ship. Swooping to the group with a vengeance, breaching the ship's windows.

Only having moments to brace, Lucius held his breath to prepare. Attempting to grab something to hold onto at the last second but it was too late. The pressure of the water felt like little needles into the skin being shoved by the violent tide.

Lucius slammed his head on the side of a counter, blacking out before being submerged underwater.

Memory I - Loose Ends

* The Lost Wanderer *

Lucius laid on the shoreline, sore all over, coughing out water, and creating an aching headache in the process.

Gathering his leftover strength, dragging himself to the shade and propped himself against a tree. He sat, watching the last of Maria's ship sink in the distance.

How'd this storm start? Lucius thought looking around with bewilderment. His vision wandered into the bright sun, making his eyes squint. The sky was as clear as it could have been.

I wouldn't have made it out... Someone must've saved me. He thought, scrambling to his feet. Tripping over a stick that was propping out from the shore. Making him land into a tuft of hot sand.

Lucius rose his face out of the beaches dry and trodden sands. Shaking and brushing off his sunburned cheeks with a swift motion.

Widening his eyes with a few weak and sandy coughs. Lucius discovered a note laying underneath a rock.

Unfolding the document, a trail of grainy sand fell from his skin and slid down to the end of the parchment. Within a glance, he recognized the handwriting.

Lucius, if you read this we went ahead without you. We couldn't find you in the wreckage.

Ernaldus went back but couldn't find you. The crash slowly drifted further away, and we feared the worst. We waited in hopes we could see you drift over to the island. We'll find a way back to Zenex soon, but we won't leave without you. I'll leave marks on our journey with our initials in hopes you'll find us. I know you're still with us.

—Maria

How did I make it out from that crash? He thought. Lucius flipped the note containing a traced copy of their map.

"Good." Lucius replied to himself. Folding the paper in two placing it in his pocket.

Before taking another step forward he felt a pain from his gut and chest as his stomach growled shortly after. Ignoring the pains bursting through his body from the wreck, he pushed on.

A wave of relief hit Lucius at the discovery of bushes bearing fruit nearby. He was way too hungry to care whether the berries were harmful eating them as quickly as he picked them. With each bite, he felt more relieved. Swallowing the gift that nature had offered him with glee. The sweet nectar revived his energy and left him more refreshed and awake.

"If they're bad, I'll pay for it later." Lucius reminded himself as he became addicted, yet selective in choosing the berries, not gathering any on the spiky branches or not fully grown.

After eating a few handfuls of berries, distant yet apparent, voices emerged. Lucius snapped a branch from the berry bush that he had emptied and hid between the shrubberies to gain a closer look. Lucius wiped off his juice glazed lips crouching down, as the two strangers headed his way. Firmly grasping the branch in preparation for a sudden confrontation, cutting his hand in the process.

"You're not alone Kain. Where's your group?" The agitated man spurted out pushing Kain back a few feet.

"We got separated... there are no others," Kain babbled cowardly. Gaining a swift punch in the cheek once the angered man caught up to him and causing him to fall onto his back.

"So you're saying, if I killed you," The man rebuked, flipping his iron sword pointing at Kain to keep him from rising. "No one would know?"

"Don't," Kain swallowed deeply. "Don't... kill me," Kain stuttered, "You can take anything."

"You have nothing of value," The man declared. "Except your life. No one messes with our community and lives to tell about it." The stranger swung his sword, after finishing his statement and was intercepted with a jagged piece of wood.

The angered man fell at the impact of the hit. He fell to his side, losing his sword. The man felt the right side of his upper lip, as blood dripped out of the freshly made, awkwardly shaped cut that reached to the top of his cheekbone. He remained in an idle and muddled state.

Lucius stood in surprise at what he did, holding the now broken branch in his hands. The stranger looked at his crimson hand and blinked forcefully snapping himself back into reality, focusing on gaining his weapon back into his grasp. Lucius stepped on the iron sword before he was able to lift the sword off the muddy ground. Lucius rose the broken branch as the man released his grip.

The stranger's hand was now in the air in a sign of defeat.

"You hit me!" The stranger snapped in awe shaking his head in disbelief. "For what cause, this isn't your battle."

Lucius remained quiet as he didn't have an answer other than being a good Samaritan.

The man now is gaining frustration watching Kain having a smile grow on his expense. "I knew you weren't alone, Kain... you'll regret this." The stranger's face shifted over to Lucius. "- and as for you rebels, I don't forget a face." The man insisted. Bolting away, catching Lucius off guard as he pushed Kain aside. The man was tripping over himself to get away.

"Come back coward and face me." Kain argued, still heated from the bout he lost his footing and got stuck in a log.

"He's gone." Lucius cleaned the iron sword with his sleeves. Watching the reflection of his long, chestnut hair in the freshened sword.

He hid his exhaustion by keeping his back to Kain. Lucius turned the blade to have a better look at Kain. The noble seemed short with black hair and clearly exhausted.

The concerned stranger seemed out of place for being isolated in the woods, Lucius thought. Should I have done that... After all, I couldn't have let him be slaughtered... right?

"Name's Lucius," He said, breaking the silence. "Who was he?" Lucius asked, offering a hand.

"Thanks, Lucius." Kain signed with relief, dusting himself off. "That was Magnus. He's a part of a bandit group."

"Be thankful I helped you at all."

"I am." Kain sighed. "Damn savages. I must find the others." Kain explained, gaining impatience. Taking off where he saw Magnus go last. A few steps before Lucius realized Kain's foot buckled. Holding his ankle in excruciating pain but continued forth.

"You're in no condition to go back from where you came without help," Lucius recalled, blocking his new friend's path.

"I'm fine. Just lost my footing for a moment. A simple walk it off will suffice." Kain grumbled.

"You need protection and aid." Lucius offered.

"I don't see why you care. I thank you for your help, but we can part ways now. I don't have gold if that's what you're after." Kain protested.

"You don't have a choice, someone in your current situation..." Lucius pointed out his injury in a joking fashion as Kain scoffed. "You won't last a night."

"That's my problem, not yours," Lucius replied, "besides, you can pay me back in the form of helping me look for my crew while you look for yours."

Kain pushed Lucius aside in revolt. Lucius stepped aside watching Kain fall into the dirt.

"I need help." Kain admitted swallowing his pride, as he was having trouble getting onto his feet.

"You jest. I'll leave you be. It would seem you have things figured out." Lucius began to walk away.

"You're right, don't leave." Kain pleaded.

Lucius came back to help him up. "Change your mind already?"

"Don't get used to it." Kain groaned.

"Once we find our people, we can go our separate ways." Kain sighed at the sun beginning to set. "Knowing Magnus, he'll be back for us in a few days."

They were ready for the night finding enough flint, wood, and berries.

The makeshift fire crackled and bursted with energy.

"That'll last for the night," Lucius explained, warming his hands. "If the weather allows."

"You say you survived a shipwreck from that storm earlier?" Kain questioned.

"I did. My friends and I were planning to land in Colosten." He said tossing a branch into the fire. "To search for the All-Seeing Eye, but I don't think we made it."

"You're in Klexta," Kain joked. "It's ironic since the All-Seeing Eye is here instead of what the rumors say, saving you time."

"How do you know?" Lucius asked.

"It's in the bandit camp, believe it or not. 'They discovered the artifact and its magnetic counterpart to help aid those who wield its power," he explained. "My group is also looking for the All-Seeing Eye, so I suppose we have that in common."

"What's your reason to obtain the artifact?" Lucius asked.

12

"I'm positive it's the same reason you have. My brother, Paul, told us about it. And so his wife, Caroline, my son, Floros, and our friends Ashlyn Colburn and Reyner Kahn. Tagging along before the bandits added to the bunch. What about your crew?" Kain inquired.

"We don't have a bandit problem unless they sunk our boat." Lucius remarked, "My friends Aelienor Cohen, her older brother Ernaldus, Gauvain Helsin and Maria Royce. We all had issues back home. We figured that this vacation would help us get away from them while inciting a little adventure," he paused seeing his wedding ring. "What about your wife, did she tag along?"

Kain's expression became grim. "Goodnight." he replied, laying down.

Why did he not reply? Lucius fell asleep shortly after the chatting ceased for the night.

* New Friend *

Ashes remained in the fireplace as Lucius awakened early in the morning from the cold.

"We're spending too much time in the open. We need to head out," Kain said, tossing the man made bowl aside after finishing off the last of the gathered berries.

Lucius became agitated, "You couldn't have saved some," he snapped, kicking the grass he stood on aside. "I saved your life, you know."

"Upset about a few berries?" Kain asked with little patience. "Go get more."

"So you'll eat them too. No thanks."

"We'd cover more ground if we split up," Lucius admitted changing the topic. "I'll go to the east of the shelter."

Lucius agreed, wanting distance to calm himself. "Meet back when the light comes to an end." He summarized entering the woods behind them.

Lucius explored the west. Time flew past knowing it was time to head back with a day's worth of supplies. Noticing a stranger rubbing his hands above the rekindled fire.

Lucius took out the sword he gained from Magnus walking toward the figure. Stepping on dead leaves, creating a crunching noise.

"Anyone there?" The trailing voice asked. Lucius revealed himself with his weapon hidden behind his back. "Who are you?"

"Paul. What about you?" Paul replied with a shaken voice. From his rough appearance and torn clothing, he knew he had escaped from a recent scuffle.

"Kain's brother, Paul?" Lucius deducted, "I'm Lucius Evans, Kain and I have been searching for you."

"Is it Kain Gordon?" Paul asked. "Where's he now?"

"He should be coming here any second now."

"Then again, you could be with those bandits." He insinuated taking a few steps away.

"You're making a mistake Paul." Lucius stated as it didn't seem to faze him.

"What's behind your back then, Lucius?" Paul asked, emphasizing on pronouncing Lucius' name mockingly.

"I'm not your enemy."

"You didn't answer my question," Paul admitted as he started to run away. "Go away... I can handle myself," Paul ordered as his voice trailed away.

Lucius lost sight of Paul. Browsing the tree's around him. Remaining silent looking for movement. Paul's stomach gave away his position."

"Your hunger is coming back and I have food." Lucius explained.

Taking a few minutes before Paul came out of hiding. "I'll be on my way after a few bites."

"As long as you don't eat as much as your brother." he commented.

Paul followed Lucius back to the base swallowing multiple berries. Leaving juice remaining on his mouth.

"When was the last time you ate?" Lucius sassed.

"I didn't trust the last place that offered food," Paul said. "That bandit camp would've made me regret it one way or another," Paul took a break eating the berries wiping his face. "Then again, There's only so much time you cannot eat." Paul explained.

"I feel that," Lucius signaled the bowl over as few berries remained after Paul grabbed a handful of berries before passing the bowl. "Is this a family thing or generally should I expect this?" He asked with a tone throwing his arms in the air.

"Expect what?" Paul asked, stuffing his mouth full of berries.

"Never mind," Lucius said with a sigh. "What happened in the camp?"

"They often blackmail their own. So they'll have a 'thriving' society."

"That's horrible."

"That's not even the worst part. If you were thought as a turncoat they would torture you until they decide that you learned the lesson.

There were times when others were killed for no reason."

"I see why Kain wanted to find you as soon as possible," Lucius said. "If Kain doesn't show, I'll look for him myself.

"Isn't it dangerous out here?" "Sometimes."

"I'll try my luck waiting for my brother here."

* Awakening *

Lucius followed Kain's footprints, going through the woods leading into a cave connected to a hill.

"Rosetta's Home," Lucius read on the side of the cave. "Huh." Watching his footing walking down broad stairs into the faintly lit cave.

"Looks scary," Paul whispered. Scaring Lucius catching himself on the railing. "It's alright. It's me." he reassured.

"Didn't anyone tell you not to sneak up on people."

"Now that you mention it," he thought. "I don't believe I have."

"A quick tip then, don't do that." Lucius said with a snark.

"Fair enough," Paul stated. "You have the torch so you go first," handing Lucius a torch.

"Oh, thanks," Lucius said sarcastically. "Where'd you get it?"

"I found it."

Lucius rose the torch with his idle hand to view ahead. Taking his sword with his dominant hand readying himself.

The stairs led into a large room. Stockpiled with books, a personal collected library of every category that interested Rosetta. Most books lay on shelves, while others stacked on other books twice the height of Lucius.

"Hello," Lucius spoke weary, turning corners until he reached the end of the room. "Rosetta?" he asked, seeing a man slumped over on a desk.

Turning the body to examine what had occurred. Taking a note off of his chest.

"To whoever finds this note, please bring me a soul tear to restore me. Without the Soul Tear, I have no power and grow weaker without it. I will be in your debt." Lucius read out loud.

"Any ideas?" Paul asked.

"We'll have to search for this Soul Tear within this library. In hopes, that it'll help.

Whoever owns this library may know the whereabouts of Kain."

"You may be onto something here," Paul pointed out. "But where to start..."

"That's exactly right," Lucius began gliding his finger among several dusty books. "This could take us hours to find this book."

"A Soul Tear you say..." Paul repeated, pulling out a book at random. "Perhaps, The History Of Soul Tears And Casting?"

"Are you serious?" Lucius snatched the book out of Paul's hand. "Volume One to be exact." Lucius scoffed. "What are the odds from an old library that hasn't been organized in ages."

"Lucky guess, are we going to open the book or not?" Paul asked with impatience.

Lucius flipped through the pages, "It's a spell to take someone out of commission. Yet still being self-aware of their position," announcing the text in his own words.

"So someone gave someone else a forceful type of comatose sleep."

"Sounds like it," Lucius said, "But where do we find a Soul Tear?" Lucius turned a few more pages.

"It commonly summons in magic forests within a circle of varied family types of flowers. The combined pollen migrates into the middle of the circle of plants creating a soul tear. Soul tears can be combined with any food and drink. Dissolving upon any contact with heat or cold above room temperature and used the same way to reverse the effects if a body detects a second dosage. Other combinations with ingredients lessen or magnify the results. Soul tears also are; if applicable turned into potions."

"Interesting," Lucius said, setting the book aside. Memorizing the example photo to look for, gathering an empty jar from the desk, and rushing outside. Paul watched Lucius exit, flipping through the book.

"Perhaps there's something here for the difficulty of rest." Paul commented.

Lucius climbed the first tree in sight.

Discovering a circle formation of flowers generating orbs of seal tears. Sticking out like a sore thumb.

"I knew it," Lucius admitted sliding down the tree. Retrieving a soul tear from among the flowers with one swing of the jar.

Returning to the cave to the weakened man. The Soul Tear left Lucius' grasp absorbing itself into the man's body.

"Rosetta Monzac is the name," Rosetta confessed, falling back to a chair regained control of his body. Rosetta set upright cracking his back. "Thank you for your aid. You've done me a tremendous favor. Anything you need, I'll do my best to help you."

"I do have some questions," Lucius said. "What happened to you for starters."

"I'll tell you what I last remember. I was guarding an artifact that had been discovered by undesirable sinful men. It didn't take long to be outnumbered," Rosetta said leading the duo to a shelf with different types of magical trinkets. "My brother led me here. He's known for his inventions."

Lucius picked out one of the trinkets on one of the dark purple shelves. A palm-sized rune glowing a weak purple with a fancy-looking x displaying on the front. "What do you call this creation?"

"He calls this one; The Rosane's Stone. A translator of sorts to understand any language spoken to you. I've mastered its use on my own. You can have it for your help."

"Thanks," Lucius commented as the world map beside the shelf gained his attention. "Do you know where we are?"

"We are on one of the seven islands called Klexta." Rosetta replied using a basic spell to spawn a cursor of their current location.

"Is there anything we can do?"

"Can you send this message to my brother that I told you about," Rosetta said, handing over a couple of parchments. "He often frequents himself on a different island. Along the shoreline of Texiel. Our friend Malyna is on the island called Edostan; she will also need to be informed. Rosetta said as Lucius seemed hesitant. "I'll give you gold for your efforts. I have much work to do."

"How much?"

"Enough for your efforts."

"How much?" Lucius repeated.

"Five hundred gold should be plenty."

"Make it for each of us." Paul added.

Rosetta's eyes widened for a moment before turning back to normal. "As you say. It will be five hundred each."

"We'll be back soon."

Lucius and Paul exited the cave, using materials around them creating a simple raft. Transporting to the next island, south of Colosten to Texiel. With calm waters, the gentle wind helped the raft onward.

"That was risky of you to do." Lucius reminded.

"Risky to do what?"

"Raising the reward."

"I don't think so." "How so?"

"I'm a people person." Paul said with a grin.

"Right..."

"Would you say no to my friendly demeanor if you were him?"

"Yes, I would." Lucius said with a scoff. "He didn't even bat an eye to part with a thousand gold."

"Must've had the spare coin." A sudden strong gust of wind came, ripping out the sail.

"Grab an oar and paddle. We'll ride this out."

"It's useless we're going to die..." Paul stated in a sudden change of behavior. Giving up before trying afraid of what ahead.

"No, we're not. Paddle harder."

Paul's eyes grew to the size of a gold coin noticing a crack within the boat. "The raft is falling apart..."

"Keep rowing." Lucius demanded.

"It's too late the raft is splitting apart now." Paul cried out as he rose to make the raft unbalanced, causing him to splash into the water. Swinging his arms wildly looking at a nearby current."

"Paul..." Lucius yelled as he grew frustrated.

"Wa...wha...what?" Paul replied.

"Stand up." Lucius said jumping out of the broken raft.

Paul rose. "I knew that," Walking onto the land drowsed. Coming back to his senses. "How are we going to find our way back?"

"We always could make another raft," Lucius reassured. Finding a house made out of dark wood. Reading the sign next to the door. "Password required to gain entry," Knocking on the door. "Is this the house of Rosane?"

No answer.

"Rosetta sent us to give you this letter."

A slot opened from the old wooden door. Rosane's dark blue eyes glowed into the outside, popping from the late-night glare.

"Not so loud. I can't let you in unless you solve a puzzle on the side of the building. To prove you're an ally."

Rosane closed the slot before Lucius could speak another word. They walked around the building to a three by three stone keypad. From the numbers one to nine. Leaving eight blank slots for the expectant digits above the pad of numbers.

"Hold on," Lucius said contemplating. "There must be some sort of clue."

"Don't you see the worn-out buttons?" Paul explained.

Lucius gave a puzzled look. "There aren't any worn out buttons..." Lucius stood aside to let Paul pass by for him to input the code.

"It's simply a reduction puzzle here. The keys two, four, five, six, and eight are pressed often. We'll have to press them correctly."

Incorrectly guessing made the eight expectant numbers reset. After a few more tries the input made the numbers glow with a short- lived ding following after.

"How'd you know?" Lucius asked. "It's awfully strange how you've been coincidental as of late."

"Thank the All-Seeing Eye for that..." Paul said, revealing the artifact before making it disappear.

"How'd you get that?" Lucius asked, widening his eyes.

Paul told the door the password to the front entrance. "Now is not the time, I'll tell you when I reunite with Kain."

Lucius entered handing the letter to Rosane.

"Thanks for the delivery. I had to make sure I could trust you," Rosane joked, "Haven't met a single soul patient enough to solve a puzzle that hasn't been an ally."

"What's this all about?"

Rosane surveyed the two men with an eager eye. "You look trustworthy enough, the artifact we've been guarding recently has been stolen."

"No," Lucius said giving a deduction of his own, "Who would do that?"

"Some bad men. I had to remain hidden until I knew it was safe. Now that Rosetta is back in action this is as good a time as any." He continued. "Before we leave, we must mask our identity from powerful people with a potion."

"Need ingredients?"

"Yes, To essentially cure us of this danger is some lavender, a few Beach spider lily bulbs, and a couple Shasta blue wings."

Paul suddenly spoke, "I know how to obtain those. We'll be back."

"Until then." Rosane said.

Paul closed the door behind him.

"These people are looking for that artifact Paul."

"Yeah, I know."

"Don't you think we should return them?" Lucius reminded.

"Anyone could say they were looking for an artifact, especially around here."

"Hear me out. The timeline makes sense," he said, debunking the mystery. "These guys lost this All-Seeing Eye from powerful men that out-powered them in numbers. You escaped from a bandit camp from the skin on your teeth then stealing the artifact during the night."

"So what if they speak the truth," Paul remarked with a tone, "I'm keeping it."

"That's stealing, I thought this was a buried treasure type of thing."

"It's not."

"Even so, I'm confident they'll reward you handsomely."

"They could," Paul thought out loud. "But something like this... " Paul tossed the artifact in the air to catch it back into his palms shortly after. "is priceless."

"So what do we tell them," He said, pacing. "Nothing?"

"Correct. What they don't know won't kill them," Paul said summoning the ingredients into his hands. "You can't blame me for being careful with something this powerful."

"I suppose you're right."

"Don't say anything to them for now," he reminded. "If the time comes then I'll give it back."

"That's impossible..." Rosane stated snatching the ingredients from Paul's hands.

"You're welcome." Paul remarked as he subtly held his head.

"Are you alright?" Lucius asked.

"Give me the materials," Rosane reminded as Paul retracted his hands to focus on his now throbbing headache, "Looks like your friend here needs a diagnostic."

Lucius took the bag from Paul's grasp tossing the ingredients onto a nearby table. Paul spoke with impatience, "Go ahead and do your thing. I'm fine."

"It doesn't seem like you are," Rosane urged.

"I'm fine." Paul snapped with anger. Paul's body turning into a static version of himself, becoming normal again after a few moments passed. Making Paul feel weak.

"What was that some type of spell?" Lucius questioned.

"That's no spell. He glitched," Rosane admitted, rushing ingredients into a mortar and pestle until it turned a light pink. Sliding the powder into a cool liquid, creating a solution. Causing a swift poof before pouring the potion into a few other vials.

Giving the last one he poured a shot. Giving a 'too sour' expression on his face for a moment before shaking it off. "That's the last time I'll take a plunderer for granted."

"What's going on with Paul?" Lucius asked.

"I think it'll be best if you send him to my brother," Rosane answered. "He told me about something similar happening to someone that we knew. Here's for your troubles." Rosane stated giving Lucius a gold pouch of five hundred gold.

Lucius put the gold into his pocket, aiding Paul to the exit, leading back to the old raft repairing itself.

"What's this sorcery?"

"It's me." Paul explained as his nose began to bleed.

"Why are you doing this if it hurts you?"

"I can't help it..."

25

Helping Paul onto the boat. Lucius hardly had his second leg into the boat before a sudden shift in wind rushed them toward Klexta.

"You mustn't use your powers Paul, you're hurting yourself."

"I don't think I'm going to make it. I just wish my child will never feel the pain of reaching the end of their life-"

"Don't say that Paul, you'll see your child soon enough. I'm sure of it-" Lucius bartered thudding into a nearby dock. Holding himself steady holding onto the supports for a moment before looking at Paul moments before slumping over on the other side of the boat. Dropping the protective magnetic seal out of his hand.

Lucius gathered the magnetic seal for the All-Seeing Eye, making it disappear with a faint blinding sparkle, in response to footsteps from a stranger drawing near.

A man with long, black hair rushed over with worry glaring on his face. Helping Paul out of the makeshift raft.

"Reyner Kahn. What happened to Paul?"

"I have no idea. He suddenly became ill..." Without a second thought, Lucius rose Paul's arm with his idle hand around Lucius' head leading them to Rosetta. Lucius handed Paul the remaining potion.

"What's going on with this man?" Rosetta asked while drinking the potion.

"Your brother said you would know of Paul's condition." Lucius explained.

Rosetta looked dumbfounded until he noticed Paul glitching, "This is the All-Seeing Eye Curse."

"What curse?" Reyner asked. "I never heard of that."

"Both of you must leave immediately, so I can concentrate on healing your friend."

Exiting the cave discovering Kain outside. "I see you've bumped into Kahn...any luck with Paul?"

"He's inside being treated." Reyner explained.

"What's wrong?" He asked.

"He has something called the All-Knowing- Eye Curse being treated in the cave," Lucius explained. Kain bolting past Lucius, being cut off by Reyner.

"No, Kain. Don't. He's being treated," Reyner Kahn explained. "Nothing worse than distracting a doctor at work."

"Where's my brother?"

"He'll be alright-" Lucius reassured.

"I need to see him." Kain powered inside.

"You must be Kain Gordon... Paul mentioned you before he passed." Rosetta stated placing a cloth over Paul's body.

"What did he say?"

"Along the lines of, Dear brother Kain don't experience power. I got a feeling I'm going to have a boy. Was his exact words. He stopped showing signs of life after that. I'm sorry."

Kain had several emotions at that moment. Sad, angry, and disgusted. "Can I at least see him one last time?"

Rosetta stepped aside. Reyner and Lucius stood quietly watching Kain.

"It's still not too late to bring you back. We could still do something, anything," Silence filled the room as Kain Gordon knew Paul was gone.

Placing Paul's wedding ring on his finger. "You dropped this," Kain admitted with his voice cracking. Holding a half-smile hugging Paul, before inevitably sobbing onto his brother's chest.

* Troubling Dilemma *

"You did your best Rosetta. Thanks." Reyner said, creating conversation wiping his tears.

"Why?" Rosetta asked, disappointed. "When you see the life drain out of someone, it changes an outlook on life." Rosetta said seeing the magnetic seal in Lucius' back pocket. "I think it would be best if the relic came back into my custody."

Lucius took the magnetic seal from his pocket.

Kain lowered Lucius' forearm. "Why should we trust him with the artifact if he doesn't trust us to know about the curse," he urged. "My brother died for this."

"It's safer in my hands than the rest of you," Rosetta argued. "You'll give Malyna a visit, and she may explain how she survived. She was the one I saved from this curse." Rosetta confessed.

"You were able to save Malyna but not Paul?" Kain asked, gaining anger.

"She was in the earlier stages," he said, "You could stay mad at me but it won't do you any good. This is your best chance to prevent this from happening to others."

"It won't hurt to see her side," Reyner counseled.

"This artifact is filled with power and knowledge, but why would people want to have it if it kills them in the end." Lucius asked, attempting to wrap his head around the concept.

"Theory is, someone can wield its full power without corrupting them from the inside out. Although it comes at a cost if you're not the chosen." Rosetta explained glancing back at Paul. "I just don't want any more loss today to find out."

Spending the night inside rooms within the cave switching between shift's guarding the artifact throughout the night.

Lucius woke to the smell of smoke coming out from below the door.

What's going on...

Lucius crouched, opening the door with a damp cloth. Getting hit with the flooded smoke. Coughing immediately covering his mouth with his shirt. Crawling his way out of the house.

Finding the entrance to exit as bookshelves fell catching on fire. Preventing him from leaving.

Lucius walked around the labyrinth of thudding bookshelves and jumping over debris as it fell. Reaching a safe distance to the other survivors. Looking back at the cave, it had collapsed with fog behind him.

Discovering a new face from the small crowd. A short hair blonde, slightly shorter than the others, wearing peasants' clothing but not afraid to speak out for herself.

"I say again I wasn't a part of the fire. It looked like it was one of the bandits handiwork." Ashlyn explained.

"A hell of a time for Ashlyn to show is all I'm saying." Reyner stated noticing Lucius wheezing, aiding him to stand. "Do you have the All-Seeing Eye?"

"I'm good by the way," Lucius admitted with sarcasm as Reyner checked Lucius pockets, making Lucius shove him away with frustration. "Personal space Reyner."

"Do you think it was destroyed in the fire?" Reyner wondered,

"I doubt it," Kain commented, "Rosetta is the last to remain and nowhere in sight. He must've taken it. We shouldn't have trusted him."

"Rosetta wouldn't have taken it. All he did was help us. Ashlyn on the other hand..." Reyner stated.

"You think I'm against you?" Ashlyn questioned.

"If the situation was different we wouldn't be this paranoid." Reyner said, grabbing some rope. "This is just to be on the safe side."

"What friends you all are." Ashlyn mocked.

"Do what you will, before we head out to find Malyna. To Edostan," Lucius said with determination.

"I know a shortcut to Edostan though Klexta." Ashlyn added.

"You still want to find Malyna?" Kain questioned bonding Ashlyn's arms. Causing her to frown.

"Malyna still has answers, it won't hurt to learn. We should also check on Rosane since he may be in danger." Lucius answered.

"Texiel's closer. Let's see if we still have time." Reyner admitted going after the raft Paul had left behind.

"You go on ahead with Kain." Lucius pointed out.

"Keep a close eye on Ashlyn." Reyner added.

Splitting up they entered woods in the north. "I helped Reyner and Kain out of that blaze and this is how I was rewarded," Ashlyn complained.

Lucius remained quiet.

"If anything," she continued, "I could be of use to you. If you untie me we'll work together." waving her arm as she complained. "Instead of becoming some sort of liability."

"It does strike me odd when you show up. Kain and Reyner are skeptical, so I'll be too." Lucius explained as Ashlyn pushed Lucius to the ground.

"What are you doing." Lucius asked as an arrow flew by his original position. Lucius lowered his voice, "What was that?"

"Do you trust me now?" Ashlyn questioned with a whisper.

"... Yes." Lucius said following a long sigh. Ashlyn moved her bonded hand toward Lucius with worry. "Release me then."

Lucius cut her bonds off with his blade. Ashlyn's bonds fell to the ground cackling amongst the wet grass, giving away their position. They ducked in preparation again without a proper look from the attacker. Ashlyn clicked her tongue before tossing a rock in the air revealing the position from how the arrow connected with the projectile. "Hand me your sword," Ashlyn ordered taking Lucius' sword from his grasp before he could process the request. Swinging the sword at the weak foundation of a nearby tree.

"Hey, that's mine..." Lucius complained. Moments later, a body fell into a pile of leaves in front of them.

"There's your weapon," Ashlyn pointed out as with sass, Lucius sauntered over to raise it from the ground swinging it a few times before placing it behind his back. "Most likely a hunter."

"Tell me the plan next time."

"Fine. We ended up getting a bow out of it." Ashlyn explained raising the weapon to test the quality of the bow and arrows.

"Now that you've had your fun..." Following Ashlyn's eyes as they widened. "What now?"

Revealing others within the woods. "Hayden's group I should've known." Ashlyn mumbled.

"Who's Hayden?" Lucius asked.

"Hayden Kristell to be precise," Hayden corrected. A Samoan with dark black hair ending just before passing his ears, fading into an extended goatee. "Ashlyn, sweet girl. If you knew who I was, why attack one of my own?"

"He attacked us first."

"I ordered out a warning but you resisted." Hayden glanced at his men around him. Each wearing a unique theme of brigandine armor from the rest. "Clearly if I wanted you dead you would've been."

"A warning shot," Lucius mocked. "If it weren't for Ashlyn I would've been hit."

"It doesn't look like you're injured to me. It was to back off our territory, stranger. Granted all the islands will soon be ours but the center of Klexta you entered is under my regulation. Or was, but it will ours again shortly. Seeing as though you attacked one of my men it won't go unpunished." Hayden's men taking out their weapons of choice inching toward Ashlyn and Lucius. "Now, now... I'm still willing to negotiate."

"What would someone like you want you from us?" Ashlyn shouted.

"Seeing as though you have armored men surrounding you, willing to slit your throat by the snap of my fingers. I would lessen the altitude of your attitude first off."

Ashlyn became quiet for a moment. Hayden in response lowering his hands as his men stood down.

"Since you are willing to oblige. I'll allow you to pass through my land freely and forget all about what has happened here if you help us with some problems."

"If it's about being attacked... We've been having that issue as well," Lucius explained, "Someone by the name of Malyna may have news on how to deal with your problems."

"We can benefit off each other then," Hayden admitted with a smile. "Follow me and I'll show you the tour of my kingdom."

Exiting the woods, revealing the entrance to Klexta's Capital. "You see before we get into the business at hand. I have a favor for you..." Hayden waving his hand in a circle.

"It's Lucius."

"... Lucius." Hayden repeated along with Lucius. "I'm sure the princess here wouldn't be a darling long enough to aid us, but you. You could be perfect for the assassination of the King, Therron." Hayden explains slowly losing Lucius' interest. "I'll allow you to use our boats as opposed to your little rafts." Gaining Lucius' attention making Hayden smirk. "We can help each other..."

"Don't do this Lucius. You're better than that." Ashlyn whispered to Lucius.

Hayden's bodyguards slowly branched off into different sections from within Klexta. Eventually remaining Ashlyn, Lucius, and Hayden to themselves.

"If at any point in time you would like to attack me while my back is turned. This would be the time to do so-" Hayden explained casually turning around observing Ashlyn rushing at him with Lucius' sword. With ease, Hayden disarmed her, punting her cheek with the handle. Crashing onto the side of a marketplace stand.

"I didn't expect you to be that naive," Hayden shook his head in disappointment paying the vendor for the trouble. "Any other attempts?" Hayden waited for Lucius to make a move as he stood still. "Aren't you the smart one," Hayden said handing a sword to Lucius. "Don't let anyone take your sword for future reference," he reminded one of his men over, "Send the one on the ground to the cells."

Hayden saw the worry in Lucius' eyes as Ashlyn was being relocated, "Don't worry about Ashlyn, she'll be alright."

Hayden led Lucius into the slums of Klexta. Filled with people who are ready for a second chance, a new and better civilization. Though the civilians that filled these streets either had nowhere to go otherwise or were paid to stay. As Lucius passed by, most of whom occupied the slums he had to hold his breath from the stench to not bother him as much.

Hayden opened the silver grand hall doors to their base. It revealed his most trusted men awaiting his command.

Kerwyn Niles, Who's Hayden's number two and closest of friends. That Ashlyn had attacked, now recovering in the medical bay. Something stuck out to Lucius about that bizarre man, could have been his mysterious nature. Who remained mute and kept to himself. Granted he was still recovering, it could simply be the strange aura Lucius felt being around him, Something that warned 'stay away'.

Stephan Dermon as the strategist. The more outgoing of the group. Ready to always help out in a pinch for those pesky last-minute plans. His long flowing chestnut hair disguised his prior battle wounds on his tan face; each scar complete with a unique story.

Hayden Lex Runtus, the battle operator who would go for the best course of actions behind the scenes. To prevent confusion in serious times. Hayden Runtus would be called by his middle name. Lex being the most built between his peers within the rebellion, it was clear that he wasn't unfamiliar with combat when it was needed.

Flynn Daxter, a scout that ran with the other mercenaries Hayden hired that has a talent in finding intel, especially against Therron. Never failing to give his daily updates, often found glued to Hayden since the fall of the other mercenaries he used to tag along with.

Finally, Nadim Tennant, The medic of the group. The rebellion wouldn't have gone far without. Being the seventh best doctor in all of Solaris Evercairn. It was a true blessing the Kristell family welcomed him in before Therron's rule. Hayden's father, Marius, saved his life when he was at a young age, he returned the favor to any of his people when he can.

"We're always in need of new people," Lex admitted, shaking Lucius' hand before Lucius could raise his hand all the way. "I'm certain that we'll get along nicely," Lex stated as he was the first to walk up to Lucius. Shaking his hand eagerly.

"Hayden brought you here, huh?" Stephan browsed at Lucius momentarily. "I'm guessing he dragged you out of some hole. There's this word called 'no', don't be afraid to use it with Kristell. You go ahead and leave if you are not willing to help us against Therron."

"All of you are fighting this King for a reason. Depending on the reason I'll continue further," Lucius explained.

"It's better shown than telling," Hayden told.

"If Therron is doing something genuinely bad, I'll help you. But if I do this you must release Ashlyn and help me find someone."

"We'll help you find anyone you're looking for, in Klexta everyone knows someone," Hayden explained. "As for Ashlyn, she'll be no issue to us once Therron's gone. You'll have her back, no problem."

Nadim spoke up during surgery on Kerwyn. "Whenever she's around it seems trouble isn't far away."

"How is he?" Hayden asked.

"He'll live. Kerwyn just needs time and some-one to tend after him for a few months to be on the safe side. Get my attention if for any reason he seeks it." Nadim said, putting Kerwyn to sleep as Hayden stood by his side.

"Permission to show Lucius around, Hayden?"

"Granted."

Lucius looked among Ashlyn's things inside a box while she was away. He rose out the bow along with a quiver full of arrows. Leading the weapons back to Kerwyn as the mute man slept with diffi-culty. Laying it beside his nightstand in good faith, despite his internal concerns.

"He'll be grateful for your hospitality. I forgot about his bow." Hayden pointed out crossing his arms, finishing his side conversations. "I made this for him after his first battle. He always preferred long-range. I knew he was good with the halberd he had but it snapped in two when we fought along-side my father's enemies. I knew the bow would be the way for him to say. Anyhow Nadim is waiting for you outside."

"I'll show you what monster we are truly fac-ing here," Nadim said waving Lucius on. Exiting the slums.

"How long have you been trying to take out this guy for?"

"Ever since the rebellion began. It was a mistake to allow his scheming. If only we knew what we do now." he rambled before getting to the point. "Usurping his throne won't be easy. We would like to take him out with minimum losses."

"Seems tricky."

"Hayden chose you for a reason. Anywhere from the way you carry yourself with a weapon to the way you deal with problems. Either way, you have a place in the rebellion." Nadim summarized with a welcoming demeanor, reaching the speech occurring in front of the castle. Watching from afar. "This is what we're up against."

"This rebellion will be handled with a swift end. Keeping peace among my fellow people. I'm here to remind every one of my true intentions today. With the same intentions I had assassinated the traitorous King before me," Therron began, "It's not about being a dangerous man doing what he thinks is for the greater good, but rather an innocuous man who can get things done, better. Which is why I brought all of you here today." Therron hoisted the All-Seeing Eye above him.

"Therron has the artifact." Lucius exclaimed.

"...this living myth will ensure victory against these rebellious types. With this tool, we can create a safe society for all." Therron finished with a scream of victory. The crowd was won over from the speech as they began to cheer and clap. Booming with a sound that can be heard from ear to ear across the island. Therron smiled at his success before he left the balcony.

* The Great And Powerful *

"How did he get that?" Lucius questioned.

"He must've got it last night. Now deeming it worthy for the public to know about."

"Something like that shouldn't be public. I'll give that King a few days before his mind melts."

"What's this All-Seeing Eye's power?"

"From what I know from a friend," Lucius said without hesitation. "Anything from your imagination."

"What happened to your friend?"

"He's no longer with us." Lucius summarized softly. "Oh-"

"Malyna held it for a time being the only survivor from the raw power."

"Let's see if we can meet Malyna a little earlier than expected." Nadim pondered reaching the base inside the slums.

"Malyna is in some way related to this ordeal then?" Hayden asked.

"Correct," Lucius answered. "Has Therron ever left the castle?"

Flynn pointed out. "Not to my knowledge, At least not to the public eye."

"We'll have to bring the fight to him then," Lex added.

"We're making an exception for you kid.

Flynn will come with you to get to Malyna." Hayden made known.

"Just one problem," Lucius stated. "What's that?"

"Ashlyn knows the exact location."

"Of course she does." Hayden slammed his fist down with ill patience.

"She always gets in the way," Lex explained, laughing at Hayden's expense. "You got to give her credit for that. Go ahead and talk to her and see if she'll reveal the location."

"Where's the prison?" Lucius asked.

"The last door at the end of the hallway." Nadim explained.

"She's a feisty one," Stephan confessed to Lucius upon exiting the cells. "She keeps yapping on and on. I'm surprised you were able to deal with her," Stephan said out loud making it known to Ashlyn.

"Don't tell me you fell into their little misfit group. The true enemies are the ones in this place." Ashlyn argued, shaking the bars.

"Calm down," Lucius reminded with a low tone, "I'll cut right to the chase. We need your help."

"We?" Ashlyn asked, raising her voice with a sudden temper. "So you did join them."

"I know you don't like these people, but they're going after the corrupt King."

"They've been saying that for as long as I've been here in Lucius. Out of these past few months, What makes this day so special?"

"Therron obtained the All-Seeing Eye."

"I thought it was kept hidden in the crypt."

"Does that mean you're going to help?"

A moment of silence ensued. "I'm not doing this for the rebels... for the record. Now, what do you need help with?"

"Where's the shortcut to Edostan?" "I'll tell you under one condition."

"What's that?"

"They'll let me out once Therron is dead, right?"

"Yes..."

"Assist them in killing Therron and while you're out and about looking for a Jack Arturo. Malyna knows him, tell him I sent you. Can you give me your word if you'll do that?"

"He's not going to be any trouble is he?"

"Far from it."

"He better not break you out of here." Lucius reminded.

"What difference will it make if Therron's dead?" Ashlyn asked. "Hayden himself will let me out after the deed is done."

"You have my word."

"The island is not too far away on the east which would be a shortcut crossing a bridge. Instead of being on a raft. You're in Edostan once you see plenty of magic." Ashlyn caught his attention on the way out. "By the way, Not many people know her last name is Kovac. You can say that I told you."

"I will," he said exiting the room, "You go ahead and watch her now Stephan."

"Did you get what you needed?"

"I did and more."

"Report to Hayden on the matter." Stephan concluded.

"Malyna is located across the bridge of Klexta's eastern exit." Lucius summarized looking at the map that laid across the table. Being the only exit that led to Edostan.

"This is a nice change of pace," Hayden remarked, "did she want something in exchange?"

"She was willing," Lucius concluded.

"Whatever made you trustworthy to her.

Ends up being useful for us."

"What made you and your crew here suspicious of Ashlyn?"

"She doesn't like me from the apparent attack. Furthermore, she gets in our way. Like she knows something ahead of time."

"Any examples?"

"In time you'll see..." Hayden said waving over one of his men, "Flynn Daxter will be going with you this time."

"Where are we going?"

"Edostan territory. Any knowledge Flynn?" Hayden asked.

"Stories, but nothing solid. Is that where Malyna is located?"

"Yes, your mission is to get information about the All-Seeing Eye. Bringing her here to us if you can." Hayden briefed.

"Will do," Flynn said, opening the door for Lucius. "I'll take point."

"You seem to know where this Edostan is then."

"It's about a half an hour walk from here."

"What's the story of Edostan?"

"The basic premise is the same. It's filled with the illusion when you enter the Edostan starting at the bridge, the theory is that you won't leave."

"Is it true?"

"To me, no." Flynn shrugged. "Few people go missing wandering off by themselves on this bridge. I think that's just the same for anywhere you go by yourself and superstition kicks into the locals."

"Are you willing to go to Edostan then?"

"If it's what we have to do for the rebellion then so be it... Hayden has saved my life by taking an arrow for me since we first met. I owe it to him to this day... I still partially blame myself that day for being reckless and wouldn't have forgiven myself if he died."

"What made you join the rebellion?"

"For most of my life, I lived on my own accord. I ventured out for anyone who would pay for my services. I eventually encountered Lex who called upon aid. Shortly after I met everyone you know now. We look out for each other since we're the best thing to a family and anyone opposing any of them is an enemy of mine."

"Strong bond of loyalty."

"Truly. It's never stopped us from achieving greatness in the past and it won't stop now." Flynn stopped at the mossy stone bridge.

"Is this it?" Lucius stopped behind Flynn.

"Yeah. I suppose we continue forth," Flynn stated, "Be watchful for traps." He recalled, slowly walking on the bridge with keen eyes.

"They say you vanish before you could say..." Reaching midway of the bridge before Flynn disappeared in front of Lucius' eyes.

"Flynn?" Lucius questioned loudly awaiting a response with no answer. Tapping his foot where Flynn stood. "The lore must be true, Is this your doing Malyna?" Lucius walked further spawning into a house filled with wealth. "... Kovac?" Lucius asked, adjusting his surroundings.

A door opened behind him, revealing a woman in her late twenties in a green, long sleeve, silk-wrapped gown.

"Willingly entering Edostan there must be something you want," Malyna said with softness in her voice.

"I just want some information that's all," Lucius recalled.

"What would you like to know?"

"Just some knowledge-"

"Many who enter want more than just knowledge." Malyna cut off. "They want revenge or riches. Is this what you seek as well?"

"Just the knowledge of how the All-Seeing Eye works."

"You had the artifact yourself."

"Not without the magnetic seal."

"You're smart for an outsider," Malyna summoned seating. "I became weak-minded and greedy."

"It didn't take long for my actions to not become my own. Luckily I snapped out of when I did. I still remember it like a forgotten dream. With my self-made medication I slowly cured my manic episodes," Malyna became lost for words. "Something told me deep inside I was chosen and I wanted to believe it but it wasn't meant to be."

"Someone new has obtained the All-Seeing Eye and could be asking for trouble. How do you stop it?"

"I sensed it, the minute he obtained it." Malyna said, "The object itself is indestructible, the only hope you have is by taking it away from him if you can."

"How then?"

"If he's willing to part with it like I was when I first obtained it, it should be simple. The withdrawal causes extreme behavior, unlike any others, have seen before. If not, that'll be up to you on how to proceed."

Lucius laid back in his chair that he found himself in, "I think I have gotten what I need here. Where'd you take Flynn?"

"He's inside. If you find him, you can leave. That's why I was willing to tell you what I have told you."

"So you're playing with me."

"You knew the precautions before coming into my grounds." Lucius rose from his seat, opening the door to begin his search. "You're looking for Jack Arturo, yes?"

Lucius stopped keeping his hand on the doorknob, "What about him?"

"If you escape, I will present you to him in time..." Malyna explained walking past his view from the chair. "Wait..." Lucius started rising to look behind him to only see a blank wall remain. Looking back on the wooden chair to see a lantern remains. "I guess I'll start my search." Snagging a lantern, lighting it, and brightening the dark hallways that followed. "Flynn, are you there?"

Lucius followed distant sounds until they became loud bashing.

"I'm coming Flynn." Lucius yelled out running downstairs. Seeing a copy of him and Maria in some type of illusion. Matching the living room from his hometown, Zenex.

"We should go travel somewhere special." Maria admitted.

"Like what," Lucius joked, "your parents' house instead of mine?"

"No," Maria said jokingly with exaggeration. "Perhaps to one of the seven islands. We don't have much but if we saved enough for a few months..."

"You're serious about this aren't you?" "Of course. Have you ever wanted to run away and not look back?"

"At times, but ideally we can't run away from our problems."

Maria and Lucius became quiet as Lucius' father, Parker walked into the room.

"Just think about it, Lucius." Maria reminded, whispering in Lucius' ears.

Lucius shook his head making the daydream in his head disappear. Back into reality from within Malyna's home.

"Flynn," Lucius yelled again. Hearing muffled voices leading him into the basement. Walking down the first few steps before the door slammed shut behind him. He turned the handle impulsively.

Locked.

Lucius walked cautiously to the bottom of the steps discovering Flynn.

"Stay your distance, feine. You're dead, I saw Hayden kill you." Flynn ordered twitching.

"It's okay Flynn, it's me, Lucius," He reminded.

"Lucius," Flynn repeated, squinting his eyes. Lucius took a few steps toward Flynn. Flynn retorted, taking out his sword. "You can't fool me, you betrayed the rebellion." Flynn swung, hitting a table beside Lucius.

"We're working together, don't make me fight back."

"What is dead should stay dead. You're the reason my friend is dead." Flynn argued running toward Lucius.

Lucius shuffled his feet dodging Flynn's attack. Making Flynn trip in confusion. Flynn extended his arm to take another jab. Flynn tripped again as Lucius disarmed the sword holding Flynn by his shirt.

Lucius slapped Flynn to make him go back into his senses. "Lucius...is that really you?"

"Are you with me?" Lucius said, waiting for Flynn's reply.

Flynn agreed. Lucius let him go, taking Flynn's weapon with him. "We got what we need."

"My sword?"

"What about it?"

"Hand it over."

"After we get back."

"Do you not trust me?" Flynn complained.

"You'll get it back." Lucius urged as Flynn gave up his steel blade.

"Are we not bringing Malyna with us?"

"We don't need to," Lucius said, finding themselves back on the bridge.

"We made it..." Flynn stated relieved.

"Did you have anything on your mind before we entered Edostan?"

"No, why?"

"Never mind."

* Feeding The Fire *

"I'm glad you both made it back. While you were gone I found out that Therron will have a private meeting leaving his castle for the first time in months. This is the opportunity we've been looking for. The meeting is located across the street from his castle inside his blacksmith." Hayden handed Lucius a dagger. "A swift death will do, I'll hold your sword until you come back. Lex will be by your side in the shadows. Try not to make a mess."

Nearing the entrance Lucius awaited for Therron to come out. "Is this the place?"

"They should be out any minute." Lex remained hidden. Lucius walked to get a closer look. Causing a guard to become suspicious.

"What's your business?" The guard asked, tapping his sword.

"I'm just waiting for a friend."

"Names Pavel, newcomer. By the way, you carry yourself. I know you're lying. Here in the upper class of Klexta, you best make yourself scarce. Unless you're looking for trouble."

Lucius back away noticing Therron exiting the blacksmith through the back door with a few guards with him.

"Runoff, newcomer." Pavel urged.

Lucius drifted forth Therron's direction. Pavel blocked Lucius from continuing with his heavy sword. "Keep your distance from the King."

Lucius walked away from the scene staying close enough without raising Pavel's attention.

"Who was that?" Therron asked, raising a brow.

"I have a suspicion the little crew of misfits recently discovered that you get your weapons here Therron. I believe Lucius was a scout of some sort, so do be careful on your way back."

How'd he know my name?

"Thank you for the warning," Therron said. " Next time attack on sight if they don't have strict business with me."

"Will do sir." Pavel saluted lagging behind Therron.

Lucius followed.

An occasional glance from Pavel made Lucius hide to avoid suspicion. Isolating Therron into an alleyway when Pavel entered a nearby pub. Lucius took out his dagger in a hesitant voice. "Am I a killer?"

"This is your chance." Lex said, noticing Lucius was cracking under pressure.

Lex took Lucius' dagger assassinating guard by guard undetected, dragging each body away from sight eventually reaching Therron himself. Therron turned around readying his freshly made sword knowing he was followed, "Wherever you are assassin you must know I'm always one step ahead-" Therron said being interrupted by Lex.

Penetrating him with one of the guard's swords through Therron's back. Sliding the sword out of Therron. Therron fell on both knees holding his chest groaning. Falling onto the cobbled alleyway as his blood filled the cracks.

"We need to escape." Lex recalled tossing Lucius Therron's sword.

"Lex." Lucius said, balancing the sword in his grasp as Pavel discovered Lucius and Lex's actions through a window finding a swift alternate exit.

"No time. We need to get out of here," Lex reminded as Lucius hesitantly followed behind him. "There's something I have to tell you."

"You're drawing attention to yourself." Lex summarized raising his index finger toward his mouth. Rushing back to the slums.

Lex opened the door for Lucius, watching his back so there are no followers before slamming the door shut.

"The deed is done," Lex confessed to Hayden. "Therron's gone and here's the proof."

Lucius rose the sword. Hayden surveyed the sword impressively and picked the sword up practicing swinging the sword.

"Something's wrong," Hayden summarized. "That seemed too easy."

"You've got to be kidding," Lex said with agitation. "He's dead. He was taken for a fool and led him to his downfall."

"Take this then, why are his guards still protecting the castle. If any leader was taken out like that, many would have fled."

"Perhaps they didn't get the news yet." Lex explained.

Stephan burst out from the courtyard. "Therron's giving a speech about the rebellion."

"I knew it." Hayden admitted.

"How is that possible," Lex admitted. "it looked exactly like him."

"I had a feeling," Hayden scoffed, "Therron's testing us but now his time is limited. That'll be an opportunity to attack while he's distracted with the crowd," Hayden stuck the Therron's sword onto the ground, "I need to know that we have an alliance, Lucius."

"About that. One of Therron's guards, Pavel. He knew my name-" Lucius announced as Lex interrupted.

"But I killed all the guards before I got to Therron."

"Pavel saw us through the building," Lucius explained.

"You let a witness get away?" Hayden raised his voice from shock.

"This is all new news to me." Lex confessed to Hayden. "Why didn't you go after him, Lucius?"

"I didn't see where he went. He burst away when you handed me his weapon." Lucius defended.

Hayden took Therron's blade stabbing the wood floor getting stuck between Lucius and Lex. Causing them to jump. "Did you say, Pavel?" Hayden snapped creating a momentary silence to ensue.

"Yeah, why?" Lucius asked.

Hayden dismissively scoffed. "Anything less than a hundred and ten percent of what I ask will result in you two causing us problems. Ashlyn and your friends will be put on the postponement of help, until then Lucius. I expected better from you Lex."

"We have the upper hand on this war. I won't fail you again," Lex assured.

"We'll deal with Pavel later."

"What will you do in the meantime, Hayden?" Stephan asked joining in the conversation. Remaining quiet until he decided to fill in the silence.

"Cause a riot," Hayden admitted. "That way the guards will leave their posts," Hayden raised his sword from the table. "They may know about you, Lucius but remain cautious and you'll be fine. You'll be tagging along with Stephan. To get a chance to get acquainted."

"I'm going with him?" Stephan questioned.

"If either of you gets into trouble, deal with it yourself. We aren't going to fail this mission because of one mistake like last time. Think of it as a test of loyalty. Everyone today will give their all or else lives will be lost. You're with me, Lex." Hayden said leaving the base.

"Lucius I have an idea for you," Stephan said tossing Therron's sword to Lucius."

Lucius caught the weapon with difficulty. Following Stephan, "Why was Hayden like that?" "Hayden's father, Marius, was the King that Therron assassinated. Many moons ago Therron used to be allies and fight beside Marius. Too many new faces makes Hayden nervous. He doesn't want to have a betrayal like what happened that frightful day. " Stephan changed the topic as they reached the checkpoint. "Now, the riot will be formed at the front entrance. Meanwhile, we'll sneak in the back. Although I don't know the layout of the place anymore, I'm sure we'll cover more ground to split up.

"Must it be me to do the killing blow?"

"I'll kill him if it comes down to it. It doesn't have to be your fight," Stephan explained reaching the back of the castle. Crowds arose in the distance with torches heading toward the courtyard. "There's the mark of our men. It's time."

Stephan led Lucius to an idle open window. They browsed their surroundings as they split up. Lucius turned to the left hallway as Stephan took right.

Lucius hid into the darkness within the hallway hearing footsteps. Guards passed by him exiting the castle.

I don't get violence, even if it's for revenge. It doesn't undo that sad fact from it happening; is it the satisfaction. Does life have to resort to bloodshed to create peace?

Continuing the way the guards came from reaching Therron. Feeling though it were invitational. Lucius glanced at the sword as he began to shake. Hearing Therron giving a speech on the second floor balcony.

"...which is why the rebellion will fall. They're weak as they have been for the longest time. As of right now we have them at their knees with their last pity act of a riot. I will do them a favor if they reveal the last of their members. I may have pity on their souls for backstabbing this fine land if they give information about their leaders. They may even have a spot by my side with triple of whatever this rebellion pays for their heinous acts."

Lucius made his way to Therron, Time became slow. The sword became heavy, lifting it up getting tackled by Pavel. Knocking Lucius out of Therron's view. Therron turned around abruptly with curiosity.

The weapon dropped out of Lucius' hand easily crashing to the ground.

"What are you doing here?" Pavel questioned with a sharp whisper, holding a dagger to Lucius' throat.

"What does it look like?" Lucius scoffed. "I'm finishing Therron's term." Lucius began to rise before Pavel used his knee to keep him down.

"You don't look like the type, even if your life depended on it." Pavel reminded. "Trust me kid, it'll be best if he stays alive. I sensed that I'd see you again but not this way. The rebellion is much weaker than I thought if all they had to bring was you... unless-" Pavel turned to watch Stephan slicing Therron's stomach.

"No..." Pavel yelled out. Therron held his stomach once Stephan retrieved his blade.

"You failed me Pavel." Therron admitted with a deep voice pointing at him before his eyes remained still. Raising Lucius to his feet, Pavel placed a dagger to Lucius' throat. "Be calm, I don't want to hurt you but I will if you give me no choice."

Stephan yelled out to Pavel. "Let Lucius go, your leader is gone. I'll be willing to spare your life this once..." Stephan bartered.

"You may want to cover your eyes," Pavel whispered once more, flicking the pommel of his dagger with his pinky. Revealing a hidden department within his dagger of a small, yet fragile smoke bomb. Detonating upon impact with the ground. Pavel loosened his grip, bashing Lucius' temple. Knocking Lucius unconscious.

Pavel slid the dagger away as he picked up Lucius, carrying him with his shoulder. Making a swift escape.

"Lucius?" Stephan asked, waving away the smoke. Stephan took to the nearest hallway to make an escape of his own. Therron's guards surrounded Stephan before he knew it. Stephan dropped his weapons placing his hands behind his head as he hesitantly surrendered.

Memory II - Around Every Corner

* Secrets *

Lucius shook his head with fatigue. Discovering his hands were bounded after a few tugs. He opened his eyes wide as he heard footsteps coming towards him. "Why'd you bring this man to my base Pavel?"

"He's an issue Jack. However, not a regular issue that the public deals with, but issues I've found you and I are having a lot more often now," Pavel explained.

"If that's the case then why haven't you killed him and be done with it. Omega has too many followers to keep up with. One of his lackeys won't know anything but the same old. You know that." "This one's different. I believe it's time to go back in time to fix the mistake Lucius inadvertently caused. Therron isn't supposed to die until a week from now according to this book of..."

"Hold on Pavel. He's listening," Jack said, glanced over sipping his tea. Setting it aside on the windowsill beside him. Walking to Lucius in a judging expression. "Do you know why you are here?"

"Pavel led me here," Lucius admitted, gathering his bearings. The name Jack ringed in his head, it immediately clicked in his head that Ashlyn mentioned him. "Isn't your name Jack Arturo?"

"Yes it is," Jack glanced at Pavel with interest. "Perhaps you did get someone worth talking to. How do you know my last name, kid?"

"Ashlyn told me to look for you."

"No kidding." Jack laughed going onto one knee. "So you're not one of Omega's people then.

That's good news but unfortunately we will have to fix the mistake you've caused."

"How was it an attempt if he was successful," Lucius said, narrowing his eyes. "Were you serious about time travel?"

"It seems Ashlyn always tells people enough on a need to know basis. Sorry about the whole being tied up and the headache you'll have for the next few hours." Pavel made known to Lucius.

"It's complicated to an extent." Jack said. "It's to make things easier on our ends, we must wait for something to happen the first time to fix it the second time around. The technology I have that's beyond your time gives me this ability to tell what's wrong and correct with certain timelines."

"But if you have something from the future within the past but don't enter the future how do you have it?" Lucius asked.

"I don't go into the future, that's Omega. Lately, Omega has been alternating the recent future and will need to be stopped. We are stuck in a loop of fixing the timelines that we don't have time to stop him from making his next move."

"A bit if ironic if you ask me." Pavel tuned in.

"Do you understand so far, Lucius?"

"A little I guess. How far can Omega go into the future?" Lucius said holding his head, "That's weird you knew about the headache."

"It's become second nature to us. The furthest I've recorded Omega's distance into the future was about a few weeks. Of which we'll have to deal with them separately if we decide to keep doing the same formula we've been. Otherwise we'll lose our minds." Pavel said.

Lucius became lost in translation. "Look, kid it's not your fault. It's pretty good, in fact." Jack said, releasing Lucius. "From what I understand Ashlyn wasn't meant to be captured but now that Therron is dead. I want you to bring her back to us, and we will fix the timeline of Therron's death."

"Wouldn't Ashlyn be back into prison with Hayden?" Lucius asked.

"No, she'll be with us. There's no such thing as duplicates of people, unless you go into the future. Figure that one out." Jack joked, elbowing Lucius.

"What?"

"You'll get it, Lucius." Pavel admitted.

"Do you by chance know where my friends are?" Lucius asked.

"By friends, do you mean Kain?" Jack questioned. "You arrived around the same period of time."

"No, my real friends before I even met Kain. One of them is named Maria Royce."

"Name doesn't strike me as familiar. I'll look into it."

"I'll be back shortly then," Lucius said leaving the building. Being across the street from the castle.

Entering the slums, he found the base in the process of packing. Bumping into Nadim in one of the hallways.

"What's going on?"

"I'm glad you're alright." Nadim hugged Lucius with joy. "We thought you died in the ambush. Therron's men are on the run and those who remain will be defeated shortly, so now we can rescue Stephan." Nadim placed the keys to the jail in Lucius' hands. "Hayden is pleased with your service. You can release Ashlyn when you are ready. If you want you can meet back up with him at the castle by dawn if you want to continue working with us. You'll be guaranteed a job in the castle if you so wish."

"What's next for you?"

"I'll do what I've always been doing with Hayden. This time I'll sleep soundly for the first time since this war. I finally have enough coin to never skip meals for my wife and I. Perhaps even start a family. Without you, It wouldn't have happened. Thanks, Lucius."

"I suppose I'll go my own way once I pick up Ashlyn. Take care of yourself Nadim."

Nadim stepped aside the hallway, unblocking the narrow corridor to continue packing. Lucius used the key to release Ashlyn as she didn't seem to pay attention until the cell door opened up. "I talked to Jack, he seems like an interesting person. Something about time travel..." Lucius began as Ashlyn covered his mouth.

"It's best to keep that a secret, Ashlyn said, exiting though the window nearest the cell.

"Why aren't you leaving though the entrance?"

"Knowing Jack he's preventing the death of Therron before we get back to him. It's best we shouldn't interfere with Hayden's plan," Ashlyn explained.

Entering Jack's base, Ashlyn was pulled into the room by a middle-aged, strict and fit woman.

"Who'd you bring here?"

"Calm down Miss Daro, Jack knows about us coming, go ahead and ask him." Ashlyn admitted.

"Helba will be just fine, little lady."

Lucius raised his hands feeling a cold tip of a sword poking his back.

"Is there someone who doesn't get you in trouble Ashlyn?" Lucius remarked.

"You'd be the way we are as well if only you knew what we deal with. Ashlyn's newer, like you-"

"They're good. Dear brother Vaughan," Jack pointed out as he appeared within thin air.

"You're back?" Helba said surprised.

"Check the window. You'll see that without Lucius there that the riot has just begun. They aren't causing fires this time around," Jack summarized as Helba double-checked.

"He's right." Helba added.

"What of Stephan Dermon?" Lucius questioned.

"He gets captured, but he'll be fine." Jack explained.

Lucius viewed the castle outside in doubt. Taking notice from the riot that bandits were giving chase to Kain and Reyner.

"We need to help those men down there." Lucius urged.

"Who?" Ashlyn asked as she made room. Pushing Helba aside, finding Kain and Reyner in mere seconds. "Jack, he knows what he's talking about. Those are my friends I told you about that were captured. They need your help."

"Why should I help you... I still don't know if I should trust you yet," Jack asked.

"You want help with Omega, this'll be your chance to have the aid you need. Combining my friends and Lucius' we'll easily have enough people to overrun Omega," Ashlyn speaking logically to Jack.

"You seem to be forcing my hand. Like you just did to make me revive Therron. But fine, we'll save your friends. But where's Lucius' friends?"

"First let's get down there before anyone gets hurt," Lucius spoke out. Storming out of the building. Finding themselves in the middle of a standoff by Kain's side.

"How'd they find you?" Ashlyn asked Reyner, causing him to jump.

"You're a sight for sore eyes," Reyner explained. "But who are they?" He admitted, pointing his thumb behind him at the new crowd.

"They're friends but I'll explain more about it once we get out of here," Ashlyn summarized hearing Magnus' voice.

"It'll be best if you come out now before I make you regret hiding. Or did you forget about

Caroline?" Magnus asked as he used the back of his hand to massage Caroline's cheek. "Such a poor pregnant broad and don't forget our new addition Floros Gordon-"

Floros yelled out. "Don't touch my aunt."

"Quiet boy." Magnus ordered.

"They have my family?" Kain whispered sharply, worried, holding back tears.

"What did you do to him that makes him want to do such drastic measures to find you?" Jack asked quietly.

"They claim that Paul stole our supplies." Reyner explained.

"Where's your brother, Kain?" Helba asked.

"He's dead." Kain said with difficulty.

"Not my Paulie..." Caroline cried out.

"No. That can't be true-" Floros preserved with glossy eyes.

"So a widow now?" Magnus chuckled.

"Don't lay a finger on her." Floros ordered.

"And what will a Fourteen year old do?"

"I'm Nineteen." Floros corrected tightening his fist to swing as Magnus twisted his arm to make him submit to the floor.

"I'll make a lesson out of your boy," Magnus tossed his arm aside to grab his cotton shirt dragging him forward. "Come out with the last of the dignity you have left to reconnect with your family before I decide that I'm not in a forgiving mood anymore." Magnus threw Floros down. Magnus used the back of his heavily scarred hand to slap Floros in the cheek that made a thunderous clap.

Floros fell backward holding his reddened cheek in awe.

"We need to show ourselves out there. I can't live with myself by just standing here," Kain focused his attention to his family as his legs became flimsy.

"Go on and go out there then. My name is Vaughan, remember that name and say it once they go too far. With us being here you'll have nothing to fear. They don't know us. We have the surprise effect on them. We'll strike them down when you say my name to get your family back. Just try to hold off from saying my name until you see us in a good place to flank."

"I told you they're impossible to deal with Drago. How will you play this in my scenario?" Magnus asked.

"In order to get a reaction you must show them that we're not messing around. Since they like to jest, I have a joke of my own. A simple smack won't do. Letting a teenager dictate your actions is pitiful. Perhaps one of them should get an arrow between the eyes to show that you're serious," Drago asked as he took out his bow aiming toward Floros at first as Caroline spoke up.

"Don't you dare hurt him." Caroline gritted her teeth pulling on Drago's arm.

"You shouldn't be talking unless you want me to kill two people today with one arrow." Drago said as he released Caroline, then aiming at her stomach.

"I have a shot." Ashlyn reminded as she aimed a bow peaking out beside a planter.

Reyner lowered Ashlyn's bow, "It's too risky. We can't chance it."

"How do you know?" Ashlyn asked as she rose her bow back up.

Kain rose suddenly to Ashlyn's right side. "Stop. I'm here," Kain announced. Drago smirked as he aimed the bow at Kain.

Ashlyn widened her eyes as Kain passed her by. "What are you doing?"

"See Magnus, that's how you achieve your goals, they just need some motivation," Drago explained to Magnus. Drago raised his voice. "You're not alone, where's Reyner?"

Reyner took a breath as he rose himself to the left of Ashlyn. "Here goes nothing. We don't have a choice." Reyner whispered as his pitch rose. "We're both here just to be rational and talk about it like men."

"If we must talk like men. Come closer instead of across the courtyard."

Kain and Reyner walked toward them as Magnus stopped them in their tracks. "While you're on your way you best be adding your other two friends Ashlyn and Lucius with you."

"Who's Lucius?" Drago questioned.

"He caused Kain to get away earlier and how I got this scar. Just as much to blame as the rest of them," Magnus explained.

"Just do what they say. If you want to trust us to trust you, you must trust us first," Jack stated to Lucius and the impatient Ashlyn. Ashlyn decided to lower her bow.

Lucius and Ashlyn got out of cover lining up beside Reyner and Kain.

"Impressive catch, Magnus. I'll only ask once and if none of you answer to my satisfaction there'll be hell to pay," Drago passed each of them by surveying them in close detail as he passed by. "Where's the All-Seeing Eye?" Drago asked, gaining anger. "I don't care who has it remaining to hide the truth you will pay the consequences."

"My brother Paul had it, I have no idea where it went after that."

Drago walked back up to Kain. "I don't believe you."

"For what it's worth I'm glad he's dead. I won't ask again, Where is it now?" Drago asked, shifting his focus to Lucius. "You must be the one who fought Magnus. Which means you must know something."

Lucius looked away from Drago dark green's eyes to Therron's balcony of which you could see the relic in Therron's hand, distracted by the people within the riot.

"You look when I speak to you Lucius." Drago ordered.

Magnus decided to follow Lucius' eyes as it didn't take long for Magnus to figure out what Lucius was distracted by. "Therron has it..."

"Wait, what... how?" Drago asked as he looked seeing Therron. Throwing away the magnetic seal as he held the artifact. Giving a speech as his eyes became crystal white.

Kain looked at Jack's progression to flank. "It would seem to be the will of Vaughan."

"Who's Vaughan?" Drago asked as Vaughan rushed toward Drago. Vaughan ran through Drago as Drago glitched. Tackling Magnus instead.

"That's new," Drago remarked as he looked at his body acting like static as it became normal again moments after. Giving off laughter. "Go ahead have this temporary victory if you want to call it that. I now have what I need. I'll be back soon," Drago chuckled, disappearing within thin air leaving Caroline behind.

Caroline opened her eyes as Floros looked at his aunt to give a faithful half smile before disappearing. "Floros..." Caroline exclaimed as she looked sporadically.

Vaughan held Magnus down disappearing with a smirk on his face. He fell into the mud that Magnus had laid searching in the mud in disbelief.

"This isn't good." Jack made known, helping Vaughan to his feet.

"Why didn't you help?" Reyner asked. "Did you see that glitch?" Jack explained.

"It's the work of the artifact, we're in more trouble than I thought."

"I'm glad you're alright." Kain admitted hugging Caroline.

"They have my baby nephew, Floros." Caroline reminded releasing Kain in a hurry.

"Then they must have a use for him." Vaughan pointed out. "-and you're getting closer to having your child. They wouldn't want to have to deal with that." Helba added.

"That's one way to look at it." Jack said. "Am I wrong?" Helba asked.

"We will get my son back soon. I know we will," Kain reassured.

"My friends are located on the path on the treasure map to get to the artifact," Lucius said handing Jack the letter he was left by Maria. "I'm glad you're alright Caroline." Lucius added.

"Thank you," Caroline stated with a smile, hugging Reyner. "I owe you all one. This is a lot to take in. Paul is gone. Floros is missing, he kept asking me if we were going to die. I didn't know what to say."

"You're in good hands Caroline. With good people like Jack and his people. He'll surely help you out." Ashlyn explained reassuring Caroline taking her turn for a hug looking at Jack with puppy dog eyes.

Jack sighed, "My brother Vaughan here will lead you into a safe place and take care of you until I come back. I'll go with Lucius to bring him to his friends. We'll be back shortly, you won't even know we left." Jack explained as he split off with Lucius.

"You know about the treasure map?" Lucius asked.

"I never went there myself but it always seems to attract newcomers on these islands. Are you positive that you'll see them there when we get there?"

"The gut feeling I have says I hope so." "I hope so as well. I get gut feelings like that many a time. I wish I was able to do all of those feelings. My life would be so much simpler if I could."

* The Hunt *

"One thing before we enter..."

"What's that?" Jack asked.

"Are you worried about Therron having the artifact?"

"The way Therron retrieved the artifact was originally different and what happened to Drago was unexpected. But now the timeline seems unchanged." Jack said. "This looks like it, this cave is ancient."

"Yeah this is it," Lucius walked to a tree next to the cave noticing the initials Maria left him. "We're on their trail. I'm just afraid of seeing something happen to them."

"I've had my fair share of losses but if something were to happen we can go back in time to fix it," Jack explained as he decided to enter first handing Lucius an extra torch.

Following the tight corners of the cave. Squeezing through sharp rocks cutting Lucius' forearm. Lucius grunted in the process as it distracted Jack who was slightly ahead of him.

"What happened, are you alright?"

"It's just a cut."

Jack looked at Lucius for a moment, continuing for a few steps before falling through the floor.

"Jack?" Lucius asked as he used his torch to light away in front of him to see Jack two floors below him on his back.

"I'll work my way back to you, focus on the directions on the treasure map."

Lucius took a long breath as he jumped over the hole that Jack fell through.

What if I fall?

"You'll get over it. You just need a little determination." a familiar voice echoed.

"Is that you Ernaldus?" Lucius questioned impulsively.

"You tell me. Maria and Aelienor are worried about you but I told them you're fine. Better not make a liar out of me," Ernaldus replied.

"Where are you?"

"Imagine if you were us for a moment, do you think we would stay here and wait for you empty-handed, leave you on this island or continue the search for the All-Seeing Eye and hope to find you in the process?"

"I'd think the last option I hope." Lucius stopped to crawl into a small opening as his heart skipped a beat as he took notice of a pair of feet in front of him. As he waited for the feet to pass by, Lucius' hand slipped.

Rosane's concerned face appeared before Lucius with a torch illuminated between them on the cave walls.

"What're you doing here?" Rosane asked first.

"To find my friends."

"Are your friends the men that Rosetta and I are going to meet here in a minute?"

"I don't know. What problems are you dealing with?"

"Kion and Fabul. They arrested Malyna for her incompetence by showing too much magic to the weak-minded. You can come with us if you like but don't make your appearance known. They're out to get us. I just know they are."

"Did you hear someone talking to me before I bumped into you?"

"No, I didn't." Rosane looked behind Lucius placing his hands on his shoulders. "Follow me with some distance, remain quiet, and listen. Can you do this?"

Lucius agreed, stepping back, letting Rosane though. Rosane picked up his pace until Lucius couldn't see him.

Only by chance Lucius was able to follow Rosane's trail successfully, was by splashes of water being echoed by Rosane's boots and deep breaths in the distance. Lucius took notice of a glowing red light nearby. Lucius distinguished the torch he had, climbing a nearby ledge.

"Are you ready?" Rosetta asked guarding the door to continue.

"As ready as I can be," Rosane said as his brother opened to the door. Showing Kion and Fabul awaiting them in a meeting room. Crossing their arms on the table.

"You two have been showing us a lot of concern as of late. There have been time shifts costing the life of the current King. However, it's much more than that. It also alternated the time of your futures. The mistakes you've made caused your death in another timeline. Understand this, you only have so many timelines before the one you're currently in runs out"

It was hard to make out either Kion's or Fabul's appearance as they would fade in and fade out from the natural dark red glow passing by them.

Fabul took out a wooden container the size of his palm placing it on the table in front of them. "The one thing that we can't see to look over though is the fact of this All-Seeing Eye device. The source of all magic that couldn't be created or destroyed with just one simple thought. It was stolen from us, from some sort of adventurer. It was supposed to be kept under your supervision and you failed us."

"The reason we weren't able to protect it was from a curse sent upon us," Rosetta explained.

"I don't care if that device required your life or my colleague. It's supposed to be here at all times. Since you made it here, I imagine you don't have the curse anymore, right?"

"That's correct sir."

"The time it took you or any other dealing with a curse. Someone would have stolen that artifact a thousand times over."

"Lucius saved our lives."

"You let an ill-minded heal you which means you had to teach them a potion or spell without our permission. Which isn't acceptable," Kion made known as he slammed his fist on the table.

"The world as we know it is in peril. Whoever took the artifact that, our founding father of us wizards and sorceresses made for a chosen, can have an idle thought to make anything a reality. Which could mean anything, even to disable our magic forever." Fabul opened the wooden container revealing a piece of metal that looked familiar to them.

"Is that..." Rosetta started as he looked closer.

"It's exactly what you think it is." Fabul interrupted with annoyance. "This here is the only way you can hold the All-Seeing Eye without it corrupting your mind becoming brain- dead within hours. Perhaps a few months if the artifact takes a liking to you. Finding this isolated in the streets of Klexta makes me disappointed in both of you. You will find that artifact and bring it back to this cave or else you'll find another side of us that you've never seen before."

"What are you going to do with Malyna?" Rosane asked.

"If you must know she'll be in mage captivity for giving an ill-minded person too much information. You all three spit in the face of what WE stand for. Unless you want the rest of the council to hear about this, you will solve this issue immediately. We will talk again soon and it better be on good terms, for your sake." Kion summarized as he and Fabul summoned green and gray auras within their hands. Generating a portal disappearing as they entered.

Lucius jumped down, "I'm sorry about giving you all so much trouble."

Rosetta looked at Rosane with annoyance. "We're already walking on thin ice here Rosane. Bringing him is dangerous." Rosetta turned to Lucius, "I get that you want to help us but due to our scenario... it'll be best for you to lie low."

"I'm serious Rosetta. He can help us retrieve the artifact back." Rosane admitted opening a magical box with silver and golden designs surrounding the box. The black and red box was topped off with a ruby gemstone peeking at the top complementing the overall box. Placing the magnetic seal inside.

"We're supposed to keep this artifact here and yet you're willing to give it to the first person you have the slightest faith in. It's like you want to have a death wish." Rosetta explained, slapping Rosane's hand away from the box.

"Sometimes faith is all I have left. Without faith, we wouldn't have magic in the first place." Rosane handed the now glowing box to Lucius as Rosetta sighed not knowing how to retort.

"I don't like that idea of yours Rosane."

"You don't have to, but he's our best chance. Think about it. You tried to get the artifact the last time. See where it ended up from your failure. In the hands of Therron," Rosane explained.

"We are behind on training." Rosetta said as an excuse.

Lucius noticed Rosetta's hesitation as Lucius decided to reassure him. "I promise you two I'll do the best I can. The least I can do is help you get out of the hole I put you in. By chance, could you tell me where the All-Seeing Eye would be if it was here."

"It would be behind a large door, a few hallways from here that consisted of a total of twelve keys. We were out of the picture for a long time. Someone found them all and retrieved it."

"Thank you for telling me. I'll be back soon with what you seek. Patience is all I ask and faith." Lucius added. He made his way to the exit meeting with Jack.

"They aren't here Lucius, but they did leave you a note that may be of interest to you," Jack said as he sat on the pedestal the artifact would be.

Lucius took the note from Jack containing another letter of progress.

We were successful in finding the treasure if it were still there. We were happy that we knew if it was there or not. We left, and we met a new group of people willing to help us go back home. But we decided to decline their offer for now. That is until we find you. We figure the best way for you to find us if you're still around, is for you to come to us. We decided to stay in a town named Quia. I hope we meet again soon.

-Maria

* Steps In The Right Direction *

Lucius folded the page placing the paper in his pocket looking up.

"Thanks, Jack, this means a lot," Lucius began. Looking up discovering someone behind Jack.

Lucius raised his hands in a surrendering tone. "Don't be irrational here."

"What do you-" Jack began receiving a tug in his throat from a muscular man's bicep.

"Where's the treasure?"

"We were beaten to the punch ourselves, we don't know. You don't have to resort to violence for us to get that serious." Lucius said calmly.

"Yeah. Lessen the grip so we can talk like men."

Jack said gasping for air.

"Who are you and how'd you get here anyway?" Lucius asked.

"Draven Foley. I'm here for that artifact to pay off some debts."

"My name is Lucius and that man you're strangling is Jack."

"Nice... to meet you." Jack spoke with difficulty.

"Quiet." Draven said, tightening his grip.

"You're not going to accomplish that goal by choking strangers. I've had my fair share of being in debt, but this is no way to act. Let him go and perhaps we can work something out," Lucius stated.

"You may be in debt yourself but the people I owe will not hesitate to hurt those I love," Draven barked out.

"Again, if you let him go we will figure something out," Lucius said calmly.

"You could be one of them and I'm not going to take that chance," Draven thought out loud.

"Don't do it Draven," Lucius as he took a few steps toward Draven aggravating him. Using the knife to stab Jack, he covered the blow with his shoulder. Failing to counterattack.

In the awe of not killing Jack immediately. Draven twisted the dagger. Jack used the adrenaline yelling out from the pain to bash Draven's head against the wall, just enough to make him fall unconscious. Jack held the dagger in place. Slighting tapping the dagger as Jack began to breathe irregularly. Agitating the thick wound. "I need to get treated," Jack explained with difficulty.

Jack took the lead until he exited the cave as he fell unconscious onto Lucius. Time flew by to Lucius as before he knew he brought Jack to base. Helba cleared off a nearby table.

"I know a bit of restoration," Reyner made known, calling off tools he needed.

"Jack," Vaughan spoke with concern. "Are you alright brother?"

"Cencil... Will be coming and he won't be happy. He'll soon meet Parker with disappointment." Jack said, going into a daze.

"Who's Parker?" Vaughan questioned shaking Jack. "Stay with me, please."

"Parkers... My dad." Lucius admitted.

"What's my father has to do with yours?" Vaughan asked.

"I'm not sure."

"You often dream about other timelines after a while being in so many. This event must've tipped him off. From what's reality and what's not. I suppose you didn't find your friends."

"We didn't, but we know where they were located. A guy Draven attacked Jack."

"Yet another person to watch out for." Helba commented.

"I think it's time." Caroline said looking around in concern as she held her stomach in pain.

"You're picking a hell of a time Caroline," Reyner explained cautiously removing the blade as Jack groaned with extremity. Reyner bandaged the wound as he took turns focusing on Jack and replying to Caroline.

"I don't exactly choose the moments Reyner. They just happen." Caroline snapped as she yelled. "Now get over here before I rip your arms off."

"Damn it," Reyner shook his head as he put Vaughan's hands-on Jack's wound. "Keep pressure here." Reyner said letting go of the bandages.

"You're not dying today," Vaughan ordered as blood-soaked up quickly. "Reyner comes back here." Vaughan bickered.

"I'll be back shortly," Reyner shouted as he focused his attention to Caroline."Just breathe." Jack began to shake uncontrollably. "Reyner..." Vaughan reminded.

"What now?" Reyner asked, becoming more stressed than before. Discovering Jack's condition. "All right everyone out. Except you... Helba."

"Why me?"

"Someone has to at least hand me supplies before I go crazy," Reyner said

"You're not going anywhere Helba. I need another woman here," Caroline ordered.

"I suppose that too. Now everyone out." Reyner ordered.

Vaughan kept pacing back and forth as the others departed. "What did you discover with Jack?"

"My friend's location."

"Lucius, I'll help finish what Jack started. To get my head off things. We need to obtain the artifact before Omega's people affect the timeline again where's your friends located?"

"They're at Quia."

"I know the way there... Perhaps they can spare supplies in the process."

"Lead the way." Lucius said.

"What about us?" Ashlyn asked.

"Stay there and guard," Vaughan ordered.

Getting half of the way to Quia the trip was with Vaughan quiet mumbling to himself until he spoke up to Lucius. "I almost lost my brother. I can't believe it." Vaughan said, shaking his head. "I don't know what I'd do without him..."

"If he did die," Lucius started as Vaughan looked at Lucius with a stink eye. "-which I'm not saying he is, but couldn't we just go back in time to prevent his death?"

"I could. But after you revive so many times in timelines. Time itself will make it inevitable. It's perilous that it's not corrected the first time around. Like hallucinations or a twisted personality. About what Jack said, where is your father right now?"

"He's across the continent. I'm sure he's not happy about me nor any of my friends for that matter, but we did it for the adventure. It sounds dumb when I say it out loud."

"Yeah, it does but I'm glad you're here." Vaughan cleared his throat. "Since we're on our way to Quia which isn't far, I might add. There's a friend I know there that can teach you on how to defend yourself."

"Like fighting?"

"Yeah. These are desperate times and you're good to have around. You'll be better to have with if you could carry yourself with a weapon. I wouldn't ask this if it wasn't such an evil world out there. Jack did tell me about you being the one Pavel caught the first time around besides Stephan. Although you were there to assassinate him, odds are you wouldn't have killed him even if you weren't stopped."

"I suppose it was better that way. I just wish that it doesn't come down to that."

"You and me both. Some people are stuck in their ways always believing that their right no matter how much they are wrong."

Reaching Quia, they had discovered the town was recently caught in flames and happened to be distinguished over the prior night before they arrived.

"Oh my Yuoki..." Lucius said as he fell on both his knees with a giving up tone.

"I'm not taking this as a loss. The Timeline Codex would notify me and the rest of the group back at the base if my informant was gone. Your friends may still be here with Wariner." Vaughan explained as he patted Lucius on the shoulder helping him back up.

"This place is in ruins..." Lucius asked as he wiped his eyes.

"This place is full of secrets." Vaughan corrected. "That's what Wariner is all about. Keep an eye out." Vaughan explained splitting off to one of the first buildings he saw that wasn't collapsed in itself.

Lucius walked to the building across the street from Vaughan pushing a large wood pillar out of the way to enter. Too much of Lucius' surprise, discovering two severely burned people lying on the ground. One of which was holding a dagger desperately. Lucius hesitantly took the dagger as the dying man grabbed Lucius' hand.

"Don't mess with the wrong people boy or else you'll end up like me," the man said, coughing roughly. The faint sun rose from the shadows burning his fragile flesh

"What happened here... are you Wariner?" Lucius asked as he waited for an answer as instead, the man's grip loosened, as his body twitched one last time before his movement stopped.

Lucius looked at the other man more burned than the person who talked to him. "He's too gone. It's too hard to figure if it's anyone I know." Lucius walked closer to the body taking notice of a bright blue light glared unto the body from a window.

Lucius followed the light coming from a well's roof. A tiny prism. He didn't account for the first time he passed it. Meeting with Vaughan to relay the news. Vaughan pointed out Lucius' discoveries before he could let him speak.

"From what I can conclude from this unfortunate event is someone was out for this town. This does seem like a random chance, it was planned the fire wouldn't have spread as far as it did otherwise."

"The building I checked contained perished townspeople inside. I thought your Codex would inform you."

"I don't have the Codex with me. Try not to let this distract you from our goal here." Vaughan looked away from Lucius as he gave him a brow. "It's mind-numbing for me too. One we find your friends and Wariner we can talk about if it's worth saving this town. All I've found is rubble and different symbols scratched into the wall." Vaughan explained as he pointed them out, one of which was Maria's initials. Lucius became blinded by the sudden bright light. Vaughan took notice of Lucius' agitation

"What is it?"

"A prism..." Lucius deducted right as the light blinded him again. "Where the well is...keeps getting into my eyes was that there before?"

"I didn't think so..."

Memory III - Dark Liberators

* Home Sweet Quia *

Vaughan grabbed the prism dangling from the well.

"We'll need to swim to the bottom." Vaughan summarized folding his sleeves.

"Are you sure this is a good idea?"

"This is our only lead," Vaughan hoisted his leg over the well. Not waiting for Lucius' response.

Lucius peaked over to the deep, unclear, darkness within the water's depth.

"Hope you're right." He entered the well, sinking a few feet before landing roughly onto the floor into the middle of civilization.

Wariner made his appearance to Lucius known. Lifting Vaughan into a bear hug.

"It's been a long time, friend." Wariner joyfully announced looking over to Lucius.

"No thanks," Lucius waved off. "I chose to breathe."

"Don't listen to him-" Vaughan said as he gained back his footing with a sigh. "Times have changed I'm afraid. I would like to ask for your aid." Vaughan explained patting Wariner's back as he gained his breath back. Turning Wariner's emotion grim.

"I'm sad to say we need the same. A successful arson attempt was made last night. The last of the survivors are here."

"That's more than half of Quia," Vaughan admitted after a general headcount.

Wariner added with disappointment. "It caught all of us off guard. We have a high suspicion that a citizen in Quia started the fire, but can't prove it. I'll show you around our living space for the time being. We're not going to leave this place until we figure out the mystery." Wariner explained.

"We'll help you piece this together. Can you teach my friend here on how to defend himself once this all blows over?" Vaughan asked.

"I'll be in your debt once again. I still know a few tricks from my dad who taught me. I can make a fighter out of anyone." Wariner summarized, leading Vaughan and Lucius to the rest of the survivors. To Lucius' surprise seeing his friends again.

Their faces lit up with joy seeing each other again as they exchanged warm and welcoming hugs. "I see you all getting along which is great, just remember what I told you, Lucius." Wariner reminded him as Vaughan led him to speak in private.

"Can't believe you're alive," Ernaldus stated he repeated to himself.

"What did Wariner tell you?" Gauvain asked.

"He just wants to figure out who caused the fire in Quia. In the meantime, doesn't want anyone to leave until he figures that out." Lucius summarized.

"He can't keep us here like this." Maria spoke out.

"I assure you that my son can, and he will," A man intercepted coming out of the crowd of people with a large brown brim cavalier hat with a matching padded gambeson. "This matter will be dealt with immediately. It's for everyone's benefit."

"Who are you?" Lucius asked insultingly.

"If you must know. Names Morrison. I'm the Lord of Quia. My son, Wariner, will be lorded himself soon. I'm teaching him my ways before I withdraw, until then, I stand by my son's actions on being a knight." Morrison explained tipping his hat.

"Wouldn't your hat have a feather?" Gauvain commented.

"Normally it would. But I don't like feathers. They're a pain and always get in your sight and just overall in my way." Morrison corrected.

"Nice to meet you, Lord Morrison. Sorry about the miscommunication. We'll get right on the mystery of Quia. We just need some time." Maria said as Morrison adjusted his collar joining his son's conversation.

Aelienor's face became worrisome leading her friends out of sight from the crowd. "I know who did the fire but you're not going to like it."

"Who?" Lucius questioned.

"It wasn't their fault mind you. It wasn't intentional as they're thinking it was."

"What are you saying?" Ernaldus asked, trying to not draw attention.

"It was me," Aelienor's face became red as her freckles. "But I was trying to stop the fire from happening." Aelienor confessed

"Who did you try to stop?" Lucius asked.

"Jousen Mercer... if we call him out on his arson. I know he'll point out fingers at me as well.

He's friends with the lord. I happened to be at the wrong place at the wrong time and now it gives me a stomach ache thinking about it."

"Why didn't you tell us sooner?" Maria questioned.

"The screams... the horrid screams. So much agony... it was horrible. It happened so fast. So much death at once. So powerless..." Aelienor confessed.

"Take a breath Aelienor, it's ok." Gauvain comforted.

"Why couldn't you try to tell me or warn someone else up before the fire started?" Ernaldus asked.

"I was too far away at that time. By the time I had the chance. You all were already awake and in that panic before we ended up here. I didn't feel safe...comfortable sharing. It's too late to do anything now." Aelienor summarized.

"I have an idea for Aelienor, but we need to prove Jousen started the fire. Do you have any ideas?" Lucius asked.

"Before the fire started. Jousen made a deal with some people. One by the name of Nolyn Kilner. Gold was involved. I know that much.

One thing led to another and it got violent. The only thing I know is that I don't see either of them here with us."

Lucius took out a dagger that he discovered earlier on. "Did Nolyn own this?"

"He did. They fought and fire came shortly after. Where's Nolyn?"

"He was killed by the fire. I found this on him."

"I feared so." Aelienor admitted.

"Let me see that dagger," Maria took the dagger with caution. Delicately rubbing her index finger across the sharp blade without cutting herself. "I don't see any clues here. No hidden compartments, initials, anything."

Jousen made himself known from around the corner. "I thought I dealt with you," Jousen began glancing from the dagger to Maria. "Hold on, how'd you get that?" Aelienor turned around catching Jousen's attention. "You were there..." Jousen crossed his arms with a smug expression pasted on his face. "I see what's going on here."

"How about we notify Lord Morrison for your arson crime?" Aelienor admitted.

"It's your words against mine. You wouldn't stand a chance. Besides, what proof do you have?" Jousen joked, waving his hands. "A dead man's dagger... You got pinned to a wall here. How about this... I finish what I started last night." Jousen reached out to his back pocket to reveal a larger dagger. "You know that I can handle myself when I'm outnumbered. It's your turn to see how you want to play this."

Vaughan subtly noticed the situation at hand.

"We just need to buy ourselves time. Make him confess to us again when Morrison and Wariner come here..." Lucius whispered to his friends as Jousen became angered by Lucius' lack of volume.

"If you're going to talk, you will talk to me. Only you knew how much trouble you've dawdled yourselves in." Jousen explained as he crossed his index and middle finger together with his idle hands.

"That they'll hang you for just looking at me the wrong way."

"Jousen, I know we met in a negative light," Aelienor said cunningly. "Perhaps I wanted you to spark that flame after all. If I knew about it sooner I would've helped you burn this corrupted city together." Aelienor's words surprised Jousen.

"I did misconstrue your timing outside his house. What about your friends here tinkering with the dagger of someone you loathe so much?"

"Sometimes it comes down to teach others lessons for their actions." Aelienor reminded. "This is my reminder of exactly that. You proved Quia from last night's performance you're not playing anymore."

"They had it all coming sooner or later. Sure we fought Aelienor and now I feel bad for not letting someone else join my efforts for the blaze that I caused," Jousen made known as he spun his dagger. Morrison took Jousen's dagger from beside him.

"Morrison?" Jousen asked confused.

Wariner shoved Jousen to the wall. Waiting for Vaughan to check his pockets finding keys to the lord's office.

"Is he supposed to have these?" Vaughan asked while Wariner stepped back to view the keys.

"No," Morrison admitted, taking the keys. Patting Jousen on the shoulder. "No wonder you always knew how to schmooze your way in my favor."

"I can explain my actions-"

"No need, causing that fire was your last mistake," Morrison admitted impulsively stabbing

Jousen repeatedly in the side. "I. Thought. I. Could. Trust. You. Traitor." Morrison exclaimed maniacally as each word became spaced out between each stab.

"I'm... sorry." Jousen cried out.

Vaughan pulled Morrison away with authority. "That's enough."

"Get off me," Morrison turned around sharply with blood on his face. Staring at Vaughan knowing a friendly face. Morrison came back to his senses. Glancing at the dagger before throwing it out of his sight.

By the time Morrison took notice of Wariner running off in the opposite direction. "Wariner come back."

Morrison looked back at Jousen. "This pitiful excuse of a man is the reason I cannot run for lord much longer. You'd think you would know someone, and then they do these horrid things." Morrison said.

The population underground watched from afar exchanging whispers.

"That didn't need to happen." Vaughan consoled.

"I agree," Morrison said with disappointment in his voice. Wariner exited opening the public exit. "This town is in your debt..." Morrison recalled extending his bloodied hand.

Lucius focused on Morrison's hand too long as Morrison discovered his mess.

"Excuse me," Morrison cleared his throat. "I need a minute with my son."

* Take Two *

Reaching the base Helba answered the door with a grave expression.

"What's going on Helba?" Vaughan asked.

"You're not going to like it"

"Tell me what happened."

"When Caroline had her baby, Jack gave his final breath."

"What?" Vaughan asked in shock.

Helba sidestepped out of Vaughan's way, hiding her glazed runny eyes.

It took only a moment for Vaughan to discover Jack's body.

"Who's Jack?" Maria asked.

"Vaughan's brother..." Lucius explained.

"I'm sorry." Maria comforted giving Vaughan a slow pat on the shoulder. He adjusted himself out of Maria's reach sliding her arm away with stubbornness.

"We're going to prevent his death. I don't care what it takes." Vaughan said.

Maria tilted her head confused, "Revenge won't fill in the void of him being gone."

"You haven't told them about the time traveling?" Kain summarized.

"I haven't had the chance." Lucius made known.

"Is that what you referred to earlier?" Aelienor asked with doubt in her voice.

"Sounds like witchcraft to me." Ernaldus said with haste.

"I don't care if any of you 'buy' it. We're going back in time whether you like it or not." Vaughan stated opening a drawer containing the Timeline Codex. Browsing the pages. "September 1550." Vaughan's eyes widened reading the pages with concern. "None of this occurred before... Jack's death, nor the fire." Vaughan thought for a moment. "Jack was supposed to stop the fire. It only makes sense."

"Just because something bad happens, you can't just pinpoint Omega." Reyner explained.

"If you knew Omega, you wouldn't say that," Vaughan explained, swiping away the tarp. Entering the time machine; a piece of technology ahead of its time. The futuristic device had a cherry wood finish on the outside.

The inside lit itself up upon entry with bright blinding lights. A few seconds passed until condensation filled on the inside leading into the room everyone stood once Vaughan entered. By the time the smoke had cleared Vaughan was nowhere to be seen.

"If you don't want him to affect your timeline you better enter that machine too," Pavel explained sitting on the windowsill.

"Will this machine affect my baby?" Caroline asked.

"I don't have a clear answer. It's your choice but if you don't enter you'll live in an alternate reality Vaughan creates." Helba explained.

One by one, entering the machine in the living room until it only left Jack.

Lucius being the last to enter, "Here goes nothing." He uttered before activating the machine.

The time machine teleported him back to the cave. Watching Draven sneak behind Jack." Watch out Jack." Lucius said with a sudden urgency.

Jack inadvertently tripped Draven before Draven could grapple him.

"You don't need to do this Draven..." Lucius said.

"How do you know me?" Draven asked confusedly. Jack smashed Draven's head into the nearest wall knocking him out.

"You used my machine, didn't you?" Jack asked, piecing the puzzle together. "Something is wrong. I feel it." Jack felt a sense of Deja Vu feeling a random pain where he was hit in the previous timeline.

"I did, he killed you-"

"I don't need to know it's in the future's past... we must only go forward in this timeline." "Well alright," Lucius admitted with a scoff, becoming blunt. "this note states my friends are at Quia, there's a fire going to happen soon, and we may still have time to stop it."

"This is a lot to take in..." Jack admitted scratching the back of his head. "I'm right behind you."

"We are going to Quia."

"I know a shortcut, there's this place underground..."

"I know."

"You do?" Taking Jack a second to process Lucius time traveled. "Right, of course, you do. This fire must've been serious." Jack commented on reaching the entrance to Quia.

Lucius swimming down the same well; not seeing the prism this time around. "We may still have time." Landing on both of his feet once he reached a certain depth. Rendezvousing with Vaughan. Vaughan hugged Jack surprising Jack.

"I must've really really died, huh?" Jack said.

"It won't happen again brother." Vaughan announced patting Jack's shoulder.

"The exit hasn't been locked," Lucius exited the underground base into the middle of Quia. Quiet as can be.

Aelienor peeked out from the corner waving them over. "Nolyn is in the deal with Jousen right now. It's going to go sour soon enough. What should we do?"

"Make sure that fire doesn't happen." Jack made known.

"I know where the fire starts. I'll wait out there to make sure that Jousen doesn't reach that point." Aelienor explained.

"I'll go with you," Vaughan added.

"Where's Maria, Ernaldus, or Gauvain?" Lucius questioned.

"They're sleeping at this point. I tried waking them, but they wouldn't wake."

A loud crash caused the group to split. Lucius and Jack followed the noise. Showing Jousen next to a broken chair. That caused the situation to be tense.

"Teigen Gervas... you know me more than Nolyn. I'm loyal and yet you want to side with him. All because of the ten thousand gold I'm willing to bet he offered you a higher cut to get me out of the picture..."

"It's not like that, you wouldn't understand..."

"That's funny that you say that. Saying that I'm the only one who understood you when you were in the deepest of holes, the darkest of times. Let those days be like the rest of them, a waste." Jousen shouted as Nolyn tackled him from the side. Jousen kicked away Nolyn.

Passing Nolyn's dagger to Teigen. Exchanging blows, Teigen picked up the dagger.

"Don't make me do this, Nolyn," Teigen stated, making Nolyn and Jousen stop fighting.

"Perhaps if you were a grown man you'd do something to save your real friend," Nolyn retorted, as Jousen slowly out powered Nolyn.

"I know my old pal is too much of a coward-" Jousen said interrupted by Teigen knocking him down.

"Nolyn... Jousen?" Teigen said as both men laid not making a sound. Teigen came closer, Jousen rushing a blade into Teigen's stomach.

Twisting the blade in the process. "Damn you for making me do this."

Once Jousen retracted the dagger Teigen fell on his knees as Jousen kicked Teigen away from him. "As for you Nolyn... you'll live but you'll be blamed for this whole ordeal. If that is, you survive the fire." Jousen explained laughing as he formed the bloodied dagger into his hand.

Jousen wiped off his hands as he moved a hidden compartment from the house to take out flint and steel. Looking back as Teigen as he attempted to get back up while holding his leg.

Jousen picked up a spear sitting beside the fireplace stabbing Teigen in the chest waiting until he gave his last breath. Retracting the spear and tossing it aside.

Jack kicked open the door as Lucius entered behind him. Catching Jousen by surprise.

"Leave before you regret it." Jousen threatened.

"That's not going to happen," Jack said as he walked slowly toward Jousen.

Jousen bolted out of the back door. Blocking his exit by shoving a chair on the outside. Jousen then tried again on creating a fire from the outside. Jack and Lucius ran around the entrance.

Reaching Jousen being held captive by Aelienor, Vaughan, and Morrison.

"I believe he has stolen your keys Morrison, an attempt of arson and murder," Vaughan explained.

"Are these things true Jousen?" Morrison asked.

"Morrison, you know me. These people are..." Jousen began to say. Interrupted by Jack frisking him revealing the flint and steel.

"He doesn't have the keys. Nevertheless, his evil intentions remain correct." Jack summarized.

"Show me Teigen's home," Morrison stated as Lucius led him there. Jack followed with Jousen in an arm lock.

Teigen laid lifeless in the living room. Nolyn woke up beside Teigen giving his statement. Being enough to toss Jousen in jail.

"How'd you know about the missing key?" Morrison asked.

"We thought he had the key. I apologize for the misunderstanding, as for the fire we didn't want to have a chance to occur." Vaughan explained.

"As much as you think you may know someone these troubling times. We need someone like you all to save our town. If you need anything from us, feel free to ask." Morrison explained with a sprinkling snow landing on his shoulder.

"We'll keep that in mind." Jack shook hands with Morrison.

Spending the night at Quia. Going back to the base within Klexta at first light.

Too much of their surprise their base was ransacked. As if it were vacant for several years. Helba tried to ease the news outside the base as Jack and Vaughan didn't have it.

"How did this happen?" Jack yelled out.

"Caroline experienced birth for the first time, for the second time. Reyner decided to get another professional to do so. Fatigued staying up for two days even though it was only one."

"I can't believe this... Omega is one step ahead of us. So many years of rivalry and now we can't prevent his next moves. We must be more cautious since he's gotten so bold..." Jack explained beginning to write. Based on the memory of the materials he needed.

Vaughan checked different drawers as he became relieved. "We still have the Timeline Codex. We need to move anyhow." Vaughan swiped through pages with haste.

"I feel that I'm to blame. I thought I was going to mess up and hurt Caroline's baby. From yesterday... I mean yesterday's today or just earlier today's today." Reyner confessed.

"You're making it too complicated, doc." Pavel corrected.

"No one's blaming you." Kain added.

"You'll get adjusted to the fatigue. Practice gains resistance." Helba retorted.

Ashlyn looked outside thinking out loud. "I remember there was a carriage parked nearby during and after the riot. Strangely, it's not here now."

"You didn't mention that to us until now. That could've been anyone. Especially Omega's men." Vaughan asked, agitated.

"With all the commotion, I didn't have the idea to mention that little detail."

"You told me that Reyner tried to revive me. Not sending me to a hospital but can send Caroline?" Jack said, stopping writing frantically about the time machine.

"It was at the moment. I failed to think about it at that point..." Reyner said as Jack ignored him.

"The nerve," Jack argued. "I died in vain. That's one less timeline where I'm no longer living. I helped you with your problems but when I need a moment of your time. I failed to be taken care of." Jack shook his head as he continued to write.

"I don't like your tone," Reyner argued. "I'm sorry that I'm not the perfect human being that you think you are. Why don't you blame this on Omega like you do when something is wrong? I wonder if this Omega even exists."

Vaughan focused his attention on reading the codex in more depth. "-In this timeline. Stephan's gotten the death penalty and will be hung later today. Can someone retrieve him, without killing anyone and bring him back to Hayden?"

"Why are we helping you again?" Aelienor questioned.

"Think of it this way, if Omega wants Stephan dead, we want him alive. It'll help you in the long run anyway." Pavel explained.

Lucius and his reunited friends left. Not taking long for Jack to argue with Reyner again. Becoming fainter distancing themselves from the hallway.

"They're an interesting set of people..." Gauvain carefully worded.

"They're good people at heart, although it's complicated to explain," Lucius answered.

"We should continue our efforts and get out of this island the first chance we get." Ernaldus summarized.

"Don't you think that the artifact will be missed if we take it..." Gauvain added.

"Remember what happened to the first boat, Ernaldus... it took off without us," Aelienor complained.

"So what...we'll wait until it comes back, ask Morrison for it, and be on our way."

"You were going to leave without me?" Lucius asked.

"We weren't." Maria started.

"We talked about it..." Gauvain added. Lucius sighed in response.

"We thought you were gone." Gauvain reminded.

"That hurts." Lucius started.

"We didn't hear from you... We had no leads. We feared the worst." Aelienor explained.

"We ended up staying," Maria confessed.

"That's just since the ship in Quia left too early." Ernaldus said.

"Ernaldus..." Aelienor said with annoyance.

"We're being truthful here. It's said and done now anyway."

"I must admit I have a confession about the All-Seeing Eye." Lucius said, gaining their attention.

"What about it?" Maria asked.

"I had it at one point but it was stolen and it has gotten into the King's hands. Therron they call him. The artifact is everything that the legends say and more. It's partially my fault, to begin with."

"That was the point of getting it. From the legends and myths. I don't see the problem... Aside from Therron." Gauvain said confused.

"Were you chosen?" Aelienor asked.

"I didn't touch it. I held the magnetic seal it came with. I know someone who did touch it, that died shortly after." Lucius explained.

"That doesn't sound good at all," Maria confessed.

"If Therron gives in and touches it and lives. I fear the worst."

"What about we leave before we get too involved," Gauvain explained.

"We're already too deep in. Besides, I want to help get Therrons' hands away from the All-Seeing Eye, then we can move onto leaving this place."

"I don't blame you," Aelienor admitted with a sigh. "I'd do the same thing. After all, we did come here for the adventure. May as well have fun doing it."

"If it exists its amazing to even think about. But if you want to continue to help Jack to get the relic away from the King then I'm with you." Maria said with a smile.

"That seems like a horrible idea." Gauvain said with concern.

"If Aelienor's in... I don't have much of a choice." Ernaldus crossed his arms.

"That's the spirit." Maria said cheerfully.

"Are you serious?" Gauvain questioned as he took a long breath. "I guess you are.

"I'm glad no one's leaving," Wariner said, intervening, wrapping his arm around Lucius and Gauvain; who flinched. "I won't say a word. Quia honor." Wariner smirked. "I know there are times I want to leave to see more of the world on what's out there." Wariner remarked rhetorically laughing "If you change your mind at any point I would like to go with you."

"We'll consider that for when the time comes. Do you know how we could get Stephan out of his rut?" Lucius asked.

"That's all I needed to hear," Wariner said, handing Lucius a map of Therron's castle. " Amazing that we were able to enter without being caught. For the exception to Pavel that is..."

"How'd you know?"

"Word travels fast," Wariner reminded. "Just swipe a map off of one of the guards like I did with this one, on my way to catch up to you. The guards are people too, which means they get lost just as often. Sure they may work here but there are constant renovations."

"Thanks," Lucius said browsing the map. Seven total entrances. "I expect there to be a lot of guards at the jail. It'll be tough to weave through with us all together."

"Vaughan wants me to teach you how to fight. That'll be the time to do so. If your friends want to learn a thing or two in the process, even better."

"Jack doesn't want us to kill anyone." Aelienor made known.

"Who said anything about killing?" Wariner asked. "A little hand-to-hand combat won't hurt."

"Won't these guards won't have swords?" Ernaldus questioned.

"I'm counting on them having weapons of all sorts. I'll teach you how to disarm while we're at it as well. I'm confident in my ability to do so. And faith that you'll get it in no time. Just do me a favor and don't bite off more than you can chew." Wariner joked.

"What if we get hurt or die?" Gauvain asked worriedly.

"If you get hurt, you'll learn a lesson about what not to do in combat. But don't worry I'll come in it if it becomes rough."

"You seem either bold or reckless." Lucius said.

"I'll let you guess," Wariner chucked. "Now stop dwindling around and let's get going." Pushing Lucius forward.

Seeing two guards, Lucius crouched by a nearby bush. Wariner whistled loud enough to gain the attention of one of the guards.

Wariner jumped out of cover behind Lucius kicking the guard in the gut. Using pressure points within the vulnerable part of the armor set. Dropping the guard without much effort. Dragging the guard into a bush.

Lucius took his turn, having trouble whistling. Causing Ernaldus to chuckle, making the guard survey the noise. Maria targeted the guards' leg agitating the guard.

Aelienor used the downed guard's shield, bashing the opposing guard in the back of the head, falling face-first into the dirt.

"That's one way to take care of it," Wariner carefully worded. "This may be more work than I thought." Wariner walked over the down guards patting Lucius on the back. "If you can't whistle, a loud noise will do. Like a laugh for example."

"I'll keep that in mind."

Wariner led into the corridors inside the castle. "Where do we go next?"

"The next two rights, and it'll lead us to the prisoners," Lucius stated reading the map.

A group of five guards blocked the path forward each with a different custom-made weapon from Therron's blacksmith.

Wariner whistled at the finely made weaponry shining into his view. "What I would do to buy one of those for myself one day." The whistle gained the attention of one of the guards.

"Time to see how each of you can take on one-to-one combat. They'll easily surrender without a weapon if they don't have each other to rely on." Wariner explained. "No waiting it out this time Gauvain." Wariner ran ahead to single out the alerted guard holding a halberd.

Using the weapon as the guard swung, using momentum against him. Hitting the guard with the halberd. Causing the guard to stumble and disarming the guard's halberd.

Wariner backed himself into a corner. Becoming surrounded. Swinging the halberd keeping the guards at bay.

"What are we waiting for?" Maria asked, rushing out of hiding to disarm a guard. The guard swung their greatsword at Maria, ducking the blow. Using the slowness of the guard's armor to her advantage pulling his arm. Colliding his helmet onto her knee knocking the guard onto his back. The guards turned their focus on Maria while she had trouble raising the greatsword.

"You're going to hurt yourself." Gauvain recalled, grabbing a guards' leg on Maria's blindside.

"Get off me filth," The guard argued, swinging at Gauvain with his dagger. Gauvain dodged the dagger getting kicked in the forehead. "You'll regret this..." Gauvain loosened his grip holding his face. The guard spun his dagger before jolting forward at Gauvain.

Ernaldus forced the blade out of the guard's hand, elbowing the guards' jaw. Picking the next guard insight into a headlock.

Lucius intercepted the last fleeing guard, shoving him into the nearest wall.

"You're naturals," Wariner complimented, watching Ernaldus drop the unconscious guard. "Loot them, one of them should have the key for the cells."

"No need." Stephan pointed out a trail of his own defeated henchmen behind him.

"You got out?"

"I was able to find my way out.".

"I wondered where you went," Stephan sighed with relief. "I thought you died..."

"Not yet, must be doing something right." Stephan scouted ahead.

"One step at a time, we aren't out yet." Wariner recalled slumming along holding his injured leg.

"Guards," Stephan whispered, going into hiding with Lucius. "Who's your crew?"

"Think of them as the rescue crew."

"Fair enough," Exiting the castle, Stephan turned to an alternate route to arrive at Hayden's base." It won't be long before they do a city search."

They discovered Hayden pacing at the base speaking to Lex. "Do you think this is how we fall? Losing men, one by one. For the sweet nectar of vengeance?"

Lex smiled upon Stephan entering. "I don't think so."

Hayden twirled his dagger in disappointment at his desk until he heard the sudden chatter. Changing from his self-pitying slouching into pure excitement to hear the latest news. Dropping the dagger onto the ground as he lifted himself from the dark oak chair.

"I hope you don't mind me bringing guests." Stephan joked.

"It depends on the occasion."

"To finish what we started." Lucius said.

"I told you Lucius anything less than one hundred and ten percent would be unacceptable," Hayden bouted, stomping over to Lucius. He shook his head for a moment before scoffing. "And yet you're here with Stephan. I don't know what to say."

"Thank you?" Lucius questioned. Hayden gave a distant look to Lucius in response.

"I'm sorry for the failure of the mission. I have no one to blame but myself." Stephan added.

"We'll have another opportunity soon enough," Hayden announced. "More recent news, Ashlyn wormed herself out of our cells."

"Any good news?" Stephan asked.

Nadim burst inside, kicking the heavy doors entering the base with excitement. "I found a certain individual of interest to us that can lead us to the artifact."

"There's our opportunity," Hayden rallied. "Are you all in?"

"Tell us everything Nadim." Stephan said.

Memory IV – Mercy

* Journey To Dorton *

"So why is this man so keen on staying in Dorton?" Lucius asked Flynn and Nadim. Rowing their way toward the distant island. Becoming impatient in the last few hours.

"It may be the only place Bishop feels safe." Nadim noted.

"Is that his name?" Flynn asked.

"It's a codename or surname to hide his identity since he gained Therron as an enemy. His real name isn't important."

"This whole ordeal is asking for an ambush," Flynn admitted. "Do either of you believe that Therron is the chosen one?"

"I hope not," Lucius said. "I'm a bit concerned that I haven't noticed much of a difference with him holding it."

"It wouldn't feel changed if Therron doesn't want us to feel a difference." Nadim added.

"Now you're trying to confuse me." Flynn chuckled with a tease.

"When Paul had the eye for a brief time. He died with strange happenings occurring beside him." Lucius stated.

"I'm sorry." Flynn consoled patting Lucius' back. "What do you mean by strange occurrences?"

"I don't know how else to say it, the world simply evolved around him-" Lucius began.

"Watch out..." Nadim said abruptly, distracted by Lucius, crashing the rowboat into a large rock. Exiting the boat and onto the large rock.

"By the size of this... We would've noticed it a while ago..." Flynn said as Nadim examined the damage to the boat.

"The boat's far from functioning now..." Nadim said disappointed. Taking Lucius' shocked expression to follow his eyes.

"How are we going to get out of all of this water?" Flynn questioned.

"I have another ordeal." Nadim focused his attention on the water transitioning to solid.

"Strange occurrences, huh..." Flynn asked as he knocked on the ice with his knuckles. "It's crystal clear and hard as a rock. I can't believe it."

"We'll have to walk the rest of the way." Lucius admitted.

Nadim cautiously put his body weight on the ice as he slipped at first. Regained his balance as Flynn held his shirt. "It may be solid here but for all, we know it could be weak somewhere else. The island isn't much further so walk slowly and spread out."

Lucius allowed Flynn to go ahead of him. Lucius eased his way on the ice after both Nadim and Flynn had a decent length apart. Each step gave chills down Lucius' spine from the sudden wind. Lucius took another step creating a crack. Lucius rose his foot away tripping into a small pool of arctic water.

"Nadim... Flynn, I ran into some trouble." Lucius warned.

"Are you alright?" Flynn stopped to question as he walked toward Lucius.

Nadim stood in concern, "Don't come any closer to him, Flynn."

"I have to help him, Nadim."

"I can handle myself. Keep going forward." Lucius stated sliding himself out of the water. Another crackling sound made itself known. Lucius' eyes followed the gap of weakened ice spreading around like wildfire.

Lucius noticed a man floating on the ice toward Lucius from another direction.

"Don't move I got you." Flynn recalled reaching out to Lucius.

"Do you see that man?" Lucius asked.

"What man?" Flynn glanced around him in denial. "You're hallucinating from the cold, grab my hand." Flynn reached out.

Lucius recalled the familiar man coming closer; Kion the mage.

"Ill minded..." Kion stated melting the ice behind Lucius. Missing Flynn's hand as he slid closer to the water.

"What do you want?"

"There are many things I want, Lucius. Like time to stop halting and alternating itself. It would seem that the ones that have been caused as of late I seem to be pointed in your direction." Kion retrieved the wooden box from Lucius' pocket. "Wouldn't want this to go into the wrong hands."

Lucius attempted to raise to his feet falling into the water holding the ice with his hands. "We can talk about this."

"Humanity as a whole is at risk and you are the pawn. The end of days will occur sooner than you realize. Tell me, Who is your leader?"

"The one who calls himself Omega," Lucius admitted speaking the first name that came from his shivering lips. Having trouble balancing himself he raised his hand toward Kion. "Can you help me up?"

"With the information, I sought. Your willingness to cooperate grants what you truly deserve. A quick death." Kion admitted poking Lucius' eyes with a flick. Lucius lost his grip flaring into the deep waters.

"Lucius." Flynn exclaimed, jumping into the water after him.

"No Flynn." Nadim yelled out running forward. Crashing into a weak patch of ice.

Lucius held his breath, squinted his eyes grabbing Flynn nearby, having trouble coming to the surface, tied up with nearby seaweed.

Lucius pulled Flynn toward him reaching an opening. Flynn and Lucius took turns coughing water upon exiting the freezing water.

"Don't you ever give the idea of walking on ice again." Flynn said with shortness of breath.

"Good idea." Lucius nodded with exhaustion.

Flynn looked around him crawling on the weakened ice. "Where's Nadim?"

Faint banging on the other side of the ice gained Lucius' attention. "Over here."

"Nadim, you'll be ok just watch out," Flynn took his sword from his sheathe to swing at the ice generating more cracks after each hit.

"Are you trying to kill us?" Lucius reminded.

"I'm trying to save my friend."

"Look for another hole for starters."

"What other holes?" Flynn asked maniacally.

Lucius scratched at the weakened ice Nadim was in front of. Lucius patted his pockets discovering his dagger was lost from the water.

Flynn attempted to gain Nadim's attention to point to the nearest hole in the ice. With one last-ditch effort, Nadim pounded on the ice before hopelessly sinking into the depths.

"Nadim no..." Flynn yelled out, shivering walking back to the hole.

"He's gone." Lucius admitted holding Flynn back.

"Let go of me. I can't leave him."

"Listen to me Flynn," Lucius reminded Flynn. "Let's get off this ice."

* Bishop's Domain *

Reaching the land, the ice behind them melted.

"With Bishop transferring the eye to Therron, do you think he took part in the water becoming ice?" Flynn asked.

"One way to find out," Lucius admitted. "Where would Bishop be located if I was him?"

"This may be a stretch, how about the only building above the hill."

"Answer me this then, why would someone betray someone like Therron."

"Feel free to ask him once we meet him."

Entering the building, Flynn looked at a toppling bowl of soup in the living room.

"We aren't alone," Flynn commented with his stomach growling. "Food does sound good."

"We'll eat something once we get back," Lucius said, placing the bowl back on the table. "Bishop must've seen us coming."

"Must've thought we're Therron men," Flynn admitted hearing heavy shuffling above them as dust fell. "I think we may have found our runaway."

"Be sure to check each corner." Lucius reminded as Flynn passed Lucius with a similar crouching motion.

A sudden creek made both of them cringe. Taking a moment to survey their surroundings before moving forward.

"It looks clear..." Flynn said continuing a few steps ahead. A soft whistle released as an arrow flew past him, scratching Flynn's ear.

Following a shattering thud into the glass behind them to mask Flynn's grunting.

Flynn rushed into cover holding the edge of his now bleeding ear. "I know we didn't ask for invitations, but we are trying to help." Flynn commented.

"We?" Bishop asked.

"Really Flynn..." Lucius recalled with a sharp whisper as Flynn shrugged in response.

"If we wanted to attack you we would've," Flynn scoffed. "You don't even know how many of us are here, we could take you down easily," Flynn said waving Lucius on. Going the opposite direction of the stairs with the T formation. "Our squad has been sent to inform us that you're not safe here and Therron's men are going to be here any moment. Now if you come with us..."

"Come with you?" Bishop rose a brow in response."If I'm not safe here, I'm not safe anywhere..."

Lucius peeked his head to focus on Bishop's path passing from cover to cover. Lucius lost Bishop in his sight from a blind spot. Entering a side room in front of him. Seeing Bishops arms reading the bow for another arrow. Bishop peaked at the door Lucius hid and turned around at another door slightly ajar.

Lucius pushed the door faintly, creaking loudly gaining Bishop's attention.

Bishop aimed his bow waiting for someone to peer through.

"If you don't want our help then fine," Flynn admitted breaking the silence when Lucius failed to move forward. "We'll get out of your way and let Therron's men do what they please. Knowing how strict they are, you'll likely get hung for your crimes." Flynn yelled out, gaining the attention of Bishop once more. More than enough distraction for Lucius to carry forward past the creaking door.

Picking his moment once Bishop turned his back. Lucius ran over to Bishop taking his main hand and chest to pin him against the wall. After a few whacks of the back of his palm to the rough stone wall. Bishop released the bow.

"Please just leave me alone." Bishop pleaded as Lucius kicked his bow away.

"We're doing this for the greater good. No matter how many times you shoot at us." Lucius explained as Flynn left his cover.

"There's only two of you?" Bishop asked comically.

"Enough to get the job done," Flynn admitted.

"I could've taken both of you."

"You didn't, so it doesn't matter," Lucius said, releasing Bishop as they guarded him.

"What do you want from me?" Bishop crossed his arms. "Is it gold... It always ends up being the wealth that people want."

"We want information about Therron," Flynn explained.

Flynn examined the window behind Bishop seeing multiple newly arrived boats on the shoreline. Multiple heavily armored guards entering the building. "I've never seen this much security before in my life. I didn't know the ambush would be this major."

"Then you must've not known what I had done. The question is how'd they find me so quick?" Bishop rhetorically asked.

"What did you do?" Lucius asked.

"I didn't receive payment for retrieving the eye for Therron after I had taken it from a resting crew of bandits..."

"Those weren't bandits, I was there." Lucius corrected.

"Could've fooled me," Bishop admitted. "Nevertheless, he trusted me to lock the safe he keeps it in when he doesn't have it in his grasp. Only I know the code, I attempted to steal it when I failed to steal it myself. I know I'm a dead man if they find me and decided to flee here..." Bishop summarized as the door began to thud.

"Open up Bishop."

"How are we getting out of here?" Bishop reminded.

"One of their boats, none of them are guarded. Quick now." Flynn reminded.

"But the windows?" Bishop asked.

"Already on it," Lucius added. "Gather more curtains as I tie this."

Breaching the door the guards flooded the room. "I heard voices in this room sir. I'm sure of it." One of the guards noted.

"Then it would seem that someone at one point in time was here." Another guard commented as he grabbed the tied curtains.

"Therron won't accept any negative results. Bishop's knowledge is vital." The heavy guard captain ordered. "We must make haste to continue the search."

"I can't believe that worked," Bishop said with excitement, entering one of the boats with Lucius and Flynn.

"Now that we saved you. Tell us about this safe." Flynn said pointing his sword at Bishop, his expression turned grim once more.

* Over The Horizon *

"Today we lost a great man, Nadim Tennant. A man who never questioned orders. Someone who believed what he fought for. With Bishop on our side, his death will be the last of many casualties Therron takes from us." Hayden stated placing a cross on a plot of land in the graveyard.

"I can't believe Nadim's gone. The other day he delivered my son." Caroline explained to Lucius stepping forward placing flowers on his grave, paying her respects as she walked back to Lucius. "Being cordial made me feel more comfortable than being around Reyner." Caroline passed by Lucius sitting next to Lex.

"I suppose it's my turn," Lex said with a broken voice. "I appreciate you all coming here, I do." Standing up to make his peace with Nadim. "You were fearless with anything life throws your way. I wish I could be half as brave as you." Lex stated holding the cross for a moment before going back to his seat next to Natasha, Nadim's wife. "Do you want to say some words?"

Natasha remained mute. Covering her glowing bloodshot eyes into Lex's shirt. Lex hugged her in response.

Lucius sat up to give a moment of silence with Nadim while Natasha was holding Lex. His wandering eyes pinpointed Ashlyn, who was subtly waving him over.

"I know this is a bad time but since you were gone. Kain's friend, Magnus, warned that if we don't retrieve the eye for them, they'll kill Floros."

"Does this ever end?" Lucius asked with a cry.

"We just have to play it out. Without Jack's machine, we have no room for mistakes. He was able to retrieve some parts, but we need more time. See what can be done to convince Hayden to work with us and tell them to meet us in Quia."

"I'll see what I can do," Lucius said, walking to Stephan, who finished making his peace to Nadim.

"This may be strange to say but I feel that I could've done something to prevent his death." Stephan explained.

"I know that feeling when I tried to save him." Lucius said.

"That's the thing. You saved Flynn, and he's more grateful to live than he's ever been. But this is different. I feel that I've cheated death whereas Nadim didn't. This makes me think that I've been given another chance but I can't shake why."

"With Therron owning the eye it's only a matter of time he'll do something like this again, and they'll be someone laying next to Nadim."

"With such loss of moral support. I don't know if we can gather the strength to go against Therron. Many of our allies we rallied were killed..." Stephan admitted with difficulty. "Back when I was in jail. Therron's eyes spelled out fear. He had doubt and withheld it to his people.

Announcing the death penalty, he knew deep down that would ignite the flame of this war... And we failed to capitalize." Stephan shook his head as he broke eye contact. "Now too much of my surprise you came back to help me out. It matters not... It should be in the grave, not Nadim."

"That's no way to talk. We'll have another opening and be greater than the last. We first must focus on the eye. The origin of his power... Without that he's just a man. We aren't the only ones suffering. This whole island is from Therron's wickedness. We just need to let the public know they can join too."

"If you're implying you want us to join. I'm in. But you and I alone will not convince Hayden. You know how he was when you started. Strange, how it wasn't so long ago. But I know you're one of us. I'll help you to convince others." Stephan said, patting Lucius' back wandering over to Lex.

Lucius laid eyes on Flynn, isolated from the rest of the funeral service. Laying beside a tree, next to Aelienor holding Caroline's baby.

"You could say Nadim filled his purpose delivering God's gift," Flynn snickered weakly as his smile depleted. "It's hard to believe he's gone."

"I understand how it feels to lose someone close. My mom passed away not long ago. It seems like it's been an eternity."

"I'm sorry Aelienor and your father?"

"He was never in the picture. If he was, my mom never mentioned him. My friends are all I have left now. I'm sure they have their reasons to stick together. My brother would say the same if he wasn't such a loggerhead."

"How'd she die?" Flynn asked as he leaned closer to Aelienor wrapping his arms around her. Aelienor dropped the topic noticing Lucius, raising. Flynn retracted his arm, scratching his head.

"How are you, Lucius?" Aelienor admitted.

"I'm alright. Has Caroline named her baby?"

"It's a boy, and she's still deciding. I'm surprised she let me have the honor of watching her son so soon. Then again these past few days I've gotten to know so many people so well."

"What did you do when we were gone?" Lucius asked, shifting his focus to Flynn as the baby cooed gaining Aelienor's attention.

"Recon around the King's castle, his estate, and learning more about him through his ranked men. I dare say I know him more than I know you."

"I promised Nadim when we first met that if we were killed in a battle that we would forgive the killer. The longer I think about it, the promise is becoming harder to keep. We were oblivious to Therron then." Flynn started wiping his eyes.

"You knew about Therron before?" Aelienor asked.

"We did. He was a small pawn at that time. If you could believe it he worked for Marius Kristell. Times change I suppose." Flynn took a deep breath glancing at the newborn. "After the ice broke. I couldn't shake the feeling when you said someone else was with us. Did you see Therron among us?"

"No, he wasn't." Lucius carefully worded. "I must have been imagining things."

"I figured."

"Times like these we need our friends to be there. Aelienor and I have friends that want to take Therron down just as much as you do, perhaps even more. The same ones that saved Stephan.

They think it's time to end his reign. Would you like to join us?"

Flynn looked away from the baby and cleared his throat. "How can I say no to restoring peace. Count me in." Flynn stood up watching Hayden pace before entering his nearby tent. "I know he'll need some convincing."

Lucius followed Flynn's meeting with Lex and Stephan before entering the tent.

"Do you want me to come back later?" Bishop asked Hayden suddenly.

"Stay, whatever they want to say you'll want to know as well." Hayden admitted.

"Lucius has informed us of a group wanting to take Therron down. I know we're close-knit and with more additions come with risk but it's about time for some reinforcements. With this new group, we will have a better chance of success. You may have noticed some of them came over to the funeral with good intentions." Stephan summarized.

"What do they want in return?" Hayden retorted.

"You'll have to follow their orders on how to proceed..." Lucius explained as Hayden cut him off.

"I have led for almost a decade. Eight of those years I've seen the loyalty of my father's men that I knew their names by heart. Meeting their families and ate side by side at dinner tables. On one strange day, those who you don't see here today betrayed my father. So asking to put my leadership aside to strangers," Hayden shook his head in denial. "Not now, not again." Hayden opened a bottle of mead, taking a chug. "This plan you've concocted is sketchy at best."

"What other choice do we have Hayden, this may be our last chance," Lex added.

Hayden passed the mead around. "Look at the bigger picture, whether they are genuine. They see us as weak and broken, they seek power. They see the truth that I'm the rightful heir and it is common sense for them to aid. But once Therron is gone then this mystery group will have only me remain as an obstacle." Hayden watched Lucius take a swig before he handed the mead back to Hayden. "I'll meet up with this group. I'm not a leader because I'm nice, it's because I make the tough calls."

"If you do decide to decline this group's offer, think of Natasha and the rest of the islands' population when you say, I'll pass," Flynn said, exiting the tent.

Hayden contemplated Flynn's words finishing the bottle. "I wish Kerwyn was here."

"When you are ready, we'll be at Quia," Lucius said, raising the tent's flap.

"Lucius," Hayden said as he turned, "Tomorrow would've been Nadim's birthday if we do strike it better be then."

* A Temperamental Alliance *

"I'm glad everyone could make it to Quia," Lucius announced. "Morrison agreed to overthrow Therron. Is everyone here sure they want to join? This will be the last opportunity to leave now. There's no going back from here."

"I'm tired of the constant thought of always being one step behind from Therron's grasp. So yes it's about time for his downfall." Hayden confessed.

"We've caught wind of your informant and it's unfortunate your losses you've had to get to this point. I hope you understand that Floros, Kain's boy, is under the threat of death. We'll need to obtain the eye itself before we go after Therron." Jack explained.

"Rosane handed me this in secret," Morrison sat down on the device in the middle of the table. "The All-Seeing Eye's magnetic seal, it's cracked but it works. Who wants the responsibility?" Morrison asked as a few others exchanged looks before Lucius took it.

"It'll buy us time to retrieve the eye from far distances but that's where Bishop comes in," Jack noted.

"Therron, will we kill him or not?" Flynn asked.

"In due time. First the eye, so he doesn't have a way out." Helba stated.

"We gathered Therron's uniforms, so we can reach the vault undetected. If we do not have to fight, we won't. Bishop will enter the codes so Lucius can retrieve the eye. Half of us will attack any opposition and lead them away. The others will protect Lucius and Bishop and meet back here when all is done. Then we do the deal to save Floros. Then kill Therron. It must be in that order." Jack explained.

"You want us to be decoys?" Hayden joked in a heckling matter.

"Think of it that way if you want. Make sure not to kill anyone, they are simply working there because of Therron. His men will abandon them if he doesn't have power..." Jack explained.

"I don't like your plan. It's one-sided. Our side would be carrying more risk."

"I assure it isn't. I've thought about this, worked out all the possible kinks. That'll be the best way." Jack explained.

"It does sound tricky to pull off but I'm up to it." Lex stated.

"I agree with Hayden." Flynn said.

"Of all the work I've done to help you all out, Jack helped me in the corner and hasn't failed me." Lucius explained.

"How do you know there are no new kinks?" Hayden asked, narrowing his eyes at Jack.

"As Bishop, Pavel can keep him busy if things go awry." Jack explained.

"Pavel Dunwell?" Hayden asked as he entered the meeting room.

"Remember me?" Pavel asked.

"It's hard not to. You were with my father during his reign..."

"I was."

"You also were one of the people who betrayed my father."

"I'm a different person now."

"If you mean a lapdog who backstabs when you find someone who pays better than the last. Then I'd believe you." Hayden corrected pounding the table with a temper. "This plan will not work..."

"That's not needed. Unless you want to stand up like Nadim, you will sit down." Jack threatened.

"I knew this was a waste of time when you first mentioned Ashlyn," Hayden said agitatedly. "We got off on the wrong foot, but we must put that aside," Ashlyn explained.

"You tried to kill me and then add the traitorous Dunwell to the mix..."

"We both need each other," Vaughan reminded. "You can disband after the deeds are done."

"What will it take for him to go on our side?" Aelienor asked whispering to Flynn holding his hand.

"What do you think about this partnership Hayden," Flynn counseled. "If we don't agree then how can we give Nadim justice?" he logically asked.

Hayden took a long breath sitting back down. "I will set aside my grievances no matter how much it eats me up inside. For the greater good and on your terms but you'll have to promise me one thing."

"What is that?" Jack asked.

"I'll deliver the killing blow to Therron."

"That's fine by us. Do we have a deal?" Jack asked, extending his hand. Hayden took a minute as he shook his hand. Jack revealed the uniforms Helba brought. "Meet us in Therron's courtyard with the uniforms tomorrow morning."

"We will." Hayden replied leaving with his allies.

Lucius began to follow Hayden as Jack stopped him. "I would like to invite you and your colleagues for supper," Jack stated.

"I can never say no to a meal." Lucius joked.

Helba lit a campfire in the middle of Quia. Morrison handed a bowl of barley porridge as it became ready to serve.

"What makes you think we can trust Hayden, Lucius?" Jack asked, thanking Morrison.

"He cares for his people. Some stubborn but I'm sure his attitude will fix itself."

"I hope you're right," Jack huddled with Lucius. "When the plan goes into motion I want you to keep an eye on Hayden, shadow him tomorrow." Jack moved away stirring his porridge with a bone spoon. Causing the heat of the freshly cooked meats and vegetables to reach his Grecian nose creating a flattering savory aroma. "The reason why we saved Therron is since his ancestry has a vital role in the future." Jack sat the bowl beside him. "Even if I mentioned that to Hayden he couldn't care less. It's a shame I'm still working on the machine."

"Once you finish this time machine... can you show me how to operate it?" Morrison asked.

"I don't mind," Jack thought a minute. "as long as I'm with you."

"How long do you think Kion will be going after Omega?" Maria asked, taking a few bites.

"Hopefully long enough that Omega won't be our problem anymore. I sure hope we can save your son... before it's too late Kain." Vaughan explained.

"You're telling me, I've been thinking about him since he was taken." Kain burned his tongue as he took a bite. "About that Codex that tells you when major events occur... Are we on the book as well?" Kain stated.

"I know that you burned yourself before you did if that's what you're asking." Jack joked.

"I never thought about that until now.

Doesn't that mean you could always pick the best outcomes?" Reyner added.

"It's not that simple," Vaughan explained. "You have to live throughout that timeline to know if it's the best outcome per se. For all of your best interests, I ask all of you to not be curious enough to look at it."

"It'll be best to get some shut-eye for the big day tomorrow," Gauvain stated.

"I hear you Gauvain," Ernaldus stated licking his bowl clean. The conversations slowly came to a halt as they laid on the ground on their sides, taking turns snoozing.

Memory V - Separate Ways

* Corruption *

"Try to keep up Lucius," Maria said in a cheerful tone. Waving Lucius over, before he was able to catch up, she continued to run further into the woods.

"I know... You're just too fast." Lucius said as an excuse.

"Let's see what Parker is up to. He never delved into his job life..." Maria said climbing a tree next to the fishing dock.

"You act like he's your dad." Lucius said as she pulled him up to the branch.

"I wish he was sometimes."

"How come Maria? I'm sure Silas is a fantastic father."

"He can be at times, it's just that Silas has been acting off lately."

"Perhaps it's since you call your dad by his first name."

"He's not my birth father, I couldn't do that to my real dad. It doesn't seem to bother Silas any."

"Like Silas, I've gotten the same feeling about my dad. He's acted strange as well." Lucius confessed watching their dad's exiting a building with their boss.

"Whatever they're talking about... They don't seem happy." Maria admitted.

The fishing captain threw a dry cloth on the ground angrily pointing at the water behind him. With the ripped nets that led several types of fish to escape from their father's fishing boats. Once the conversation ended, Silas and Parker left the site.

"We should follow them," Lucius confessed as Maria agreed. Remaining in the outskirts of the woods they followed their fathers into a bar. Lucius stopped himself from continuing. "Why would they go there?"

"Mom says that Silas only goes when bad things happen. Do you think they got fired?"

"I hope not. They've had trouble as is keeping things afloat."

Maria and Lucius waited for their fathers to come out of Gauvain's fathers', Dorian's Pub. Hours passed too much of their surprise Gauvain exited. With fresh blood on his shirt, Gauvain began to weep on the corner.

Maria rushed to him, "What happened Gauvain?"

"Silas and Parker entered then the attack began..." Gauvain said out of breath.

"The attack?" Maria asked.

"So much blood it was hard to keep up on whose blood was who's..." Gauvain's voice cracked as he looked at Maria taking a deep breath. "I'm sorry, it was a bloodbath."

"I must go inside," Maria stated as Gauvain and Lucius held her back. Holding back tears of his own. "Why did this happen?"

"I don't know... Don't go inside. I don't want you to see that dramatized experience I went through." Gauvain explained as they left, people passed them by entering the bar behind them to discover the aftermath. "I'm going to go home and be alone for a while. I believe you two should do the same."

"I can't believe it," Maria said watching Gauvain branch off to his home.

"I'm here for you Maria," Lucius said embracing Maria.

Maria repeated herself with an echo. "Lucius... I can't believe it." Lucius awoke as Maria finished. "Look at the sky..." Lucius rubbed his eyes seeing the violet sky and dark nimbus clouds forming within minutes making Lucius speechless.

"It may look beautiful but with how quickly it formed. This means that Therron time is coming to an end," Jack explained waking Caroline. "Are you sure you want to tag along Caroline?"

"I'm fit and able," Caroline retorted quickly as her baby began to whine. "Never mind. I'll stay with him. "

"I'll stay with you Caroline to make sure everything goes well," Morrison stated. Thunder roared near their location.

"That must be a sign," Vaughan explained. Morrison led Caroline inside as Jack led everyone to the courtyard.

"Where's Hayden and his people at?" Ernaldus asked, looking around as rain started to pour.

"We're here. We just needed to gather some last-minute precautions." Lex explained coming out of hiding as the rest of the group came into vision.

"Where's the rest of your group?" Hayden asked.

"Back at Quia, we do have a baby over there needing to be taken care of." Jack explained.

"Where do we go, Bishop?" Hayden asked dismissively.

"No matter the disguise, the guard will notice me." Bishop admitted.

"Do not fret, focus with the vault and you'll be fine." Hayden stated.

Bishop entered Therron's castle with fright.

"We found Bishop. Report to entrance zero-two." One of the guards remarked immediately as he passed through the front doors.

"You must protect me. I knew it wouldn't have worked." Bishop reminded.

"Just run to the vault we can follow," Lex explained. Bishop made his way through the castle by memory as he saw an opening. Reaching downstairs that was surprisingly quiet. "It's somewhere down here."

A faint tinkling noise gained Lucius' attention. Seeing a plaque with a sword on it glimmering. He decided to poke the sword, causing a mechanism trigger opening a hidden wall revealing the vault. "Here it is."

The group huddled together guarding Bishop. As he fidgeted with the locked safe.

"I need some room." Bishop started waving them away.

"This is easier than expected. Why do we need to divert Therron's attention anyway?" Hayden asked Jack.

Jack pointed to the stairs as if on cue seeing Therron and his best guards come down the stairs. "That's why."

"Have you done this before Jack?" Hayden asked confused.

"This is the first time. But after doing the work that I do after a while you just know these things." Jack said as the thud of the safe opened. Lucius turned to the noise as the magnetic seal flowed toward it.

Therron pointed down at the men downstairs glitching in the process. "After those men. Kill them all." Therron ordered as Jack's team rushed toward an alternate exit as Hayden's team remained. One of the guards shot an arrow, whizzing by Hayden. Hayden moved his head in time entering Bishop's back.

"Bishop's down." Flynn reported with udder shock.

"It's our time to strike." Hayden snagged the magnetic seal from Lucius, bee lining at Therron. Shooting beams at Therron and his men. Therron fell back before Hayden had a clear shot.

"We need him alive Hayden." Lucius bickered as a heavily armored guard blocked his path.

"You've got to deal with me now. Without you the rebel group will surely end." The heavy guard stated shoving Lucius to the ground while holding Lucius down with his foot. The guard swung as Lucius rolled away in time.

Unbalancing the guard momentarily for Lucius to retrieve his sword from beside him. Clashing swords, this time the heavy guard had more force than the last. The guard let go for a moment before meeting steel once more.

The guard's sword jolted down to the beginning of Lucius' blade. Resulting in Lucius' ring finger falling to the ground from a clean chop. Lucius fell on the ground in agony.

"Goodbye so-called hero." The heavy guard chuckled maniacally.

Gauvain rushed to Lucius' side, knocking the guard into a wall bumping him into the concrete wall. Something in Gauvain snapped shaking the guard head back and forth to the wall until the guard fell to his side, not fighting back. Gauvain looked at Lucius' injury briefly.

"Are you alright?" Gauvain asked as another guard tackled him before he could give a thorough look. Taking out a dagger toward Gauvain. Gauvain held the dagger in place before it could enter his chest, kicking a sword to Lucius.

Lucius attempted to raise the blade as the burning sensation of the cold blade agitated Lucius' finger. Lucius dropped the blade, holding his throbbing and pulsating bleeding finger.

Aelienor came to Gauvain's aid, kicking the guard in the stomach. The guard bent over and kicked him in the side of the temple. Aelienor and Gauvain helped Lucius up.

"Lucius... your finger," Aelienor said out of breath looking around the room to discover Therron's graveyard of defeated men.

"I'll live." Lucius admitted gritting his teeth. "We need to make sure Hayden doesn't kill Therron."

Lucius explained escaping Aelienor and Gauvain's grasp, opening the door to the upstairs. Mid twist of the door made his hand impulsively twitch with pain. Watching the blood pouring down the door-knob, it occurred to him how much blood he had lost. "We need to get your hand looked at before it gets any worse." Maria admitted.

"I'm sure my finger is... Fine..." Lucius said in annoyance hitting the door with his shoulder falling forward.

Time went slowly as he heard Ernaldus speak, "How can it be fine if it's..." seeing Ernaldus mouth the word 'gone' but not yet say it realizing he tele-ported to Therron's quarters from the corridor. Once Lucius landed in front of Therron, he locked the door behind him.

"Like my powers?" Therron asked. "Teleporta-tion, I just now thought of it."

"This is crazy, you don't have the eye in your grasp anymore... how is this possible?" Lucius asked, holding his hand under his armpit.

Therron glitched in front of Lucius, now beside him... "Once you touch it. The power doesn't leave you although it's limited."

Therron glitched, teleporting over to the balcony looking at the view. "You always want the Eye by your side like a bad itch," Therron glitched again, this time spawning in front of his desk. "I'm not as bad as they say I am, Lucius. This relic is the real enemy here, mir-acle or curse. One thing is for certain. People say I was chosen. Yet, I know now I'm not, only another victim."

"Do me a favor and never have this power."

"What did the Eye do to you?"

"It breaks you down and eats you up inside," Therron yelled out holding his head. "You are always left wanting more." Therron confessed marking tallies on the wall in fast motion. Filling the wall within a few seconds after a brief glitch. "You make things up to fill that void inside and eventually crack under the pressure... all I want to do now is rest." Therron said discovering the lock on the door flying off.

Therron braced from the lock colliding with his forarm. Once Therron gained a clear view ahead he was interepted with Hayden's blade.

The artifact crashed onto the table beside Lucius.

Therron felt the blade that now rested inside his stomach. Attempting to wiggle away backward before Hayden shoved the blade further to appear on the outside of his back. The sword now having a crimson highlight as it dripped fresh blood. Therron let off a brief hoarse squeal before his voice cracked.

"Hayden, what have you done?" Lucius asked.

"Heed... my... warning." Therron urged out to Lucius before his pain-filled eyes became languid.

"You deserve worse than death Therron, but consider this a debt repaid." Hayden slid the blade away before shoving Therron away.

Hayden looked at Lucius with sudden concern. "Anything he may have told you Lucius was filled with corruption. I couldn't have let him continue with his evil ways. Jack will see. Everyone will see." Hayden announced opening the nearest window detecting the clear skies. "This is a step into a new community. A better world to live in... Lucius watched the sky clear as he noticed Jack from down below the window mouthing the words, 'All-Seeing Eye'.

Hayden began to survey Therron's office. "He had a purpose," Lucius uttered sauntering over to the idol eye.

"And you think I don't?" Hayden questioned pointing his bloodied sword at Lucius. "Look at all of these clues that Therron's term was up. You were lucky he didn't do worse than cutting your finger. In my eyes, I saved your life." Hayden exhaled, lowering his sword. "This will be a new era, Lucius. Soon I'll restart my father, Marius' work before that let's get you patched up." Hayden said as he raised his hand to help him up as Lucius hesitantly grabbed Hayden's hand.

Hayden placed down Lucius' hand on the desk nearby as Hayden wrapped Lucius' hand.

"He knew you were coming, Hayden. He wanted you to kill him." Lucius confessed.

"Of course he did. He knew he had it coming."

Being wrapped up, Lucius reached the magnetic seal, dropping the seal out of the window. Jack caught it below as he summoned the artifact flying past from behind Hayden. Hayden glanced back as if he had heard something.

"What?" Lucius said impulsively. Hayden scratched his head. Looking at

Therron's corpse. "All that matters is that the so-called King has perished." Hayden closed the dead man's eyes before moving on.

* Sticks And Stones *

"Hayden patched you up pretty good. No more bleeding as long as it remains untouched." Reyner admitted opening Lucius' wound at Jack's base. "I know Drago and Magnus are waiting for us to bring the eye to them. You should lie low until you fully heal. It doesn't exactly grow back but be wary that you won't be able to lift things as well as you used to. " He explained replacing the bloody rags.

"Those carriages are back..." Ashlyn recalled watching the window.

"How'd those pesky bandits discover our location?" Vaughan asked.

"They must've followed us." Jack assumed.

"It's because of All-Seeing Eye." Helba explained.

"If these people are anywhere close to as bad as Therron. They'll get what's coming to them." Lex explained.

One of the henchmen breached. Hitting Kain in the nose from the impact.. As each bandit entered the base; the leader Drago entered last commenting. "This was only supposed to be a simple transaction between us, Kain."

"I see that we both don't trust each other enough for that. Look at how many people you've brought with you." Kain said holding his bloodied nose with a raspy voice.

"This was purely for security. Do you have the eye?" Drago asked, glitching. "I know you do, I sense it."

Hayden checked his pockets confused as Jack stepped up.

"I've seen how this could play out." Jack placed the relic on the table with its seal.

"How'd you obtain it?"

"I couldn't take the risk Hayden, I had to be sure this goes the way it has to happen," Jack said as Hayden narrowed his eyes.

"You don't trust me then?"

"You can't blame Jack." Drago reminded. "He's afraid, he knows what I'm capable of..." Drago said with a smirk. "bring out the boy."

Appearing the most wealthy out of all his bandit kin. Chain armor protecting him from beneath his clothing, Omega appeared walked out from the crowd with Floros, holding on his collar.

"It's been a long time since I've seen you, Jack," Omega commented. "Wish it were under different circumstances."

"I never see you in good scenarios. What do these people have in common with you Omega?" Jack asked.

"Straight to the questioning aren't you?" Omega crossed his arms. "I respect that, but let's do one thing at a time. This isn't about me, Drago has a deal to do." Omega looked at Floros. "You can go now." Floros ran to hug Kain.

Drago reached out for the eye. Absorbing the essence in his hands. Vaughan interrupted the flow using the seal to retrieve it.

"Block the door," Drago ordered. "That was a mistake. Hand the eye back before you regret that choice." The bandits took out their weapons awaiting orders.

"My men are good at what they do. Don't you agree?" Omega joked.

"You don't threaten me or my family." Floros took the eye out of Vaughan's possession. Aiming the eye at Omega.

"Watch what you're doing boy," Omega warned, raising his hands.

"I'm not a kid." Floros burst to grab the eye out of its magnetic seal.

"No," Drago yelled, running toward the eye as Floros charged a beam of light; having everyone stop in awe for a moment before he fired. Causing Drago and his men to fly across the room.

"Floros...why did you do that?" Kain asked, blistering with anger.

"To save you..." Floros answered in a classic attitude from a teenage tone. "We have a chance to leave now. Thank me later." Floros started as Omega remained in his path.

"How'd you resist?" Jack questioned gaining Floros and the rest's attention.

"I have my ways, Jack. You'd better do more research next time." Omega started wiping the debris off of him, snatching the magnetic seal from Floros, retracting the eye. "This is no toy. You have no one to blame but yourself. We will meet again soon. I'm certain of it." Omega stated as Hayden tackled Omega disappearing.

"What just happened?" Ashlyn asked. "I'm not sure but I feel strange," Floros admitted.

"You shouldn't have done that," Kain explained.

"Something told me I had to. To protect you, it was the only way. I don't feel hurt but I do feel different." Floros took a few steps before he fell to his knees, holding his head.

"Malyna would know how to heal your son. Floros is gaining the beginning stages of the curse." Jack informed.

"Rosetta and Rosane told me that she's in jail for helping the Ill minded," Lucius stated.

"That's not good," Caroline admitted.

"I just got my son back, I'm not losing him again," Kain said.

"What do we do with the bandits scattered around here?" Helba asked knocking on one of the rising bandits to make him fall back into unconsciousness.

"Capture them and offer them back for Hayden," Flynn explained.

"That could work. We didn't exactly pass with flying colors with this deal." Maria stated.

"Do you have a place for them?" Jack asked.

"We can keep them in our base while we move slowly into Therron's castle," Stephan explained.

"In the meantime, Jack, Helba, and I will help you out. We will try to find Hayden's location. As stubborn as he is, he's still useful." Vaughan explained.

"What should we do?" Ernaldus asked.

"I trust you to visit Rosane and Rosettas. There's a church nearby that Morrison talked to them in earlier. Church of Nortell. They may still be there." Jack said as he made sure to tie the bandits up before they were relocated.

Knowledge Of Time *

"They knew all of this was going to happen," Gauvain confessed as he, Lucius, Ernaldus, Aelienor, and Maria left Jack's base.

"Using time travel, sure. But what makes you say all of it?" Lucius asked as Gauvain revealed his hands to show the Timeline Codex.

"I know he told us not to but... He does know a lot more than he lets on. Everything from the actions that we do when we do it. It updated itself as I turned the pages that I'm even reading this book." Gauvain explained as Aelienor took the book to close it.

"This is too dangerous Gauvain," Aelienor said.

"Why'd you take this Gauvain..." Ernaldus asked.

"It states to the specific detail of Lucius' loss of finger to Omega getting captured." Gauvain pointed out.

"Are you serious?" Aelienor asked as her curiosity gained the best of her as she looked over Gauvain's shoulder.

"Jack and Vaughan always ask us to trust them, but not once have they trusted us," Gauvain explained.

"What do you mean he's trusting us right now..." Lucius asked.

"He knew you were going to hurt. I know he can't go back like I'm sure he has before. He didn't give a damn about healing you. Only cared about himself. We cared. We remained by your side. He wants us to contact Rosane and Rosetta for help." Gauvain read ahead from the present. "He's going to send Helba to follow us."

"He did say... he didn't see us in that book." Maria confessed.

"It's for the best that we didn't look at it," Lucius said, trying to calm Gauvain.

"I've held my tongue since both Maria's and I's fathers were slaughtered in front of my own eyes."

"What happened?" Aelienor asked surprised. "I didn't know that..."

"When did this happen?" Ernaldus asked.

"The same day I convinced Aelienor to buy that treasure map that led us here. Which is why her dad didn't notice the boat going missing, he's long gone." Gauvain said, exhausting his breath. "I'm feeling bad about Jack, I just have a hunch. I don't want this hunch to be left in the air like I did last time."

Maria began to run away from Gauvain from him, hurting her feelings.

"You know I'm speaking the truth, Maria.

I'm trying to guarantee our safety." Gauvain said, upset.

"I'll get her. Meet us in the church." Lucius said paying attention to Helba in the distance exiting the base with Magnus. "Hide the book and go on your way. I'll catch up."

Gauvain hid the book upon leaving with Ae-lienor and Ernaldus.

Lucius caught up with Maria. Sitting in the shade. Watching ships docking from down the hill.

"This may be our last chance to leave." Maria reminded.

"We need to help out Floros before he gets worse. Then we can leave I promise."

"You act like you know Kain as you do us. If it wasn't for us leaving in the first place. You wouldn't have even met him." Maria snapped as she rested her head on a tree. "There's always going to be another predicament to keep us here. Let Gauvain do his own thing with Aelienor and Ernaldus. We could leave without them...they don't have to know."

"We can't leave our friends here..."

"You use the term friend loosely," Maria admitted focusing on the clouds instead of the ships. "But I know you're right." Maria held her arm nervously. "All I have left is you. In this journey, I feel... Disconnected from everyone else. Like I don't belong. But I don't feel that with you..." Maria sauntered her eyes over to Lucius. "I don't want to always run away from problems. But I'm done fighting with the constant fear of pain from losing someone."

"If I recall, that's the reason why we left. To get away from it all; a distraction."

"I didn't expect this...all these problems sent our way all of a sudden."

"None of us do. It's what we do after that matters."

"I guess you're right, it's just the fact that it never ends. One problem is solved the next one is harder than the last. Making the current issue feel that the previous one was nothing. I was free when we left. I can't stop thinking about what my mom thinks of leaving shortly after dad died. Does she think I died as well...or does she think I ran away because she did something wrong? That feeling of freedom... Ironically left when I stayed here. All I want to do now is go back."

"We will see them again soon. I promise you. But the way you want to do it isn't the way. We should save the day first per se and leave with good terms. Otherwise, Omega could just suck us back in before we know it."

"What's to say after Omega is dealt with. There'll be another Omega out there that makes him look like a simpleton?"

"We won't know. What I can tell you is that once the adventure is complete, we save the day..."

"-We aren't heroes, Lucius. Once we stop Omega if that's even possible. Who's going to undo the death and destruction that has happened throughout. Without Jack's machine, the answer would be that there isn't. That's if we should continue helping Jack if Gauvain is right... All Jack does is lie to us. What else will he lie about to get what he wants?"

"I may not have all the answers, Maria. But what you do have, is my never-ending support to get through the ruts we'll find ourselves in. We can question things all day and may never get the answers we want at the end of the day. But what can happen is if we stick together, anything is possible..." Lucius said as Maria interrupted Lucius by connecting her soft lips to his firm chapped lips. Lucius allowed Maria as he moved his hands around her back. Maria wrapped her arm to the back of Lucius' neck in response.

"You always knew what to say. Someday we will discover that this was some sort of distant bad dream."

"If this was a dream... I wouldn't want it to end." Lucius commented as Maria blushed.

* Kralans' Request *

"Where have you two been?" Ernaldus asked impatiently.

"I just needed some time alone. Lucius helped me figure some things out." Maria said.

"I'm sorry about your dad Maria. I never knew that happened. Perhaps if I was with you, I could've made a difference." Aelienor said comforting Maria.

"There wouldn't have been much you could've done. That whole ordeal was life- changing. I didn't mean to offend you, Maria." Gauvain confessed.

"We checked The Church Of Nortell. Rosetta and Rosane weren't there but there was a man inside. Claiming that he's expecting you." Ernaldus said, glancing into the door to make sure the man was still here.

Lucius checked the door detecting Fabul in an instant. "He does know who I am."

"Did you want us to come with you?" Aelienor asked.

"If it wouldn't be too much trouble. I'd appreciate the backup. He didn't seem to be the nicest person to talk to." Lucius said.

"What did he say to you?" Maria asked.

"I didn't exactly speak to him, but he was giving Rosetta and Rosane a hard time for not guarding the eye." Lucius summarized as he took a deep breath entering the church.

Lucius came closer to Fabul and he began to speak. "You want Malyna, yes?"

"I do."

"I expected you did. She's on many Ill minded as of late. Why should I let out Malyna just since you want her out? She broke our law and will need to be punished."

"Is there any way you could look the other way?" Lucius asked.

"We need her help," Gauvain explained.

"Perhaps there's a way. Why should I trust an Ill minded..." Fabul explained.

"If you wanted to talk to me. Speak up about it and not waste my time." Lucius stated.

"Since I have you all here in front of me. It'll be a shame for me to waste this opportunity." "What're you trying to say?" Lucius asked.

"We both have something that may be of benefit to each other. I have Malyna and you want Malyna. I want you to take part in killing my comrade Kion. He's a traitor to the cause. I have proof of his wickedness. You may have seen me and my comrade speaking to Rosetta and Rosane. That enough could be punished by the law of my people. It's also illegal to kill another mage but not illegal to have a suspicion of being involved in a murder case in the mage land."

"So you want us to do your dirty work?" Maria questioned.

"You want me to aid you in risking my abilities of mage work. You must prove your usefulness to me. I know about the under table work Rosane and Rosetta have been doing and I've been ignoring them until now. You should feel lucky that I've been letting Kion take over in that area. If you want to place a label on this work, you should name it as a test. As is watching your tongue when speaking to a high ranked mage as I am."

"We know someone like you. Someone who everyone seems to praise until they find out how much of a criminal you truly are underneath.

You talk about trust, it goes both sides. Why should we trust you?" Aelienor asked.

"You'll have to take my word. This is only going to either hurt you badly or benefit me greatly. Think of it as, without Kion, our people will not cause any more harm than they have in the past. You can leave this church not accepting these terms but you'll find it harder to get Malyna out any other way as you will find me as an enemy who knows a lot of information instead of an ally no one will need to know about."

"How do you expect us to find Kion?" Lucius asked.

"A man who enters the mage realm and this realm the Ill minded are in. Frequently switching between the two. Calling himself Hunter. He knows about my business and wants something from me as much as you want Malyna. You can find him in Quia. I would've thought I lost a good ally from that fire but it would seem as much as it agitates Kion from the time shifts that we've been having. He's now alive, there was a silver lining in it if you will."

"It'll take time." Lucius explained.

"I have patience but I do expect results. Or else." Kion said as he sat down crushing a skull with his fist. "That'll be one of you."

"I can't believe we accepted that." Gauvain confessed after he closed the door behind him.

"We didn't seem like we had much choice," Ernaldus remarked.

"Since we're going to Quia anyway. We should question Jousen in prison. Before you deal with a prick one must understand how a prick acts and works." Aelienor said.

"Should we visit Kain to tell him about our progress?" Maria asked.

"We'll waste our time if we go to him without any good news." Lucius admitted.

"How may I help you?" Morrison asked.

"Where's Jousen?" Aelienor asked.

"I'll show you he's in jail in this town. Still awaiting trial. We're starting the trial once my son comes back. Speaking of which, where is Wariner?"

"He's with Jack, he'll come around soon," Lucius said thinking back as he spoke. With doubt from his friends on Jack.

Was *he*?

With a swift answer, Morrison didn't become worried. "Let me show you the prison,"

Morrison said respectfully as he walked a few buildings over.

"Talk to him as long as you need. He still needs a trial. It's sort of a Lord custom."

"Funny enough, you seem to be more so a Lord of action to me," Lucius muttered.

"What's that?" Morrison asked confused.

"Nothing."

"Come back to me when you're done," Morrison said as he left the prison.

"The last time I recall Wariner was with us when he helped us break Stephan out of jail. Then it's a blur." Aelienor confessed scratching her head.

"We'll figure that out soon enough. I'm sure he's alright." Lucius said as they entered the jail. Inside the jail they discover Jousen cutting off a conversation with Draven. "I didn't know you were here too..."

"I don't belong here. You just happen to make things worse. That Jack guy I swear bribed Morrison to lock me up here. I didn't even do anything wrong." Draven explained.

"You and me both," Jousen added.

"You killed someone... What do you mean you don't belong here?" Aelienor questioned.

"It was self-defense. I was fighting two people at once. But you wouldn't know anything about that."

"Try me." Aelienor explained as Jousen rolled his eyes.

"What do you want?" Jousen asked, narrowing his eyes.

"Is that Ashlyn that you were talking about," Draven asked.

"Yeah, isn't she an angel?" He remarked sarcastically.

"She's with the same guy who knew my name," Draven confessed.

"It would seem that wherever either of them is around trouble follows," Jousen confessed.

"Do you two know each other before or have you recently become prison pals?" Ernaldus asked with a scoff.

"If you must know. Draven here needed gold to pay off some debt. That debt just happened to be enough that I could help him loan him those pushovers. I knew they were just lackeys but since I killed Teigen. Nolyn and his people backed off from me but still haven't paid up. I'll come up with a way to get it once I get out of this place. If you knew the people Draven owed money to you'll know why paying them off would be something you do asap." Jousen summarized.

"Who does he owe money to and why?" Lucius questioned.

"Why would you care anyway. It's not like you would help anyway..." Draven said with impatience.

"With that attitude, we won't." Gauvain snapped.

"Alright, fine. The Nolyn guy works with this guy named Drago who I thought was a big fish. They owed me a big sum of gold since I did a lot of work for them. I became angered by that fact they wanted to kill me when I was tired of waiting for payment. That is until Draven informed me he did a deal with one of the mage realm counselors; Iiokio." Jousen asked.

"The deal was that Iiokio was going to revive my friend that died recently. I did some of Iiokios work for him and in return, a reward. That you beat me to, thief."

"It's Lucius."

"It matters not," Draven said waving off his hand. "I thought it was another test. I knew the artifact was there. I didn't want to disappoint Iiokio. Although now... it's too late and I'm to blame for the missing eye. I don't even know what this artifact looks like."

"Is everyone connected to some type of shady business?" Aelienor asked.

"You can think what you want but it's how most of this whole island runs. Especially Quia, if this place would be destroyed I would imagine you'd at least of a few corrupt people. Even perhaps worse than us. But since we're the low people of the group we're getting all the blame." Jousen said as he took notice of Hunter entering the jail. "Speaking of the devil. You know if I ever catch you doing something offish you'll be dead "

"Good luck with that Jousen. Sorry if these guys have been causing you an issue. Maintain distance from them and they're harmless." Hunter sat at his desk, discovering Morrison's missing keys. Rising as he spun the keys. "Did Morrison leave his office keys here in jail again. I'll bring them back to him. Care to walk with me to bring them back to him?"

"Sure, I believe we got what we needed here," Aelienor said as he exited first with Hunter. As Lucius, Ernaldus, Maria, and Gauvain followed.

"I knew they weren't going to help," Draven confessed.

"They'll pay they all will. We just have to find a way out of here." Jousen stated as they both frantically scavenged around their cells for a possible escape.

"So you're Hunter..." Lucius asked.

"Yeah, if you want to talk about what I think you came back here for we should discuss this with Morrison by our side. He tries to know all about what's happening throughout Quia. But with all the people here it's hard to keep up. We haven't gotten around to teach Wariner about this, but he will get the scoop when he comes back." Hunter explained. The group was silent going back to Morrison's office. "All of you look so tense. Lighten up a bit, you are not in trouble." Hunter joked.

Opening the door to Morrison's office. Lord Morrison scavenging his office for his keys. "Where are they at?"

"Are you looking for these?" Hunter asked, tossing his missing keys.

"I was," Morrison said as he sat them down at his desk. "Thanks. It's been on my mind since arresting Jousen. Where were they?"

"On your desk in prison again."

"I need to get better at that... My apologies, how can I help you today?" Morrison asked.

"Fabul wants Kion dead. He sent these four, able people to help us out."

"This is a tricky ordeal then. Omega and Jack from what I understood have been feuding for the longest time. Same for Iiokio and Omega. I don't want Jack to get involved with Iiokio but if we fail in Iiokio's eyes, It'll be an issue." Changing the topic at hand. "So, you're Jack's people. I'm considered part of Jack's people as well. I personally despise both Iiokio and Omega. My wife left me for Iiokio one month ago. Leaving me with Quia and leaving Wariner behind. She's selfish. As for Omega, I'm just fine with killing him for the headache he gives so many of my people. Unlike Omega, I'm willing to give Iiokio a chance to a truce to off Omega. To do that both sides are at a standoff until one side attacks first. We must kill Kion, looking like Omega or his men did it."

"That's tricky," Maria commented.

"Indeed it is. How do you want us to pull that off?" Hunter asked.

"This is to release Malyna right?" Morrison asked rhetorically with frustration. "That's typical of them to take one life to save another. We'll need to use magic against their people, which is where Hunter comes in. I'm sure you're familiar with a masking potion. One of the good ones from the black market too, not those cheap ones. You four can disguise yourself as Omega and his men who you captured that Jack informed me about. Act like you're them and you'll be able to maintain the disguise."

"Back when we were in Therron's castle we only knocked people out when Wariner taught us. We aren't exactly familiar with killing." Lucius confessed.

"It's time to get yourself familiar with it. Wariner isn't too fond of it, I've done it before and didn't enjoy doing it. Sometimes it must be done. It's the only way to get things done. When you find yourself in a fight and you discover how menacing the fight can become it ends up becoming the only choice you or them." Morrison explained as he noticed Lucius' finger. "The wound could've been worse. I know Jack doesn't want you to kill. I know he doesn't know about this either but only kills Kion and doesn't leave a bloodbath. The message will be crystal clear when the people guarding Kion couldn't stop Omega."

"I know we've been partners for the longest time. You scare me how fast you make up these plans. Morrison, you should become someone higher than just a lord." Hunter explained.

"I'm thinking about it myself Hunter but nothing sticks out to me. Any questions?" Morrison asked. Morrison waited as he took the silence as an answer. "Hunter will lead the way." Morrison picked up his keys surveying outside before locking the door.

Hunter took out from his pocket a cylindrical device containing a silver piece used as a controller. Containing lines sporadically scattered throughout the rest of the tool. Of which were glowing a dark red and orange. Hunter twisted the silver trigger from the device turning it on. An electrical shot flared into the air a few inches ahead of him as he drew out a line down that created a portal.

"A lot of the time when traveling to the mage realm the higher-ranked mages like I am would typically blind you so you don't see us get a clean getaway. I'm just showing this to you to ease you in the mage realm. This will disorient you at first seeing a portal being drawn in front of you by a Portalatrix. But your mind will adapt to two different locations quickly. You all can go ahead and go in first."

Lucius' eyes strained to process the tear in the air. Looking from the other side, as he first entered his arm. Slowing entering with the rest of his body. Lucius looked at Morrison's office. His friends followed behind on the other side. The portal made them look like they had left a pool. Oozing out within the tear without being miraculously wet.

Hunter entered last. Morrison gave a signal to Hunter patching the portal. Hunter began to push a bookshelf. Hunter's wife walked around the corner helping him move the bookshelf.

At first, Lucius and his friends heard gibberish from Rehiba as the Rosane's stone levitated out his pocket to teach him and his allies the new language within seconds.

"I see you've brought a Rosane's stone with you. Good thinking. Must've cost a fortune." Hunter commented.

"...what ill-minded did you bring back home now hon?" Rebiha asked. Rebiha smiled as Lucius and his friends looked at her strangely as they didn't expect to meet a shamrock colored alien.

"Just some of Morrison's friends Rebiha, How's Lukin?" Hunter asked as he pecked Rebiha on the cheek.

"He's doing well, but he's missing his father. You know he's more of a father's boy. He often cries when you're gone."

"I know. I'll take a vacation here soon to spend some time with you and Lukin soon enough."

"Your business friends don't seem to be familiar with my appearance dear."

"Oh, yeah it's their first time being in the mage realm. It'll take a few minutes for them to adapt. Rebiha meet Lucius, Ernaldus, Maria, Gauvain, and Aelienor." Rebiha shook their hands as he spaced their names out as she shook all of their hands.

"Gaveen?" Rebiha sounded out chuckling. "That's a unique name. Not that the rest of you don't but yours is funny."

"It's Gauvain." Gauvain corrected.

"You can understand me. I'm not used to newcomers with runes so early on." Rebiha chuckled. "Wouldn't they be illegal?" Rebiha recalled with concern. "They'll need to sign in to the Codex Of Population Hunter..."

"They aren't supposed to be here. I must admit Rebiha. It's part of the mission for Morrison. Just keep it between us alright..." This is important." Hunter explained.

"What do I say if anyone asks?"

"No one will ask."

"I just don't want them to take Lukin away from us..."

"They won't." Hunter replied giving Rebiha a calming kiss. "They won't."

"I'm trusting you," Rebiha said, hearing Lukin cooing. "Continue with your business."

"I will, but by chance do you have any left over some cloaking potions?"

"Are they for your mission?" Rebiha whispered with concern as her shoulder perched up.

"Yes."

"It'll take some time..." Rebiha confessed as she scratched the side of her neck. "How many do you need?"

"Four if you can."

Rebiha explored a few cabinets before sighing with defeat. "I'm fresh out since the last mission."

"We'll have to visit the black market again then."

"Those are expensive Hunter. We're having trouble making ends meet as it is." Rebiha sighed as she inevitably smiled. "I'll see what I can do."

"I'll come with you. Some of those people are evil." Hunter said as Rebiha smiled with relief.

"What about Lukin?"

"The Ill minded can watch him. We won't be gone for long." Hunter said.

"If that's ok with all of you." Ernaldus didn't like the idea as he began to wave the idea off as Aelienor beat Ernaldus to the punch as she spoke. "Sure we can watch him while you're gone. I love kids."

Rebiha smiled as she retrieved Lukin from his bed. "Thank you for doing this. You'll be noticed by everyone here if you don't have these potions. It's for your safety."

Rebiha handed Lukin over to Aelienor, wrapped around a light blue and furry blanket. Rebiha and Hunter put the bookshelf back in place as they left.

Memory VI - Last Strings

* Supply Run *

"I wonder how long they will take." Lucius explained as he looked around the room with more depth.

"We may as well get comfortable," Gauvain said as he sat down next to a fireplace. Warming his hands.

"This baby reminds me of Caroline's baby," Aelienor said as she gained a brow from Ernaldus. "Besides it being an alien and all, It's still pretty cute." Aelienor sat next to Gauvain.

"You better not hurt that kid or our chance to help out Floros is blown," Ernaldus explained.

"Thank you for your concern Ernaldus."

"What happens if it gets hungry, what would you feed it?"

"We'll deal with that when it comes. I'm sure they'll be back before then. Besides, I would think they would eat human food, right?" Aelienor asked.

"Your guess would be as good as mine," Maria admitted.

"Where would they keep the food around here." Lucius began.

"Be quiet," Gauvain whispered sharply. "I hear something."

"We shouldn't compromise ourselves out here in this realm, it could be anyone," Lucius whispered back. Easing his ears to the bookshelf.

"You know where the Amiri's were going..." An intruder explained.

"There is someone here." Lucius admitted

"I knew it."

"How many?" Aelienor asked softly.

"There's two of them," Lucius said, focusing his eyes to the peephole.

"There's no way that they were going anywhere else but the black market. You know that this isn't the first time that they went there. Who's watching their boy?"

"With the havoc going on lately I wouldn't be surprised if they left him alone. Do you think it's a smart idea to invade their privacy to find out?"

"You wouldn't have told me in the first place if you didn't think this was so important. Think of it like this, we're doing Kralan a favor."

"I didn't know you would resort to this. If we find anything sure, we're local heroes, otherwise, we're breaking the law."

"Let's be real, Hunter has been on our watch for the longest time. If we get him for isolation for leaving his kid at home it'll be all we need." The man said as Lukin began to cry, making the talking silent.

"Shh," Aelienor whispered to Lukin as she cradled him, rocking him back and forth.

"It came from behind this wall."

"I bet he's the type to be cliché with bookshelves. Start pulling books."

Lucius noticed as the books started to be pulled there was a peephole that was sticking out like a sore thumb. Lucius covered the hole with his hand. With a few minutes of them pulling books to clear out the shelf. One of the people began to move the shelves over in curiosity.

"They're back, we need to get out of here." One of the invaders exclaimed darting toward the back door. Lucius reached at one of the men's collars, being just out of reach.

Hunter rushed inside with Rebiha in shock from the messy house.

"What happened here?" Rebiha asked, noticing glass spread throughout the living room.

"We had visitors... They trashed the place." Aelienor exited the room handing the sobbing baby to Rebiha. Lukin immediately stopped crying.

"The important thing is no one was hurt. Did they see you?" Hunter asked with relief.

"I'm positive they didn't. They would've if you waited a minute or two longer." Lucius explained.

"Good. Go ahead and drink these potions. We were only able to get enough for the mission. I wanted to tag along but it seemed it would be best if I stayed here with my wife. To make sure these harassments don't keep occurring. I'll hear the progress over time through the town's rambles."

Lucius drank the potion, raising a brow. "I don't feel any different than before."

"I would hope so. It shouldn't affect you in a negative aspect." Hunter reassured.

"So I'm guessing Omega is an Ill minded?" Ernaldus asked after he swallowed the potion followed by others drinking in silence.

"No. He's strong-minded." Hunter joked. "Ill minded are known to be ones with no knowledge of the magic arts. Omega is a legend in these parts. No one who has value in Kralan hates him and his opinion is highly valued. He was the person who trained Iiokio before they went their separate ways. Omega and Iiokio helped make what this town is what is today. He'll visit once in a while. It's rumored that they haven't been seeing eye to eye." Hunter explained.

"You look like the same people to us. We saw you drink the potion. You won't be known out there and you should be safe for the rest of the duration of your visit. Just be sure to not blow your cover." Rebiha added.

"Do you have a map or something we can use?" Maria asked.

"Omega and his men don't know Kralan well so it'll be alright if you look around the town at the maps stands around the city."

"Any advice before we go out there?" Gauvain asked.

"Since you don't know much about this town it would be best not to trust anyone beyond our house. Sometimes I don't even know who to trust anymore. It'll be better that way too since Omega is a hard person to talk to when he does pop in. You'll just be befitting your characters well if you only talk to those who talk to you. The black market doesn't judge our purchases which are good for our intentions but it scares me what other magic they offer to others that I don't know well out there."

159

"Good luck with your adventure. I'm sure you'll do fine in your endeavors. I have faith in all of you." Rebiha said as the crew left, seeing the environment dramatically different from what they're used to. Futuristic tech connected to houses while different tame monsters passed by cobblestone roads that they've never seen in their life before. Buildings with turbines powering machines that were unknown to the common man. Lucius and his friends took a few steps heeding the green sky as airships passed by. A Steampunk wonderland. Decades beyond the Ill minded lands.

"Omega..." One of the townspeople shouted threateningly. "Die, scum."

An Unlikely Meeting

"What the...?" Omega questioned landing roughly on the ground with a couple of rolls onto the dark oak floors with Hayden landing beside him with a slide. Omega rose first. "You've got some guts, Hayden is it...aren't you supposed to be killing Therron or something?"

Hayden rose to his feet feeling his jaw. "He's already dead. I don't care what it takes, that eye your holding doesn't belong to you and I ask, no order you to hand that over or else..."

Omega laughed in response. "Impressive you killed Therron. But what will you do if I don't hand over the eye to you, you'll kill me?" Omega scoffed. "I get threats daily and I deal with each accordingly. I spit at the spirit you appear to have, this full of action persona. It's all an act to impress but no one is here which means you'll do nothing." Omega turned his back to walk away from Hayden shaking his head.

Hayden took a blade from his scabbard rushing at Omega. Omega levitated the artifact into the air as he caught the blade with his hand snapping the metal in half. Throwing the metal to the side. Omega pulled the remaining part of the weapon toward him to lead Hayden to him as Omega headbutted him. Omega looked at each bloodied hand as he healed himself by closing his hands together for a moment. Seeing the blood drip as his hands had a faint purple glow for a moment before his wounds disappeared.

Omega lowered the eye back into his hands pointing the eye to Hayden. Shoving Hayden into a wall with his elbow. "I've mistaken your courage. That much is clear but I'm not surprised. Your attempt was adequate at best. Too typical of an attempt like Ashlyn has done to you. I sense... potential."

"How do you know so much about me?" "You're an open book, sort to speak." Omega smiled. "We both know Jack wanted to get you out of the picture, as we speak he's finding a way to kill off the rest of your friends. I'm not talking about your new friends but the friends you've had since day one of your father's reign that's still by your side today. However, with enough time by my side, you'll know the truth and I'll just hand this over to you without caring what you do with it. But until then..." Omega released Hayden as he made the eye disappear. "We'll just imagine it doesn't exist...your feelings against Jack were ideal to have. Imagine the lack of trouble he had gotten into following his lead and the fall you had in comparison."

"How can I trust you?"

"I like your spirit. There's a fire that awaits to be let free. This new relationship between us you'll find both of us have a lot in common. Are you with me?"

"I'll tag along for now. Don't expect miracles."

"That's all I ask. Jack thinks he's a step ahead with capturing my men that I don't trust that well myself. He can celebrate that victory as much as he wants, I have more people where that came from. Like Iiokio's whole realm for example would join in if I simply asked. Speaking of Kralan. I've caught wind of someone in Iiokios realm becoming sketchy. It's either Kion or Fabul, if I get enough information they'll be a visitation for confrontation."

"Didn't you just say you had a lot of enemies?"

"It's complicated. Most of my enemies switch out as fast as an emotion. I always do something myself to either make them forget about why they hated me or do something for them that they'll love me for it later. Or they end up in some ditch." Omega put his hand on the doorknob as he stood in place thinking out loud. "You haven't been here in Kralan before haven't you?"

"Not at all."

"I'll get you set up then. Call it a treat of mine."

Exiting the abandoned house. "You won't go far into Kralan without one of these," Omega revealed a Rosane's stone.

"What does this do?" He asked. "It looks like a rock."

"It's a rune."

"A rune?" Hayden repeated confused.

"Yes, A fancy rock," Omega explained with a scoff. "I forgot I'm talking to an Ill minded," Omega said, changing his language to some sort of tongue that Hayden didn't deduct, understand, triggering the rune causing the symbol on it to glow brightly. "And by now you should hear me with clarity. You also learned in this time to speak among Kralan's people." Omega said, taking the rune away from Hayden.

"What happened?" Hayden asked, scratching his head.

"One of my proteges' created this to impress me in his potential. Violence doesn't always get the point across to be useful. We both learned something that day. Since then Rosane and his brother Rosetta; who's also talented, joined the council." Omega summarized. "Understand Kralan may astound you at first. Just don't take one of the domesticated animals and try to escape at night. I took notice of someone doing that last time I was here and it didn't end well for them."

A middle-aged man gained Omega attention as he was on his path with a weak stance, slumped on a wall wearing ripped leather armor with a pale face. "Are you Omega?"

"What happened here?" Omega asked with

haste.

"I'm ill from defending the outskirts of this town from poisonous snakes and I think I may not last much longer in this timeline of mine. Can you go back in time to give me more back up?"

"What can you do for me in return?"

"The man is dying..." Hayden huddled to see what he could do.

"I know what I'm doing."

"I can join your ranks... You can have my gold." The dying man thought up. "I figured you'd say something along those lines. You'd want to join me but I don't need anyone and I don't want your gold."

"What do you want from me then?"

"Hmm..." Omega glanced seeing a couple enter the black market. "Send someone to check out Hunter and Rebiha and tell me the results in your next timeline. I'll be back soon."

"Thank you kindly." The man said with a smile as his face became still.

"He's dead."

"Not for long."

"Can you bring him back from the dead?"

"In a manner of speaking, yes."

"Who are they?" Hayden asked, struggling to keep up with Omega's speed walking. "Hunter and Rebiha, I mean."

"Suspicious people. That'll be all you need to know." Omega changed the subject. "Since I know that stranger will be successful I'll prevent his injury, you can come along."

Hayden expected Omega to teleport again but

instead kept walking. "Where are we going?"

"You're considered ill-minded here. Without you getting in trouble you must follow me somewhere isolated and lucky for you, I know a place." Omega led Hayden to the council's castle. Next to it is a shed with Omega's name on it.

"What's this building have to do with anything..." Hayden asked as he entered. Omega closed the door behind him.

"Open that door again Hayden," Omega said.

Hayden opened the door. A layer of impassable, yet clear protection laid beyond the door. Planets in the distance made Hayden step back in awe.

"That big circle you see is our planet. Solaris. I had a funny conversation about this person saying he claims the planet is flat."

"It's spherical."

"Some people aren't always believing. Now close the door I'm getting a draft."

Hayden closed the door as he turned around seeing the shed become as wide as a mansion upon entry. Omega began typing on a futuristic device. Hayden glanced back behind him seeing the door locked this time around. Hayden walked back to Omega. "What is that?"

"I'll tell you about a lot of things but this isn't one of them. I'm done teaching you things for now... You've already learned so much at once. Explore if you want Hayden but make yourself scarce I'm having a meeting." Omega said, beginning the transmission once Hayden was out of sight. Hayden acted as busy eavesdropping from afar.

"Sir Raullin, How's Iiokio?"

"He's currently teaching me as you wanted. There's much to learn but lately, I've discovered my training may come to an end shortly. He wants me to test my wits."

"Don't kill him Raullin. Put him out of commission for a while." Omega ordered. "This is important that he's not an obstacle but not useless either. Once you do that, notify me of your results." Omega ordered ending the transmission.

"I thought Iiokio was your ally?"

"That's me keeping tabs with future Iiokio to make sure he doesn't go out of the line. Now go ahead and open the door for the last time. I got what I needed here."

Once Hayden opened the door he revealed they're back at Kralan, this time at night. The shed disappeared when they exited. "This should be the time that man should be getting attacked any second.

"Where do you think his men would be?"

"This late at night, the best bet would be drinking which would be useless to call on for..." Omega walked up to some mercenaries handing them gold. "Help out the lonely guard over there. He doesn't know he's going to be messing with poisonous snakes."

The hired hands pocketed the gold rushing over to the snakes that roamed among the town.

"We're done here," Omega said.

"Those men didn't even question you."

"They fight for gold." Omega corrected.

"Where are you going now?"

"Am I going too fast for you?" Omega joked.

"We're isolated, so I can teleport away now."

Within a blink's notice, they exited back into the Omega shed opening the door to be outside. Omega waited for the man to come back with the news.

"They bought four masking potions of good quality for what reason. I'm not sure. I thank you for helping me out."

"No, thank you. You've done me a great service...what's your name?"

"Around these parts people call me Thex The Knight. Rewarded for the service I've done here."

"I'll call you Beta for short-"

"But that's not my name-"

"It'll grow on you." Omega patted him on the back placing a device on his back of his neck. "I'm sure we'll meet again."

Hayden broke the silence leaving Thex.

"What did you place on him?"

"Nothing you should worry yourself about. Now before we have any more distractions. Let's talk to Iiokio. If he knows about the possible turncoat... and to get you registered. " Omega explained as he walked up the stairs to meet Iiokio on the main floor waiting for his entry.

"I knew you were coming." Iiokio made known shaking Omega's hand.

"Before we get started I need this Hayden..." Omega started snapping his fingers.

"Kristell." Hayden replied.

"To get a realm license."

"That'll be no problem. I can get someone to do

that as soon as they get a chance."

"Any strange problems lately that you've noticed?"

"Not that I can recall. Everything has been smooth sailing so to speak. Nothing that I or the council can't deal with ourselves. Why?"

"I'm here for the greater good Iiokio. I suspect something big will arise. I can't pick out how. Even the slightest detail that you looked over could have a major effect on you, your council, and perhaps Kralan itself."

"You've been traveling in time plenty. This Draven was dumb enough to do chores for me and expect me to give him the All-Seeing Eye in return. I finished him off recently. He may be someone you could check out since I've gained word on him cheating death. If it's anything bigger than that...why can't you just go in the future and find out what's going on tell me who or what's going on now."

"Plus let's say it was that simple. I wouldn't see change unless it was significant, and I have plenty of research before I go altering timelines. All I'm saying is to keep an eye out on your men and Kralan itself a little more. Now if it isn't too much trouble I would like to speak to the rest of the council."

"You know where they are, Omega, help yourself. I'll give Hayden Kristell what he needs." Iiokio explained.

"What's this realm pass do?" Hayden asked.

"To be in this realm whether you're visiting or living. You'll need a realm pass. Not just to this realm but for all realms. It's universal. We'll give you little information on magic to get by here like healing and simple defense spells but nothing compared to what you can achieve if you stay here a long time like the council."

"I thought Omega only visits."

"He does. But all the magic I learned he knows as well. In case Kralan falls he's my plan b. Omega and I only talk business now and I'm afraid he's doing this both for our sake but I want the old Omega back. For that to happen I must fix what bothers him so much. Of which I can't figure out without him telling me. I dislike time travel. So many secrets make me think there's some sort of disconnect."

"Do you know Raullin?"

"Not at all. Who's that?"

"Ask Omega. He talked about him like you know him."

"I know his crew-" Iiokio scoffed with a half laugh. *Sure you do.*

"That's his friendly side. I wish I could see more. I slowly get more concerned after each visit." Iiokio stopped by a vendor, handing the vendor a slip to give Hayden his beginning supplies.

"The more often you visit the better you'll be at magic. Just by seeing magic performed in front of you, with enough patience and practice. You'll learn it in no time." Iiokio said as he raised his hand as it raised Hayden's hand to come up causing a spark to come out of both of their hands.

"What was that?"

"Don't fret. I forced you to cast magic. To expand your knowledge. It feels strange to cast for the first few times but once you can master it, it passes you by without a second thought. Welcome to Kralan, Hayden Kristell. For whatever reason, you decided to join us. We're glad to have you, follow me to meet the rest of the council. Omega attends meetings from time to time. It's best to talk to them one on one as you can get to know them personally and how many ways you can use magic."

"Who's in the council?"

"Rosetta, Rosane, Malyna, Anne, Kion, and Fabul. Omega and I. We're all good at certain types of magic. Malyna has the power of conjuration. Rosetta majors in restoration magic, his brother Rosane does environmental. My girlfriend, Anne does Astrology, Kion does destruction, Fabul works in Mysticism. I work with Nature. Omega was taught none other than the creator of magic himself, Yuoki. Which class of magic interests you?"

"I'd like to learn more about Omega"

"I'm not sure what class Omega knows but maybe someday you may be lucky to learn from him, does any other class interest you?"

"I'll try destruction instead."

"Destruction magic, the best in combat.

They're often on the front lines defending Kralan borders Let's see what Kion is up to. As we head that way, what makes you decide on that type of magic?"

"I want to make a difference. Not a difference that refers to behind the scenes but if someone hears my name they knew I was a fighter. Fighting with what he believed in."

"With the fiery passion in your voice, I believe you." Iiokio gave off a half-smile. "Fight the weak and conquer the strong. That's the motto in the destruction school. You'll soon earn a burning sigil where your magic comes flowing though like I do." Iiokio opened his palm to reveal his sigil of a tree as it disappeared shortly after with green fire. "Any more questions you want to know about magic?"

"Not at the moment but I'm sure I'll have plenty to learn here."

"Oh, you do. Don't let it overwhelm you, take a breath when it becomes difficult as we all will be here for you. We'll know you'll have success in all of your endeavors." Hayden was led into the council's castle.

Iiokio pointed out the other rooms to different types of magic if he changed his mind or wanted to learn another class later on and become one step closer to be like Omega. He stopped in his tracks with his cheery attitude when blood dripped off Kion's door from the inside.

"Something is wrong, take a step back Hayden," Iiokio said as his hand had a green overlay pushing the door open. Witnessing the crime scene of Kion's bloodied body and two Omegas. Iiokio's hands turned into vines as he grabbed both legs of both Omegas.

"It wasn't me, I found him like this." The left Omega said.

"He lies, The double kills him." The right Omega retorted.

"Hayden, take the memory plant from the corner of the room. It saw what had occurred and told me which Omega did this to Kion," Iiokio ordered.

Hayden grabbed the plant relieving the past. "Oh my Yuoki." Hayden stated looking at both Omegas.

"Who is it?" Iiokio asked.

"It's that one." Hayden pointed out. Iiokio teleported who Hayden chose to the prison. "What should we do with the double?"

"We needn't worry about that Omega," Iiokio explained as he left the room.

Hayden doubled back to retrieve all Omega's belongings at the prison's entrance. Hayden followed Iiokio with an eagerness by the time once Iiokio entered the cells. The All-Seeing Eye laid on the desk retrieving it as Iiokio's back was turned. Teleporting back to Therron's castle seeing Wariner in one of the cells in a secret cell isolated from the rest of the others.

"You have the artifact of all people. You know what, get me out of here. I tried to escape back when Stephan got out of jail, but I was caught." Wariner confessed.

"You're useful to me. We'll help each other." Hayden explained with a smirk as he teleported Wariner with him back to Kralan. Making the relic disappear before Iiokio noticed he was gone.

Wariner stood still in a confused manner as Iiokio walked up to him.

"Follow my lead or you'll regret it," Hayden whispered to Wariner, making him gulp. "So is this all of Omega's belongings?"

"It is." Wariner spurted.

Iiokio looked around Omega's belongings. "I can't believe what he did. I thought he was such a content man."

"It surprises me as well."

"You must be new here since I don't recognize you but there are so many new faces it's hard to keep track." Iiokio joked as Wariner's and Hayden's face became stale as they laughed when Iiokio did. "So what should Omega's punishment be?"

Wariner glanced at Hayden as Hayden's eyes widened. "He should have a trial as everyone does. No matter how bad it is." Wariner guessed.

"I suppose you're right..." Iiokio said. "I'd like to see him."

"Go right ahead, take your time," Wariner said in hopes Iiokio knew where he was as Iiokio walked away. Giving Wariner a breath of relief. Wariner waited until Iiokio left his sight. "Are we even now Hayden?"

"No, but close. I have plans for you and you will obey them." Hayden noticed the warden Wariner was replacing came back from break as Hayden teleported away with Wariner.

"Was that Wariner..." The warden asked. Knowing based on belongings on the desk Omega had been sent to jail. "This isn't good."

* To Start A War *

Lucius' eyes widened as Ernaldus caught a sword, inches away from Lucius' temple. Knocking the angered man to his knees as Ernaldus kicked the sword away from him.

"You should kill him, he's a traitor to Kralan." One of the standings by civilians spoke out.

173

Lucius decided to raise his sword to swing to practice for Kion but couldn't swing down as he lowered his weapon.

"I knew you were weak..." The man on his knees confessed as he was met with multiple stab wounds by Gauvain.

"Enough Magnus." Lucius admitted keeping his cover.

"He almost killed you..." Gauvain said with anger.

"I know you're in charge, Omega...but no more chances." Gauvain confessed.

"Since you killed him I suspect you to clean the mess. Go with him Drago to make sure he doesn't continue to be reckless." Lucius said, looking to Ernaldus.

"You know I'm right Omega. It took me this long that I don't need to be by your side and be such a liability." Gauvain explained as Ernaldus focused his attention on the dead man.

Fabul took notice of Omega walking up to him. "Iiokio said you'll take his place in the meeting today. Follow me before you get distracted like you always do."

"Do you remember my friends here?" Lucius asked.

"You know they can't come in, they'll have to stay outside the meeting room like usual. Keep this meeting between us and the council." Fabul explained giving a tour around the council's headquarters. As they saw Omega talking to Iiokio and Hayden.

"I'll be at the meeting briefly, I need to go to the restroom." Lucius made up on the fly shifting Fabul's attention so that he didn't discover both Omega's in his line of sight.

"Fine, be swift. This is important." Fabul entered the meeting room as Lucius grouped up with Aelienor and Maria. "When did Hayden get here?"

"I'm not sure but I don't trust him here," Maria explained.

"We need to find a place to listen in to the meeting," Aelienor said as Lucius found a window to creak open listening into the room as they hid.

"That was quick Omega." Fabul summarized as Omega entered the room.

"What?"

"That was inappropriate. My apologies." Fabul said as he changed the subject. "Due to Ill minded as of late learning magic faster than our populace averages and having the Ill-minded pop in as often as they are now. It only raises questions on what to do with those Ill-minded. We need to focus on security. Kralan as a whole needs to focus on fewer teachings on magic since the Ill minded are learning magic faster than the rules that apply with them." Fabul explained.

"Since its recent loss from Rosetta and Rosane. We do not want this in the wrong hands again. What are your thoughts going forward Omega?" Anne summarized as Omega summoned the All-Seeing Eye in the air to deconstruct it for observation.

"Iiokio sent me here today to convene what makes the eye have so much interest in the common mind. Not one mind, whether they're ill or not, cannot withstand the power for long without corruption without the magnetic counterpart. I propose we store it within Kralan for the time being, but we need a more discreet location in the long run."

"Why are we trusting you with it Omega?" Kion asked.

"I say this with the utmost respect possible. Who else?" Omega asked.

Kion sat back in his chair speechless.

"Where in Kralan should it be?" Rosetta asked.

"It's been safe for the last few decades." Rosane worded.

"Malyna would know a good place..." Kion thought out loud as it made the room silent.

"She's a traitor, why should we trust her?" Anne asked. "Perhaps I shall guard it since the last guards didn't do well enough and it's time for a change."

"I didn't follow Malyna's case and it matters not she shouldn't be trusted," Omega configured the All-Seeing Eye back into place making it disappear. "I believe if Iiokio makes the decisions for all of you he should also make this decision. I'll keep it until then."

"You'll regret not putting this into Malyna's hands..." Kion said as he slammed his hands on the meeting table.

"I would like to meet you in your office to speak more about your outburst here. This meeting is done." Omega said walking out into the hallway murmuring to himself. Lucius held his breath to not make a noise as he walked outside. Following Kion to Aelienor and Maria, reaching the door behind him. Kion sat on a chair facing his back to Lucius.

"You want to talk about business. My word has never meant anything to you, so why am I even in the council?" Kion asked as he turned to Omega and his two guards.

"Don't make this harder than it has to be," Lucius said.

"I know what you're planning to do here Omega. I'm not an idiot, you want to kill me. Tell me why you want to betray your cause, you and Iiokio built up."

Lucius was speechless.

"Actions speak better than words. Eh, Omega?" Kion took out a knife to stab his hand. Causing Lucius to flinch as the knife went into the table. The potion acted up to show Lucius' missing finger.

"What the hell?" Kion looked down to discover the knife got stuck in the wood as Lucius moved his glitchy finger away from the shock. Aelienor took the knife out of the table jabbing toward Kion.

Kion fell back from his fancy chair as he charged his power to make his hands glow a dark purple to begin forming an orb toward Aelienor. The power of the orb forcefully made Aelienor levitate into the air and form pains across her body.

Maria rushed by Aelienor's side stabbing Kion's side as he flinched slightly. Summoning another orb to attack Maria with his other hand. "Who are you?" Kion asked as he revealed their real identity. "Aelienor and Maria... So who is Omega?"

Lucius twisted the knife inside him. Making him drop his orb to lose control of Aelienor and Maria. Kion tapped his side to feel the blood as if it were the first time he saw the red liquid. "You're Lucius. I knew you would've been an issue. You're halfway there Ill-minded," Kion confessed giving a weak smile. "You may as well finish the job and discover what true fire you have lit." Kion said, slumping down the wall while holding his stomach.

Kion coughed up blood looking up as he laughed. "Good luck explaining this one to Iiokio." Kions voice trailed as his cocky smirk became empty as his magic aura left his soul.

"A part of him wanted me to kill him. What a sick man..." Lucius thought to himself looking at the blood on his hands washing his hands in the bathroom as he entered back to the room where Kion laid seeing his friends Maria and Aelienor lying unconscious in the corner of the room. "I'll get you two out of here soon enough."

The real Omega opened the door realizing Kion laid lifeless with his spelt blood staining the marble flooring.

"Who did this?" Omega asked as he looked up with hatred in his eyes seeing Lucius. "You're that kid that got the shield masking potion from Hunter and Rebiha didn't you..." Omega admitted. Running up to Lucius being surrounded by vines in a sudden flash before he was able to grab him.

Memory VII - Familiar Faces

* The Bigger Picture *

Once Omega disappeared with Hayden and Iiokio. Lucius' legs were sore from the vines. "Why vdidn't Hayden pick me?" Lucius asked as he picked up Aelienor and Maria leaving Iiokio with caution as he dropped them off at Hunters.

"What happened?" Hunter asked.

"It didn't go the way we wanted it too. Kion's out of the picture he hurt Maria and Aelienor. But Omega knows you bought the potions for us." Lucius summarized.

"This isn't good at all." Hunter admitted as he called upon Rebiha to use her conjuration to heal.

"Omega was sent in mage jail for Kion's murder."

"It won't last long. We're going to have to move out before he breaks out." Hunter sighed.

"Move again?" Rebiha asked with disappointment.

"It's for protection," Hunter explained.

"I know."

"Where's Ernaldus and Gauvain?" Hunter asked as they entered after he asked.

"We heard what happened but Lucius-" Gauvain began catching up behind Lucius as he was cut off by Ernaldus.

"What happened to my sister?"

"Things got a little dicey." Lucius carefully worded.

Ernaldus threatened. "I'll dice you if Aelienor's isn't alright."

"They were choked. You can see the markings on their throat. I know some remedies..." Rebiha explained.

"We must inform Morrison of our progress right away," Hunter explained.

"What were you guys doing?" Lucius asked.

"You told us to bury that guy." Gauvain said in a what do you mean tone.

"Did it take that long?" Dragging the word 'that' until it aggravated Ernaldus. Which surprisingly enough, took longer than Lucius expected.

"Did you bury Kion?" Ernaldus insulted.

"No, but we need your help." Lucius stated.

"We would've helped if you didn't want us to bury that guy. We did notice Hayden has the relic now." Gauvain explained.

"That's why he wanted Omega to be captured." Lucius massaged his temple for the headache he gained.

"The more reason we need to talk to Morrison. Rebiha will inform me of the progress of your friends." Hunter said as he drew the portal back to the Ill-minded realm. Back into Morrison's office. As they found out as they drew the portal that Morrison was arguing with Jack and Vaughan. Hunter entered the portal with haste. As Lucius, Ernaldus, and Gauvain followed.

"What's going on?"

"The Timeline Codex. We want to know where it is." Vaughan explained.

"They're blaming Wariner. That's preposterous. I thought Wariner was with you all for the longest time." Morrison explained.

Gauvain decided to give back the book as he checked himself whispering to Lucius. "I lost it."

"What?" Lucius raised his voice.

"Did you know who took it?" Jack rephrased with a short tempered nose flare.

"I don't." Lucius said as Jack continued back to Morrison. Lucius looked at Gauvain with agitation.

"Wherever your son is...I'm willing to bet all of my gold, it won't be too far away." Jack complained.

"Watch your tongue. If it weren't for me you wouldn't have gotten as far as you did without me by your side. You better remember that before you point fingers without proof. All you're doing is throwing accusations as fast as you could make them." Morrison explained as a knock silenced the room. "Come in..."

Nolyn entered as he explained. "Wariner is in the mage realm. I work in the mage realm as the warden in the jail on the side. Once I came back I noticed Jousen and Draven escaped. It appears by the explosion..."

"Oh, my Yuoki... How didn't I hear it?" Morrison asked with a sigh.

"The mage realm?" Vaughan asked.

"What's that?" Jack added.

"It's where I had Lucius and his friends go." Hunter explained.

"-And who are you?" Jack asked.

"I'm surprised you don't know much about Malyna," Lucius said.

"She didn't say anything about a mage realm. I knew she was in jail, if Wariner's in the mage realm I need to talk to him." Jack explained.

"You're not talking to anyone until you calm down," Morrison explained. "I've been worried about some time when he's been. But we have two escaped convicts to worry about."

"Those two convicts can wait for the book is a higher priority than those two mistakes. They'll find themselves in jail again in no time." Vaughan explained.

"Fine. I'll go with you then." Morrison stated. "To only make sure you're not going to do anything rash. I'm going with you." Morrison looked over to Lucius. "Lucius, Gauvain, and Ernaldus do me a favor and help Nolyn to find whatever Draven and Jousen are doing." Morrison said leaving with Vaughan, Jack, and Hunter.

* Q&A *

"What a time to be meeting up like this. I do owe all of you for saving my life. I do suppose now's not the time for this speech." Nolyn said as he exited showing the explosion to them. "Do you have an idea of where they could've gone?"

"I'm positive they went to save Drago to gain some trust, so Therron's castle," Ernaldus explained

Lucius entered the castle. Lacking Therron's guards made it look empty. "They should be somewhere around here..." Gauvain said as he searched the cells.

"Are you looking for me?" Draven asked looking down at them from the previous floor. "If you're looking for my boss, they're free."

Out of anger Nolyn took out a bow and aimed it at Draven.

"Go ahead Nolyn. It won't end well for you." Draven said with a smirk as he was met with an arrow in the throat. Draven grabbed his throat as he fell beside them.

"Now that's over with let's find-" Nolyn explained taking a step forward as he was met with an arrow of his own to the back of the head.

Lucius lowered his weapon at the sight of Jousen's bow.

Drago and his men appeared behind Jousen.

"Nice to see you, Lucius." Flynn explained as he appeared in front of Lucius.

"Are you going to let this happen?" Lucius asked.

"What happened to Draven and Nolyn was nothing personal. It took a while discovering Drago was on our side the whole time. He was lenient with us and since Hayden is now back in charge it's time to follow him and his ways no more following others." Stephan explained as he took out his sword.

"I saved your life, Stephan. Yours too Flynn. Why are you doing this?" Lucius asked.

"This is the rebellion's highest point. We have accomplished so much this is only the beginning. Hayden claims you as an enemy, so I'll be damned if I'll let you get away. No matter how much you've helped us. I'm not going to let him down." Lex added.

"Hayden's a smart man, I'd like to do business with him." Drago said.

"I'm sure he'll be more than glad to help," Stephan said as he and the newfound allies started to surround Lucius, Ernaldus, and Gauvain before they were able to close enough to fight. Kain, Reyner, Ashlyn, and Pavel gained his attention with weapons of their own. Scaring them off. Lucius grappled Magnus before he was able to escape.

Magnus placed his head down in defeat as he dropped his weapons."If you expect me to give you information. You've picked the wrong man, you'll only waste your time."

"Good, I like a fighter." Ernaldus confessed punching Magnus.

"I'd figure we shouldn't have trusted Hayden. I didn't think we would've done what he did today." Ashlyn explained.

"Their personalities changed. I know they tried to convince Hayden to join Jack. But something must've happened that they decided to combine forces." Reyner confessed.

"Hayden has the eye," Lucius answered. "I suppose they don't want to be on his bad side. We didn't do anything to make him hate us." Gauvain explained.

"As much as he wouldn't want to say it. Hayden is afraid, you can make more change than what he can. Look at all your accomplishments here Lucius, It took less than several years to finish what he planned." Fabul said coming out from the shadows with Malyna.

"If it's not too late, can I see the one who calls himself Floros Gordon?" Malyna questioned.

"You must be Malyna. He's in the infirmary." Kain explained.

"How'd you manage to bust Malyna out?" Ernaldus asked.

"It won't take long to discover Kion's death isn't the only issue around here. From what I gather Malyna's crime was never proven. Only speculation I'm sure you're in the same boat. I'll do what I can do to help." Fabul summarized as Kain led them to Floros, who laid on a bed.

"He's starting to glitch..." Caroline said as they entered.

"It'll be tough. I'll do what I can." Malyna explained.

"My brother glitched before he died." Kain said dryly.

"It's all a matter of how long you hold it without its second part. He may still have a chance." Malyna said.

"No, wait...I want to help-" Floros said as Malyna put him to sleep.

"I know you wanted to and you did..." Kain sighed with an abrupt end. "What did you do?"

"It'll be best if he doesn't think much. There's a higher chance of being corrupt that way which is when the glitch happens. I learned to control my glitching." Malyna glitched to prove a point. "I'm not corrupted but you must glitch once in a while to maintain sanity. While glitching you may have trouble with your memories or an occasional colliding with memories of others that held the artifact before. You snap back to reality quick-"

"It took until now you wanted to explain this to us." Kain remarked with concern.

"It's a side effect, for his safety he shouldn't be close to the artifact."

"She'll need some time to do what she does to help Floros. In the meantime, I would like to set Hayden and Omega a few steps back while they'll be busy if you're up to it." Fabul summarized.

"Anything at this point. What do you have?" Ashlyn asked.

"We'll gain access to Omega's base. His magic is disabled for the time being which means all of his supplies and devices have been left idle." Fabul explained.

"Can I come?" Caroline asked.

"I suppose so. Be careful with that boy." Fabul admitted.

Everyone left to follow Fabul to the mage realm to let Malyna work with Floros as she waved her hand over Floros speaking a spell.

"This is the mage realm?" Ashlyn asked.

"It is. People are going to recognize all of you are ill-minded, so we must be quick. Stay your distance from me but keep up from within the shadows." Fabul summarized rushing out of his house checking the streets to make sure they were clear. Lucius bumped into Jack, Vaughan, and Morrison as they were following Fabul.

"Wariner wasn't here. It would seem that we missed him." Morrison said with disappointment.

"I'm sure you're glad that you didn't find him." Vaughan remarked.

"I'm not and I'm willing to prove you wrong with your stupid book. I think you happened to overlook it."

"You three should follow us. Fabul's bringing us to Omega's lair before he escapes. It'll have a lot of information about all of what Omega does. I'm sure we'll find what you're looking for." Lucius said.

"What about the Draven and Jousen deal?" Morrison asked.

"It's dealt with. We'll tell you later." Gauvain said.

Vaughan and Jack followed Lucius' lead with Fabul.

"This is it." Fabul pointed out the shed.

"It's tough for even two people inside." Caroline said with doubt.

Fabul gave a slight chuckle. "Meet me inside."

"This guy must be joking..." Ashlyn scoffed discovering no one on the other side.

"I'll try it then." Jack said entering next.

"He shouldn't be too far." Vaughan commented before he followed, one after another after the door was shut. They would vanish to the other side before the next person would grasp the handle.

"This is engineered like my time traveling machine..." Jack took notice first thing as he looked at the devices Omega used within Omega's base. Jack placed a part in the machine that he had brought with him. "If my research is correct he has the updated device here somewhere..." Jack started as he matched a sketch with a piece he was searching for. "Here's his future time travel piece. I should've figured out future time travel compatibility would've been this simple. I must've overthought it years ago."

"This base is now yours. I transferred the ownership in my hands, giving you access any time you want." Fabul said with cheer in his voice as he messed with the terminal.

"Lucius I want you to do the honors of being the first person to use this finished prototype." Jack as he laughed. "I still can't believe it myself." Jack placed a goblet in the middle of the pad as he sent it back within a few seconds picking back up the goblet seeing it unaffected.

"I thank you, Jack, for the invitation as long as it is alright with you, I don't want to mess you up." Lucius said.

"I feel you deserve this more than us all. " Vaughan said with confidence.

"I believe you should do it, Lucius. If this is true, we'll accomplish so much more." Gauvain confessed as Lucius decided to walk into the time travel machine convinced.

"Are you ready?" Morrison asked.

"I am."

Jack pressed the button from the outside to trigger the time machine. The machine sparked, making a sudden electric stir to power off.

Lucius' confidence plummeted before Lucius was able to leave he was teleported.

"I sense you in my time machine, Lucius," Omega confessed. Omega rose from his prison cot in response watching Lucius levitating in the air outside of Omega's cell.

"Did you do this to me?" Lucius asked as he looked down, seeing nothing keeping him up. Looked back at Omega to not try to dwell on it.

"Whatever you did to my machine was your doing. I knew it was going to be taken away someday. I didn't figure it would've happened this way but I know it's my time to get out before anything else happens. Tell a fellow escapee Malyna, I said hello." Omega said grabbing a patrolling guard, bashing him against the bar until the man slid down to the ground. Omega slid the key out the guard's pouch leaving his cell with rage-filled stomps.

Lucius had teleported again.

This time seeing Lucius' mom, Bella sobbing back home. Lucius attempted to comfort her as she didn't budge.

Piecing together he could warn her writing on a piece of paper. "We went to find the All- Seeing Eye." Bella rose to see the paper floating into the air watching the paper start writing itself. Her expression on her face changed to immediate joy. "Parker, I know where they are..." Bella yelled out. Parker came out from another room with multiple healed wounds.

"Dad, you're alive?" Lucius said shocked.

"What're we waiting for..." Parker said with a raspy voice.

Lucius teleported once more.

Seeing Hayden and Wariner talking in a group with Helba.

Helba walked up to Hayden with the future book. "Here you go, Hayden. I stole it from Gauvain when I followed them into the mage realm."

"Good, progress with Lucius?" Hayden asked.

"He and his friends escaped, but they killed Nolyn from the loss of Draven." Wariner explained.

"Little fish... Little fish. I don't care about them." Hayden turned to look at Lucius. "Wait a moment I feel watching eyes." Hayden walked closer, aiming the relic at Lucius. "There you are..." Hayden said as he began to charge the artifact.

"Is there someone there?" Helba asked.

"It's nothing." Hayden said as he shot Lucius.

Jack waved his hand in front of Lucius' eyes. Lucius rose in sudden urgency covered in a heavy sweat.

"What did you see?" Ernaldus asked.

"His mind shifted with a glitch as he teleported. This has never happened before..." Lucius looked at his hands glitching. "Oh, no."

"We need to get you to Malyna," Jack said as his eyes widened.

"There's something I need to tell you. Helba isn't with us anymore." Lucius said as he glitched again as the glitch caused him to spaz making his vision become black.

"What'd he mean, will she die?" Vaughan asked.

"She may be in trouble. We need to look for her..." Jack said.

"No." Lucius mumbled knowing it was too late.

* Back To Reality *

"Dear Yuoki, Chosen of the All-Seeing Eye. The master and creator of magic, leader of legends. Save this poor soul for it has been corrupted. Lucius has a purpose, therefore, has life." Malyna's voice repeated around Lucius.

Before long Lucius came in and out of consciousness.

Floros stood in front of Lucius in an array of light.

"You're here too?" Floros asked.

"I am."

"But you didn't touch the eye. I have a mark on my chest from my mistake." Floros showed Lucius the artifact's mark.

Causing Lucius to look at his chest discovering the same mark. "What does this mean?"

"Your guess is as good as mine. When we get out, I mean if we get out. We have to work together to take down Hayden. He's the reason this happened to us. He corrupted me as much as you. Promise me you'll do that for me. It's the least I can ask you to do."

"I promise," Lucius said as Floros smiled as he woke up in a bed in a house he wasn't familiar with. "We must be in Omega's shed?" Lucius guessed. Taking a look in the mirror at his chest.

"The mark..." He uttered to himself rubbing his newfound scruffy beard. "How long was I out?"

Exiting the guest room. Discovering Caroline entering the time machine with her child.

"What are you doing," Lucius asked, interrupting Caroline.

"I'm going out. It's great to see you again. Your voice is deeper than I remember." Caroline said.

"I don't recall you like doing time travel."

"You got me," Caroline smiled with sadness. "We figured out what you meant by Helba. She's changed. I don't want that to happen to me or my son. Which is why I must go away. You understand. Things have only become worse since you've been out of the picture. Hell, some of us thought you died. Please, let this be a secret between us."

"You can't leave. We need to get through this together..." Lucius admitted.

"You're a fighter, Lucius. I'm not. Which is why I know you can do it. I'm tired and I don't want any more wickedness." Caroline entered the time machine.

"Wait..." Lucius said as Caroline turned around entering the machine.

"No more waiting, Lucius. I want to remember this, a good memory as our last memory. Unlike Magnus Almon who has caused me to get pregnant again to carry his 'legacy'. That hedge-born cumberworld. And if you're wondering, the name of my first son is... Blade Kentrell Almon. I'm sure he'll be a fighter like you." Caroline teared up as he lost her in a cloud of fog.

"Caroline..." Lucius rushed as he looked at the time machine to not see any history of where or what time she left. "Magnus... I can't believe it. I'm sorry Caroline."

"You're awake. Were you talking to someone?" Malyna said, rubbing her waking eyes.

"Yeah, I'm awake, and no, I wasn't," Lucius said, taking a long breath feeling like he was punched in the gut.

"I'm sure you have plenty of questions." Malyna said.

"That's an understatement."

"Take a seat, I'll answer anything you want to know to catch up," Malyna said as he pulled a chair for Lucius.

"Thanks," Lucius sat pushing himself in. "My first question is where is Hayden?"

"He's at where you remember Therron's castle being. With the renovations, he's made a bigger and worse fortress there. He's captured, Kain and Reyner." Malyna said looking up. "Jack, Vaughan and their dad; Cencil is planning to assault their base once they get some rest. Hayden 'invited' us to dinner which I don't like since we all know it's a trap, but we have to try. As massive as it is, there's only one entrance. They're forcing our hand. I'd figure you would want to join and I wouldn't stop you. I'll stay with Floros and Pavel."

"What about everyone else?"

"The rest of us are fighting a war with Omega. Taking turns to escort the others to safety. Its absolute chaos there. We'll join the fight there once we gain our friends back."

"How long was I out?"

"At least six months if I had to guess. It may have been longer than that. Maria visited you every day, longer than the rest of your friends right until she went to bed. I figured you wanted you to know that. She left with Aelienor to help defend Fabul. The council isn't what it was anymore."

"Do you know what this symbol means?" Lucius asked as he moved his collar down to show the mark.

"The same mark Floros and I have," Malyna

said as she showed him her mark. In the middle of her chest holding her collar down as he was hesitant to look.

"Don't make it weird," Malyna said. "It means that we have built resistance to the All- Seeing Eye's power. It doesn't make us invincible, but we're on the magnetic seal's list now. It's not going to show a ping of our location but what it will do is make Hayden or whoever is holding it next to see us as a threat... We have resistance to fight back, but we must be strong and to expect anything."

Cencil walked out from another room gathering two pots to wake up Vaughan and Jack. "Wake up. It's time to settle the score with Hayden. You don't want to be late."

"Five more minutes." Vaughan cried out.

"Is Cencil always like this?" Lucius asked.

"Ever since I've known him he's been like this. We need him for his army skills. He owns an army, but they're our plan b if we need them." Malyna explained as she drank tea as she passed him a cup as well.

"Don't five more minutes me. That calls for more loud noises." Cencil said as he clapped the pots faster and louder making the brothers get out of bed.

"Morning," Cencil said smiling as on a dime he changed his voice to bark an order. "Now get ready."

"Aye, aye. Sir." Jack joked as he saluted.

"You think this is a joke. I don't see it funny." Cencil said clapping pans next to Jack's ears, as his son flinched from the noise.

"I get it." Jack reminded himself with irritation. "I think this joke is pretty funny myself," Cencil said, sitting the pans in the middle of the table between Lucius and Malyna. "How're you doing Lucius?"

"I'm doing well."

"Don't you lie to me. Not a good first impression of someone being known as leader material."

"I am doing as well as one would be under the experiences I was given." Lucius corrected.

"Don't mind Cencil, Lucius. He gets under all of our skins." Malyna explained.

"Hey, that hurts. At least Lucius' up, alive, and doing alright from what I can tell."

"Lucius isn't like Helba." Malyna stated.

"I didn't say he was. But you never know when someone would betray you. Be wary of who you trust Lucius. I mean it. Now Lucius I know you came back from a coma just this morning but did you want to depart here with us for a little visit to Hayden?"

"Yes, I believe Hayden does need a surprise visit from me."

"I like your spirit. I took you as a coward at first. Then your recent feat of taking down Kion... I knew then that I misjudged you."

"They wanted to die."

"Bloodthirsty are you?" Cencil asked laughing. "You have a lot of courage."

"Not what I meant. They didn't fight back." "In this case. You should come along so Hayden will want to die as well."

"I doubt it works that way..."

"It may not." Cencil looked around confused. "Where's Caroline?"

Lucius avoided the question as he went upstairs to ready up as Jack and Vaughan passed him as they went downstairs. Walking upstairs he noticed a door ajar enough to spy inside, seeing Magnus. Tied up waiting with a joyful demeanor hiding under utter malice.

"I see you." Magnus reminded. "You're free to come in," Lucius entered Magnus' room with curiosity. "Did you have a good dream?"

"I know what you did to Caroline."

"I'm sure you do. But you also need me to tag along since Hayden wants me back. Henceforth, this invitation I hear about. You could tell everyone but if you even lay a finger on me it won't end well for you in the long run."

"They're looking for Caroline now. How could you?" Lucius asked, gripping his fist.

"She left?" Magnus asked. "It was a matter of time I suppose. She couldn't look me in the eyes anymore. What you want me to say in response... Paul had good taste in women?" Lucius punched him in response.

"You're a sick man."

"I'll allow that to be a freebie. I'm sure you're planning on a conclusion to this fiasco you put yourself in. They'll take your word over mine. But now I'm an asset. So what'll it be?" Magnus asked as Cencil walked up to Lucius.

"Are you ready to head out... Wait why'd you hit Magnus?" Cencil asked, noticing how Lucius reddened Magnus' cheek.

"Why did you hit me, Lucius?" Magnus raised a brow.

"I don't like the way he spoke to me. I flipped." Lucius confessed holding back.

"Save that strength for Hayden." Cencil said as he untied Magnus.

Magnus held his wrist as he rose. As he whispered to Lucius, "Caroline was the same way. I'd say you made the right choice. You're scared." Causing Lucius chills of loathing and disgust. Magnus passed by Lucius with a wink as he exited the room.

"Caroline went on without us," Malyna said, checking the last room downstairs.

"I didn't expect her to leave. She'll come back when she's ready. " Vaughan said with hesitation.

"She's not coming back, isn't she?"

"Let's head out," Vaughan said dismissively. "We have a lot to do."

* Dealing With A Madman *

Jack led them outside the base to Hayden's castle. On the route, Lucius looked at the castle surprised by the surrounding changes. "This used to be Therron's castle?"

"He has been busy without much trouble from all of you. Not that I blame you for not doing much." Magnus explained.

"It'll be best if you don't speak unless you're spoken to or-" Jack said as Magnus interrupted.

"Or else. You kill me?" Magnus joked. "I don't take threats nicely."

"I'll find your weakness and exploit it so much that you'll wish you were never born. Only then will you realize that there are worse things than death." Cencil threatened, making Magnus forget how to breathe for a moment.

"Fine, tough guy. I'll stop, for now."

Reaching the entrance, The door opened itself. A long line of different men working for Hayden on either side. Lucius glanced around the throne room feeling like an eternity until reaching Hayden.

"I see most of you received my invitation," Hayden said, glitching to make his words echo. "I expected more of you to show but instead I'm surprised that you've brought Lucius with you. Which is a treat for all of us I'm sure." Hayden raised as he led them to the dining room that was composed of several guards around each corner. Reaching the dining room it revealed Hayden's crew awaiting the guest.

"Where's Reyner and Kain?" Jack asked. "They're here but didn't want to take part in this magnificent event. You'll see them after," Hayden explained as he walked to his seat. "Now sit before the food gets cold."

"I don't believe that for a second." Vaughan burst.

"Watch your manners. Cencil, have you not taught your sons respect?" Hayden corrected.

"The nerve of some people." Magnus shook his head as he sat next to Drago.

Cencil held his breath as he pointed out a seat to Vaughan, sitting down after swallowing his pride.

"It's good that most of you made it out. Lucius, I must apologize for my actions of putting you in your coma-like state. It wasn't anything personal." Hayden explained.

"Is that the only thing you want to apologize for?" Lucius asked.

"I'm being civil and I don't want to be anything less than cordial on this great day."

"I told you this may not have the greatest idea." Flynn explained.

"You know Lucius I do give second chances. This is not too late to come around."

"I don't know about anyone else but this whole ordeal is making me uneasy. Something will happen, I know it." Drago explained.

"I feel the same feeling but the reason you're here is for support which is what you're going to do. I've helped you out more than enough."

"You're right, my apologies." Drago explained.

"They mean well." Lex added.

"Are Kain and Reyner alright?" Malyna asked.

"They're well and without a scratch. Only scared." Stephan summarized.

"You want to know why I've invited you all here today. I would like all of you to join us to take out Omega. The mage realm is in shambles and it's up to us to be their saviors. We both know we'll be successful if you accept. I've joined you when you were at perilous times. Only fair to pay that forward."

"You didn't go through the plan to take out Therron. Why should we trust you?" Jack asked.

"You'll have to take my word. You have to." Hayden answered.

Vaughan took out his sword pointing at Flynn. "Just kill me, Vaughan. I know I can't beat you so why should I live?" Flynn said with a fake giving up tune. "But I do know who can beat you. Would you be so naive to give up your life for mine?"

Hayden froze time with the All-Seeing Eye. Everyone's eyes looked at Hayden as their bodies still. Hayden was surprised when the artifact didn't freeze Lucius. "Why can't your men and mine get along?"

"It's the food you've brought." Lucius remarked.

"I knew I should've made the beef stew," Hayden chuckled briefly sauntering over to Vaughan and Flynn with a closer depth. "I don't get how minds work. I've lived through multiple timelines but certain results always end the same."

Lucius looked at the kitchen knife as he sauntered over as Hayden interrupted. "Don't even think about it," Hayden said as he teleported the knife away. " Hayden shook his head with annoyance as he resumed time as Vaughan picked up Flynn.

"I'll kill him, Hayden," Vaughan explained.

"Let him go, Vaughan." Cencil ordered.

"No, dad. I'm not allowing this to go on further."

"Then kill Flynn. Prove your point."

Drago jumped out of his seat to intervene Vaughan. "Is how you treat your people?"

"Sit down Drago, I will only tell you once," Hayden explained as Drago went to swing at Jack.

Hayden adruptly shot Drago with the All-Seeing Eye. Twitching for a few seconds before he became limp.

Jack was surprised by the relic's power. "Drago... Drago Endri?" Magnus asked, concerned feeling his pulse. "He's gone."

"I could've told you that. I said I would've only warned him once. He's not your boss Magnus, I am. Do you have a problem with that?" Hayden asked.

"No, sir."

"Is this what it takes for us to get along. Needless violence... I'm serious about our alliance. I've been more than patient with all of you. Drago drained the last of my trust. First was on his side, Omega then mine. Not a loyal guy."

"Is this what we should expect if we join you, an unexpected death?" Cencil asked.

"Not at all," Hayden said as Lex interrupted him with a goblet over the back of his head. Sliding it over to Jack. As Jack reached over Hayden teleported over to beat Jack to it as he forced Jack, Lucius, Cencil, Vaughan, and Lex to their knees with the power of the artifact. Hayden glitched with anger flashing like a strobe light.

"It's endless with all of you..." Hayden scoffed. "It's comical how much you want this artifact. I was going to give everyone a second chance but now that Lex is joining you, I'm appalled. One of you will never see the light of day again..." Hayden said, giving off a chaotic glare, rushing toward one of the members of the group.

Memory VIII -
The Confrontation

* Casualties *

Vaughan fell back, screaming with agony from a sudden rush of different slashes on his cheeks. Vaughan fell back blocking his face as best he could. Having his hands penetrated by the blade.

"Vaughan..." Jack yelled out as his veins from his neck began to bulge. Struggling to break Hayden's spell. As opposed to Cencil who was too weak to raise his head once the stabbing began.

"Look at me." Hayden ordered.

Vaughan weekly raised his bloodshot eyes using the strength he could muster kicking at Hayden. Hayden laughed watching Vaughan crawl toward his family. Groaning with urgency leaving a blood trail behind for Hayden to follow. Hayden grabbed Vaughan's leg back to the middle of the room an arms' length away from Jack.

"No. Please..." Vaughan urged out as his shirt curled over from the carpet, giving off rug burn.

"Your time is up. Such a waste of potential." Hayden announced as he continued to slash at Vaughan. Hayden stopped to raise Vaughan by his hair, facing him to his prisoners. "This is a message." Hayden finished with a jab into Vaughan's forehead before kicking Vaughan to the floor.

Releasing them from their paralyzed spell.

Cencil ran to cradle his lifeless son. Hayden rose his bloodied dagger to Cencil as Lucius intervened.

"No more death Hayden. It's time for your term to end-" Lucius explained during mid- breath feeling a dagger enter his stomach.

"Noble to pick yourself to die next but not smart."

Lucius took a grasp of air as if it were the first time breathing.

The room became silent.

"Goodbye Lucius," Hayden retracted the blade with force. Taking a few steps forward before cleaning his dagger's blood discovering no new blood on the dagger. Hayden made a firm grasp stabbing again.

Looking at the blade's entry into Lucius' glitchy body. "Impossible."

Lucius looked into Hayden's now wide and fearful eyes, "You've made your last mistake." Lucius announced the building began to shake, tearing itself apart.

"We need to get out of here..." Magnus said as he stepped aside from being crushed from part of the ceiling giving way.

"This isn't over." Hayden said as he teleported away with his remaining council.

"Are you alright?" Lex asked.

"I lost control for a moment. I thought and it happened. Sensing Kain's and Reyner's location made the building shake. We should go there while we have this chance. What about you, Lex?"

"What about me?"

"You did betray your friend to be on our side. How do we know you won't do it again to us?" Jack asked with a crack in his voice. Looking up at Lex as he hugged Vaughan with his father.

"My actions were controlled. Like many other he's around. In good faith I'll tell you about Hayden plan... Project Silverstar."

"Project Silverstar, you say?" Cencil asked.

"I don't know much about it myself but one thing for sure I know it's dangerous and is to end Omega's reign and us if we stand in his way which is why we need to go after him."

"I believe you, let's see if Kain and Reyner know of the project." Lucius rushed out of the nearest door revealing Floros.

"I want to help." Floros started.

"It's too dangerous." Malyna explained. "It's always too dangerous. I'm not useless."

"No one said you were... Just keep up with us." Lucius said with a rush in his voice.

"Thanks, Lucius." Floros said with cheer in his voice.

"Are you sure about his Lucius?" Malyna asked.

"Let's go." Lucius said dismissively.

Lucius led the group where he last sensed Reyner and Kain. They found them in cells looking for ways to escape themselves.

"Floros... What are you doing here?" Kain asked.

"I'm here to help. Do you know where the keys are?" Floros asked.

"Helba had them last. She's changed. I'm sure Jack and Cencil will see to that. Where's Vaughan?"

Kain asked.

"I'll tell you later." Lucius said as the room was silent.

"Where did you see Helba last?" Floros asked as he changed the subject.

"She does patrol, I suggest you should hide as she will pass by here soon," Reyner explained.

"There's nowhere to hide," Malyna said as she began to cast a spell charged up her hands. As her hands became yellow as Floros slapped her hand away.

"Magic will give away our position. It's not the mage realm." Floros explained.

"Any better ideas?" Malyna asked.

Floros ran ahead to the cells, attempting to rip it apart.

"That won't work..." Lucius started as Floros stepped aside with the bars parted away.

"I suppose that kid shouldn't be taken for granted." Cencil thought out loud.

"Stop calling me kid." Floros complained.

"You'll always be a kid," Kain added as he exited the cell patting Floros on the back. "My kid."

Floros turned around shoving his dad to the wall. With his shoulder to Kain's throat. Changing Kain's expression.

"You left me in Hayden's hands. I blamed him for all the things that had happened. I realize it was you that was the problem the whole time." Floros said with a glitchy voice. Lucius grappled Floros away from Kain. Kain held his throat, gasping in desperation for air.

"I'm sorry. I didn't know... I'm trying my best." Kain said.

"It wasn't good... Enough." Floros said as he rushed toward Kain.

"You have nothing to be sorry for Kain... It's the artifact speaking though him." Lucius said intervening as he had Floros in an arm bar with his face against the ground.

"I know it corrupts but does he also speak the truth and believes I am the one to blame?" Kain asked.

"It's hard to tell, but we need to get out of here," Reyner explained.

Lucius looked up to Reyner and Kain he noticed Helba waved at him before Teleporting away with her prisoners.

"No." Lucius yelled.

"What happened to me... Is Kain ok?" Floros asked as he stopped resisting.

"They took Kain and Reyner again." Jack summarized with disappointment.

"We still have a chance for an upper hand with project Silverstar," Lex explained.

* The Cold Shoulder *

Back in Omega's old base, Jack looked up the codename Project Silverstar in the terminal, "Corrupted?"

"I'll decrypt it, but it'll take some time," Lex explained.

"Can this revive my brother Vaughan?" Jack asked.

"I don't think so..." Lex explained.

"I need to go back then," Jack said as Lucius stopped him.

"Don't you remember he did the same thing for you?"

"What's your point?"

"He may have foreseen it to happen, think about it. Vaughan knew about you stopping the fire in Quia. I know you're sad about his death but you shouldn't go back. That's what they want you to do. Hayden even said to himself he relieved moments like that before. It could've been worse. It should be me if anything since I can do things you couldn't. Give me time and I'll bring Vaughan back."

"But Lucius the same thing can be said about him. Perhaps it's my destiny to save him."

"It's suicide to go back there. Who knows what else could happen if we alter time in a dangerous place like that."

Jack sighed. "Once we get your friends back and finish Omega. I want you to do that for me. I know you won't fail. You haven't yet." Jack explained.

"If you do plan on taking out Omega... you better do it now this encryption will take longer than I anticipated but it's doable," Lex stated. Floros created a portal to the mage realm. "I'll stay back and lock myself up, I never wanted to hurt him."

"It was the artifact's doing. It may have also been Helba's idea of a distraction... Where'd you get that portal...stick?" Lucius asked.

"You mean the Portalatrix?" Floros corrected.

"Answer the question," Lucius asked with impatience.

"I took one from Quia," Floros confessed as Lucius gave him a look. "Worry not. I'll give it back soon." Floros said as they entered the mage realm. Lucius stopped as he spoke up. "Lex watch Floros for us."

"I will be careful. We all haven't forgotten about the glitch that happened in front of us. You should've been dead." Lex reminded.

"Perhaps I was given this second chance for a reason," Lucius said as he left.

"You've missed plenty of action. Taking plenty of time. No matter what, I'm glad you're here. Kralan is falling. We have to work together before Omega finishes us all." Fabul explained looking outside. Lucius followed him watching a dark purple, upside-down tornado in the sky forming to tear apart Kralan.

"This is worse than Therron's reign." Lucius said.

"Since the new threat is an experienced mage I'd say so. We don't have much time here to dawdle before this building collapses from the pressure, and we're forced to fight."

"Where's everyone else?" Lucius asked.

"They're all scattered across Kralan. Either fighting or hiding to recover. I've never seen this side of Omega before, I don't think anyone has. He's unpredictable." Fabul said, being lost for words as the roof was sent flying off with the fierce wind.

"This is our time to fight. Gain his attention as much as you can. Avoid obstacles in your way and let us do the rest of the work. Good luck." Fabul explained as he rushed up to Omega as the rest of the house was knocked down.

"What did we get ourselves into?" Jack asked.

"It's best if you follow his directions," Malyna said as she summoned a flying bird to fly toward Omega.

"Watch out." Cencil yelled out as Malyna flew past Omega's meteorite. Malyna was successful at dodging, it came at a cost. Crushing Rosetta and Rosane underneath instead.

"Rosane... Rosetta..." Malyna said as she released a tear with her newfound rage rushing back at Omega. Lucius was helped up from the blast by a familiar face, Hunter.

"Where's your family?" Lucius asked. "They need to be out of harm's way..."

"There are other mage realms out there, aside from Kralan. We need to be fast. Those meteorites are the mages only way of transportation. I need to catch up with my wife and if you can lead me to her I'd be most grateful." Hunter summarized.

"Lead the way," Lucius said as lightning struck nearby mercenaries who helped Thex. Lucius, Jack, and Cencil picked up the freshly fried mercenaries' weapons.

Blocking stray arrows and challenging anyone who had gotten in Hunter's way. Lucius looked at his hand as his missing finger seemed to hologram itself back. Giving Lucius a better grip on his sword. Hunter was able to enter a functioning meteorite with his family waiting in hiding to leave.

The Meteorite took off with a flash. Lucius noticed Maria and Ernaldus getting overwhelmed with Omega's henchmen. Lucius, Jack, and Cencil made the odds even as they attacked them from behind. Killing them without much effort.

"I knew you were alright," Maria said as he knew the coast was clear hugging Lucius.

"No time for celebrations. We have work to do." Ernaldus said.

"He's right. Be on your guard." Cencil said.

Omega headbutted Iiokio. Kicking the stunned Iiokio into Fabul. Twisting Malyna's arm pushing her into Anne. "Feel some of my wraith Lucius," Omega said as he shot an arrow at Lucius when he had idle time. During the distraction, Iiokio blinded Omega with poison oak within his palm strikes.

Ernaldus pulled Lucius away as he walked into the arrow in the process getting shot in the stomach. Ernaldus took a few steps forward as his eyes widened coughing up blood. Swiping a couple of fingers onto his crimson filled lips. Falling to his knees. "Watch my sister for me, Lucius." Transitioning to become flat on the ground giving off a longing and final sigh.

"Ernaldus..." Lucius said, having trouble breathing. "You'll die you bastard," Lucius screamed out to Omega. Cencil grabbed him away from the open. As Maria, a crying mess was picked up by Jack following Cencil.

"Let me go. Omega will die by my hands." Lucius yelled out. Cencil let him go. Entering a building blocking him from leaving the building that hasn't been destroyed.

"Not this way. Your vengeance will happen soon but this anger will not make you successful. I loathe Hayden for killing my son, but he'll get what he deserves." Cencil explained as Lucius punched Cencil in the nose to rush outside picking up a bow nearby. Shooting at upon an opening.

Omega took the arrow to his left hand as he dodged attacks from Anne, elbowing her throat before kicking her a few feet away.

Omega used the arrow in his hand slapping Fabul into the temple. Fabul became still giving Omega enough time to realize he was gone. Omega retracted his hand with anger as he kicked Fabul away.

Iiokio rushed to attack once more. Omega turned around snapping the arrow in half. Iiokio took a dagger to stab Omega. Omega disarmed the dagger slitting Iiokio's throat.

"You forced my hand Apprentice." Omega admitted with guilt.

"Iiokio," Anne exclaimed coughing with difficulty. She rushed toward Omega. Omega dodged her attack. "You'll pay for your crimes!"

"You flee now and I'll give you mercy." Omega bartered as Anne fired several astral beams into his leg. Leaving multiple burn marks on his legs.

Omega rose his hands to force the Astral plane from her hand to close. Paralyzing her posture long enough to stab Anne in her back three time before he noticed the paralyze spell begin to ware off.

Omega rose Anne with her neck snapping it like a twig.

Shifting the dagger out of Anne. Parrying Malyna's attacks with ease with Anne as a shield. Thrusting the knife into Malyna's chest. Omega tossed what was left of Anne to the wreckage of Kralan below.

A storm grew above Omega, growing darker with each minute. Before lone fog began to form. Omega felt his bloodied and slimly hands before tightening his fist as he looked for his next victim.

"They're gone. All the coucil...gone." Lucius said in awe as he was turned around. Cencil returned the punch to Lucius. Lucius fell to the ground as Cencil accidently made Lucius dodge a shot from Omega.

"No one punches me and gets away with it. This is for your safety. " Cencil said as he looked up in the sky, knowing it was over. Cencil looked back at Lucius as Cencil helped him to cover.

"You got a good hit kid. Next time make sure you swing at the enemy. Your recklessness could've been your end."

"Sad times are with us this day but I believe our struggles with Omega have come to an end for now. We need to leave."

"I want to see Omega's dead body," Lucius ordered with tears generating in his eyes. Watching from a distance Pavel coming with Aelienor and Gauvain.

"Where's Ernaldus?" Aelienor asked.

"No time." Cencil said.

"We'll buy you time..." Rosetta explained meeting up with Lucius with his brother handing him some armor. Both beaten up with scars and several burn marks.

"That's suicide." Lucius yelled.

"It'll be your only chance." Rosane explained as they both readied magic.

"Thanks for everything," Cencil explained as he forced Lucius and the others to follow as Omega entered the building with Rosetta and Rosane.

"Out of the way." Omega ordered.

"Not happening," Rosetta said as he and Rosane shot out a beam of combined magic at Omega, reflecting with a beam of their own.

Exiting through the portal. Aelienor slugging along as the portal disappeared. "He's gone. Isn't he?" Lucius babbled. Static grew in his head confessing Ernaldus' death. Aelienor bawled into Lucius' shoulders, something deep inside him changed. Snapped. Hoping it wasn't the same feeling as everyone who had exposure to the artifact.

Only once Aelienor left his shoulder, Lucius sensed a bad vibe from Gauvain. Not being able to shake it. Lucius grappled Gauvain seeing as he wasn't upset from his or any others

"What'd you do Gauvain?"

"What's going on with you Lucius?"

Lucius looked at Gauvain with suspicion as he pushed him away giving Gauvain concern.

Gauvain waited for Lucius to turn his back as he left after Lucius.

* Risky Business *

"How's the progress with project Silverstar?" Jack asked Lex.

"It's all finished. I'm ready to show what I have but I have a confession before I continue." Lex said.

"I'm not a fan of surprises. Spill it." Cencil explained.

"Project Silverstar. It's Hayden's project for time travel... He's sending an army of people in the future to attack the past. We can stop it from happening but it'll be tricky." Lex summarized as he as Helba popped up on the screen.

"You want Reyner and Kain, come to my location. Hayden has plans for you but I have my own incentive. I have your book right here. You wouldn't want a particular Hayden to bump into this information. You have a few hours to decide." Helba ordered stopping her broadcast with a bratty smile.

"How'd she get that?" Jack asked.

"I don't know but it'll be simple to track her location. I don't like this at all." Lex explained.

"It must be a trap." Jack thought out loud.

"I know it is. We better not keep her waiting." Lex said pointing out her location from coordinates on her broadcast. "She's at some sort of temple. It looks like she has company but no Hayden."

"I know what temple it is." Cencil asked.

"You know this temple dad?" Jack asked.

"I should've figured she'd want to meet us there. It's the Temple of Prophecies."

"How'd you know she would be there?"

"That's where my old base was. I should've locked everything down."

"We'll get to the bottom of this." Lucius reassured looking around him.

Where's Aelienor and Gauvain?

* Price Of Failure *

Gauvain stood outside seeing a ship land next to the docks. Starting to head his way out of the island as Aelienor stopped him. "Where are you going?"

"I'm going home. I can't handle anymore of this craziness. Ernaldus' gone... The whole mages' guild, Lucius' out of his mind. I want to remember everyone when they were doing well. It was bad enough when my father was killed in front of me. I have to leave Aelienor."

"What do you think everyone will think if you leave now? We have to finish what we started. Wariner wanted to leave with us once all of this was over, this isn't the time to leave. Trust me there's been times I've wanted to leave but I haven't, no matter how much I wanted to, I've been fighting. It is what Ernaldus would've wanted."

"I'm not as strong as everyone else. I'm going to stand in everyone's way, it'll be best if I was gone."

"You don't mean that. We need you."

Gauvain raised his voice as he spoke, "Stop making this harder for me, I'm leaving and this is the only thing I'm confident about."

"Gauvain." Aelienor yelled out.

Gauvain rushed down the hill ignoring him, hijacking the ship. Aelienor rushed to follow Gauvain to stop him from getting distracted by seeing Lucius' parents, Bella and Parker.

"It's been a while, Aelienor. Where's Lucius?" Parker asked as he looked around the foreign land.

"How'd you know where we were?"

"Everyone from the town pitched in to help find you. I'm happy that you're alright and subside my anger for now about how irresponsible you all were..." Bella started.

"Lucius is ok but Gauvain..." Aelienor stated in disarray pointing out at their ship.

"He doesn't even know how to operate that. He'll get himself killed." Parker reminded. "Gauvain..." He yelled out rushing downhill with flailing arms, before reaching halfway down the hill he had left the dock.

"I can't believe he left." Aelienor said as Parker calmed her down.

"Bella, talk to the people around this town and see if you can borrow one of those traders' ships to bring Gauvain back whenever their deliveries are done," Parker explained.

"How do you know about the traders' ships?" Aelienor asked.

"We did plenty of research before we left," Parker explained.

"I know a lot of the ships are active at the moment but fingers crossed for Gauvain's sake. You've missed a lot and there's plenty to talk about...

I thought you were killed at the bar." Aelienor confessed.

"It would seem I have some things to talk to you about as well. Now, send me to your friends, and we'll go from there..."

Once Aelienor brought Parker back to the base she had been informed that Lucius had left with Jack and Cencil to meet up with Helba.

"I'll wait here until they come back." Parker explained.

"Who are you?" Ashlyn asked.

"I'm Lucius' father. It's time for him to go home."

Memory IX - Déjà vu

* Helba's Plan *

Cencil kicked open the door knocking it off its hinges.

"So much for subtlety..." Jack thought out loud.

"She knows our every move with that book. It doesn't give us an advantage." Cencil said.

"Why'd she pick here of all places?" Lucius asked to change the subject.

"I have a general idea. You'll find out soon enough." Cencil confessed as they entered the temple.

Helba awaited leaning against the wall, glancing at the book from across the room. Guarded by Jousen and Magnus. "Like the book says. Not like I'm surprised but the magic from this book astounds me every time."

"Where's Reyner and Kain?" Jack asked.

"They're here being held in a cell. The key is somewhere in the temple but before I tell you or hand over the book. I would like to explain my actions." Helba stated.

"I'm curious about the reason for your deceit." Cencil said.

"You say I'm a traitor that was under Hayden's control. I followed orders since I was young, although never taken seriously for my work. Hayden had the answers I sought for... until Hayden changed. I retrieved Reyner and Kain behind Hayden's back in good faith." Helba said as she laid the book on a nearby table.

"Hayden killed Drago..." Magnus scoffed. "I didn't know I was dealing with a psycho."

"I know I'm the last person to trust. I'll bring myself back at Quia after all of this is over." Jousen said.

"I wanted to clear the air. To undo all of this negativity of what happened the last time I was here." Helba explained.

"Helba..." Cencil said with a tone.

"What happened here?" Jack asked.

"A similar ordeal with different circumstances. The reason I joined ranks with you from the beginning was because of Cencil. To swipe everyone's memory once Omega was gone. I believe Hayden isn't an exception. The All-Seeing Eye should be forgotten and we needn't worry." Helba explained.

"I believe there was a time and place for that as a new beginning." Cencil explained.

"Dad, you knew about this?" Jack asked.

"This wasn't what I meant, Helba," Cencil explained as he turned to Jack. "Look Jack, time travel is too dangerous no matter who does it. It doesn't matter how much good you do. It's all subjective. I would've said the same to Vaughan."

"What kind of plan is this... It'll never work." Lucius said.

"Vaughan wouldn't have stood by this either. Does his life mean nothing to you?"

"You're thinking about it all wrong. We're telling the truth, it'll keep death from occurring. To prevent more death-like Vaughan."

"Your memory won't be wiped out. Cencil will keep the book taking it from Hayden. You'll remember everyone and everything that you would in your normal life." Helba said in a positive light.

"I'm not going to allow this." Jack yelled out as he took his sword out.

Helba's expression turned grim.

Jousen and Magnus took out weapons of their own. Helba took out her memory fogger.

"All I need is a minute. One moment of it to scan your eyes and a handprint. I don't want to hurt you but if you don't comply. I can't stop what'll happen." Helba explained.

Jack and Lucius stood side by side as Magnus and Jousen ran toward them.

"Please don't hurt my son. Helba, he doesn't see the truth as we do." Cencil explained.

Lucius ducked a swing from Magnus being able to disarm Magnus as he raised his arms in surrender glancing at Jack.

Jack took a gash into the forearm by Jousen. Jack fell back toward Lucius; now on the other side of the room.

Magnus used the time to take the fight back to Lucius. Lucius in ill preparation lost grip of the sword, twisting Magnus's arm before he could gain an advantage. Gaining time to gain a firm grip of his sword. Jabbing toward Magnus backing up, dodging each blow. Losing his balance over a bench hitting the wall near it.

Magnus kicked Lucius in the gut with his knee once Lucius took a look.

Magnus swung the sword. Lucius grabbed his upper arm under his armpit, headbutting Magnus.

Losing their weapons from the confusion. They both were groggy from the attack; coming to first, Lucius raised pressure on Magnus' arm. Lucius swung at Magnus with his elbow to knock him unconscious.

Jousen had picked up Magnus' sword swinging at both Jack and Lucius. Jack swung at Jousens side of his stomach before Jousen could follow through the attack. Jousen fell on one knee holding his wound as he swung back at Jack. Cencil pulled Jack away from being stabbed holding Jack down into a headlock. "Let it happen, son. It'll be fast."

"Your plan won't happen," Jack said squirming. Helba worked her way to Jack seeing a clearing.

Lucius capitalized as Jousen was distracted with Jack. Kicking Jousen's chin, knocking Jousen back. Lucius dodged each swing Jousen swung, Lucius swung which each opening he found. Yet it wasn't enough. Up until they were at a standstill with a test of stregth between blades.

Lucius recalled the last time this had happened he lost a finger. He decided on swiping at the same time Jousen swiped up. Resulting in Jousen's right hand being cut off.

Lucius flipped his sword and hit Jousen with his pummel before he could hear Jousen whelp.

"No..." Cencil cried out.

Jack escaped his father's grip to be met with Jousen's blade. Lucius looked at Jack falling back with an exposed chest. Jack reached out for Lucius. "You must... stop this..." Jack said before he became breathless.

"That was a shame that happened, Cencil.
I'm still a person of my word."

"You're a monster Helba."

"At least we have one person around to test this new technology," Helba said as a bright white flash occurred.

* Reliving The Past *

"Try to keep up Lucius..." Maria said in a cheerful tone waving him over.

Lucius began to catch up. Maria started to run further into the woods once more.

"This is familiar." Lucius said under his breath.

"Stop talking under your breath and catch up. Let's see what Parker is up to. He never let us delve into his job life." Maria said as she climbed up on the largest tree next to the fishing dock.

"This already happened," Lucius said as Maria pulled him up to the next branch.

"I don't know what you mean by that. I mean sure we go out in the woods more often lately but..."

"We both have a second chance to stop this all from happening," Lucius confessed as he noticed Silas and Parker exiting a building with their boss.

"You're acting strange Lucius. Are you alright?" Maria asked with concern as she glanced away from Lucius after he gave off a slight smile. "Whatever they're talking about their boss doesn't seem happy," Maria admitted.

"I know they're going to the bar nearby soon. Trust me." Lucius explained as he pointed out the boss throwing a dry cloth on the ground angrily. Causing Silas and Parker to leave the site.

"We should follow them," Lucius confessed as Maria agreed with hesitation. While remaining in the woods they followed their father's tracks as they ended up seeing them enter a bar. Lucius stopped himself from continuing. "I believe they were fired from their jobs... We need to catch up to them."

"I had a feeling myself but how do you know this?"

"Let's say I was given a second chance for whatever reason and this time I will make this right."

"You don't think we should wait here until they leave the bar. They may be mad at us for following them..."

"I'm counting on it," Lucius said as Maria gave Lucius a look. Entering the bar seeing Gauvain in the entrance cleaning tables.

"What are you two doing here?" Gauvain asked.

"We followed our fathers back here." Maria said.

"They passed by like they were in a bad mood... It's strange." Gauvain explained.

"I have a similar feeling..." Maria added as she glanced at Lucius.

"Can you lead us to them, Gauvain?" Lucius asked.

"Follow me," Gauvain replied, continuing. "I must ask what's the hurry?"

"It's hard to say who it is, but something is going to happen soon. We need to keep an eye on them." Lucius summarized.

"If you're worried about the fights that have been happening as of late. You needn't worry it's all under control." Gauvain summarized as he stopped at their booth. "Here they are."

"What are you two doing here?" A raspy voice asked behind Lucius.

The stranger Lucius couldn't put his finger on. "I don't believe I've seen you here before and I for one have been here for a while." The mystery man announced.

"Don't worry about him Thex. He's checking up on his old man." Parker explained.

"No, he's not." Thex explained.

"What do you mean?" Parker began as Thex picked up a glass from the table clashing it against Lucius' head as he fell. Blood oozed out of the new cut he had gotten.

"What the hell... Thex?" Parker asked, jumping up shoving Thex.

"Your son knows too much Parker." Thex explained.

"Are you alright Lucius?" Gauvain asked, waving his hand in front of Lucius.

"Protect..." Lucius mumbled. The bar fight had started upon Lucius blacking out. Lucius opened his eyes like a bad dream of discovering several injured within the bar. Blood poured onto the floor from major open cuts. Smeared on the walls attempting to get away from the scene. The injured in havoc attempting to heal their wounds.

"Why are you doing this?" Lucius impulsively kicking Thex as he passed by. Causing Thex to trip temporarily fighting the crowd.

"Lucius' awake. Are you alright?" Dorian asked as he helped Lucius rise.

"I don't quit easily. Feel lucky for all of your life you still live these days whereas hers ends as a lesson." Thex yelled out. Recovering from stumbling out of the riot he created. Bringing Maria with a broken glass holding her hostage. "Nice seeing you sweetheart. You and your friend Lucius aren't supposed to be here."

"Let her go..." Silas ordered.

"You don't have to do this." Lucius said calmly as he moved toward Thex running on adrenaline.

Thex matched Lucius' steps, going backward for each time Lucius came forward. Up until Maria was up the stairs.

Maria adjusted herself out of Thex's grip long enough to bite his forearm.

"Arrgh." With impulse Thex jerked Maria out of his grip and down the stairs.

Lucius' view became limited to follow Thex trail as a crowd within the bar hovered over Maria.

"My little girl..." Silas cried out holding her. "Stick with me, honey."

"Maria..." Lucius yelled outreaching her lime eyes losing life. Lucius took a few blinks before he was able to catch up in a chase with Thex. Grabbing his arm to realize he was back in the cave, holding Jack's biscep.

"You look pale..." Jack said with concern having difficulty taking Lucius' hand off his forearm.

Lucius let go willingly as he shook his head in denial.

Draven sneaked himself passing by each shadow until reaching behind Jack. Lucius instinctively slid his note from Aelienor into his pocket.

"Behind you Jack." Lucius said with sudden impulse.

Jack turned around before Draven was able to grapple him. Jack dodged the attack, having trouble to take the weapon away from his attacker.

"Do you feel the insanity yet Lucius?" Hayden asked as he stopped time looking at the struggle between Draven and Jack. "You're losing control of your body, It's a sad sight to see, yes?" Hayden chuckled. "It's happened to Therron, now it's you. Face it, Lucius, Let the fire happen in Quia, some say that where most of the problems originated. Some good people have to die before history ends up fixing itself. It's up to you Lucius, I still can't believe it, of all people it's you, a living time traveling machine." Hayden disappeared as time resumed.

"I need some help here Lucius." Jack said as each word seemed to wind him.

Lucius used his hand to slam Draven's head into the wall as Jack became surprised as he was more than content with the result.

"That was my iconic move." Jack said with surprise. "and you didn't even look behind me to know this man was here. You used it didn't you?"

"I did, he killed you in a previous life. We need to stop a fire in Quia." Lucius summarized.

"He could do that if it wasn't for you...wait, a fire... Did you even look at that note?"

"Don't need to," Lucius explained as Jack shook his head looking at Draven. "We can't let this man continue to be a problem down the road."

"What do you mean?" Lucius asked.

Jack temporarily glanced at Draven lying unconscious as he got madder looking at Draven. Stomping on Draven's jaw hearing a loud crack.

"Jack?"

"It needed to be done. I'm not a big fan of killing but the gull of that man kills me. Let's keep this between us. Don't let it bother you. Lead the way."

Lucius's life sped up blinking a few times before reaching Quia.

"What is going on with Lucius?" Vaughan asked.

"He's feeling the side effects of time travel. We'll help him out with that shortly as long as he keeps strong for us. Let's focus on Quia for now." Jack explained. They quickly left out of Lucius' view. Lucius attempted to follow them, bumping into Aelienor across town.

"Did you drink a bit before coming here?" Aelienor asked.

"Not at all. Where's Maria?" Lucius asked, trying to process time passing him by.

"She never left home, remember?" Aelienor sighed. "I wish I was there myself... I could've helped but try to not let it bother you. Are you sure you're alright?" Aelienor asked, biting her bottom lip. "We need to stop this before it gets any worse..." Aelienor summarized as she took a few steps before a fire broke out.

"Too late?" Lucius asked.

"It may not be too late for the town itself.

We need to save anyone we can." Aelienor rushed into the burning building.

"I'm not letting you die Aelienor." Lucius raced into the burning building as she discovered Nolyn lying dead with a sword wound to the chest. Teigen left, coughing from the smoke.

"What a monster..." Aelienor thought as she and Lucius aided Teigen out of the house as wood fell blocking the entrance.

"The window," Lucius quickly remarked using a chair to bust open the window clearing the glass. Lucius allowed Aelienor to go first while listening to Teigen who had kept mumbling the whole time.

"What happened?" Teigen asked, dazed forming a question Lucius couldn't answer.

"We're getting you out of here," Lucius answered, raising Teigen's leg out of the window. Lucius jumped up from the collision of a knife landing in the wall next to him.

"Hey, I'm not done here," Jousen admitted. "Tell me where Morrison's keys are or I'll kill you." Jousen grappled Lucius, pulling him away from the window.

"Let me go." Lucius urged as more of the house fell apart.

"Speak now before I lose my patience," Jousen explained.

"On the chair in the prison." Lucius confessed.

"Good." Jousen shoved Lucius away from the window.

Landing roughly on his side, Lucius kicked a loose plank in the flooring; hitting Jousen in the back of his leg. Bouncing his face in the flame for a moment as he rose too quickly. Giving off a yelp.

Lucius quickly rose to his feet, jumping out of the window as the building collapsed upon exiting.

"Are you alright?" Vaughan asked.

"I'll live... But Quia?" Lucius asked.

"It can still be contained," Morrison said as he waved over Hunter. Using the Portalatrix to bring Anne from Kralan and into Quia. Dissipating the fire with three pillars of light coming from the stars above.

"It's a good thing I was told about this. I live right next to Teigen's house in this realm. I fear I could've been next. The thought of leaving Rehiba and Lukin..." Hunter thought out loud.

"Worry not Hunter. We caught this right on time." Morrison explained as Anne made eye contact with Morrison. "It's been a long time Anne."

"It has. Remember I'm with Iiokio, so don't let me defend your town make you think I still have feelings for you. This is for the town's sake." Anne summarized as she dissipated her spell.

"Thank you, my lady." Hunter bowed respectfully before leading her back into Kralan Morrison put on a half-smile as the portal dissipated taking a sigh as he looked at Lucius.

"Was there anyone there?"

"Jousen was asking me about your office key..." Lucius explained exhausted. Morrison signaled his men to surround the jail to look for Jousen.

"You did good Lucius. You've altered more timelines than I have, you must be proud." Hayden asked as time stopped once again with an echo. Lucius looked away from Hayden in spite. "Tell me how you feel Lucius... I'm not the bad guy here that is, not anymore. That's you. The timelines make you feel something that no one else fully understands, regret."

Lucius woke up and wondered if the mind games were finally over. Rising to his feet with fatigue and agony. Knowing deep down it's not over. Lucius walked to a mirror seeing his scruffy beard. "What's going to happen now?" Lucius walked outside the guest room feeling out of breath. Noticing Caroline holding her baby boy as she walked to the time machine getting stopped by Lucius.

"Don't leave Caroline..." Lucius said as Caroline jumped.

"You're full of surprises, Lucius but it has to happen. Kain in the other room, and he can't know what has happened."

"Kain's here?"

"He is. It's fruitless for him to protect me with the power Hayden has. I must depart before anyone does anything reckless. We're not simply visiting with Hayden's for a peace treaty, especially after what Magnus had done."

"I know what you mean. I didn't know you looked at the book but I don't blame you. Sometimes knowing the truth hurts. Leaving here will break Kain's heart. You're the last he has, apart from Floros."

"I know you're trying to help Lucius. But one thing's for certain, some things don't change Lucius. Goodbye." Caroline said as she entered the pod to leave.

"Caroline... No." Lucius rushed over to open the machine. Opening the doors to know for certain; she was gone. "I knew what had happened to you, I'm sorry," Lucius said with a sigh as Kain peaked out nearby groggy.

"Oh hey, Lucius, You're awake. What's going on?"

"You need to know the truth, Kain."

"We already know about Helba. I wish we were able to find out sooner..."

"It's about Caroline."

"What happened to her?" Kains' voice changed on a moment's notice with a deeper voice that partly scared Lucius.

"Magnus did something bad to her..."

"What did he do?"

Lucius confessed to Kain. Kain wasted no time to charge to Magnus' room pushing Lucius out of the way. Lucius lagged hesitantly Kain as he yelled out to Magnus.

"Is it true?" Kain asked with a breaking voice.

"Oh, you caught me killing a bird when I was a teenager. Drinking the public and passing out in the streets of rugged slums in Colosten. Be more precise than that Kain." Magnus' sarcastic remarks made Kain punch him.

"Did you rape Caroline?"

"I did and every thrust..." Magnus admitted with a smirk. Changing his expression immediately as a dagger slipped into Magnus' gut. "But... you need me." Magnus urged out gasping desperately.

Kain's eyes twitched as he spoke. "No one in this world needs you. This is for Paul..." Kain retracted the dagger as he stabbed him again. "Floros..." Stabbing once more going as far as the blade would allow. "-and Caroline. Let the agony of the blade make you think of what you did. How worthless of a human being you truly are..."

"He gets the message, Kain." Lucius explained.

"How long did you know?" Kain asked.

"A few minutes ago when I woke up before Caroline left in the machine. There was no track of where she went; she must have deleted the history."

"Caroline left?" Kain said as he began to tear up. "It's a good thing you told me, Lucius. I don't trust much of anyone nowadays, you're a good friend." Kain admitted patting Lucius on the back. "I'll find her again wherever she is."

"Of course."

"I will." Kain said, clearing his throat

"Screw you," Magnus grunted, coughing roughly. "You all will pay."

Kain opened the door to leave. Leaving Jack in shock.

"Ah Lucius, hey..." Jack said as he discovered Magnus. "What did you do?" Jack bewildered.

"Gave him what he deserved. I told you, we will wait on Hayden to come to us. Let Magnus be an example of what happened to who messed with us." Kain explained.

"This is wrong..." Jack admitted.

"This is like the Draven deal, Jack." Lucius explained.

"It is?" Jack asked.

"Who's Draven?" Kain asked.

"Nothing," Jack said dismissively as Kain looked at Jack confused. Jack sighed in response.

"It's something that I'd like to keep between Lucius and me."

"I think we should let Hayden come to us as well. Trust me on this Jack." Lucius explained.

"I sense that we've lived this before." Jack explained. Hearing pans being slammed together. "Cencil's awake, better get down there and see what he wants before he gets angry."

"I don't like the secrets but I suppose I can keep this one." Kain explained as he left with Jack. Lucius stopped Jack from leaving.

"There's one more thing I have to tell you, Jack. It's about your dad."

"What about him?"

"He's working with Helba to relieve others of the memory of the All-Seeing Eye. Which explains why he decided to show up so recently to gain your trust back."

"He's helped us so much while you were out of commission. I want to trust you Lucius but this is my dad you're talking about. He's the smartest one here of this group. He's got a militia to help us take out Hayden. Why would he throw that away?"

"You have to believe me on this Jack. The timing couldn't have been better for him to return in your life since he's blinding you with being family. I'll prove it to you." Lucius said.

"I'd like to see this proof." Jack crossed his hands as a glitchy Hayden appeared wrapping his hands around Jack.

"It's a shame Magnus is gone but I suppose he had it coming. I won't stop you from telling Jack the truth, see how good it works out for you. Check your pockets, Lucius." Hayden said as Lucius took out the device Helba had with her. Looking back up seeing Hayden disappear.

"Is that what I think it is?" Jack asked as he looked at it with a shock.

"It's what you think it is."

"I've seen dad with this before when he taught his soldiers. It looks tweaked enough for a different purpose. I can't believe this..." Jack heard pounding on the door, hiding the device before answering.

"Are you coming down or what?" Vaughan asked.

"We need to talk to Cencil." Jack said with urgency.

"He's still our dad."

"This monster isn't my dad."

"Do you think that's a bright idea?" Lucius asked.

"With what we have against him he'll tell us what we need to know." Jack said.

"If you say so." Lucius said as he followed Jack and Vaughan downstairs.

"What do you mean monster?" Vaughan asked.

"You'll see."

"It's about time you boys got down here. We're going to Hayden's base." Cencil explained.

"I have a different idea." Kain explained.

"What might that be?" Reyner asked.

"There's not a reason for us to go there. I mean they only have the book, and we all know he won't give that away. There's another reason he wants us there, but we all know he's too corrupted to think." Malyna explained.

"We're not going anywhere dad until you explain what this is," Jack said as he pointed out the device at Cencil.

"Watch where you point that, boy. Where'd you get that anyway?" Cencil asked.

"What is that?" Vaughan asked.

"It's to clear our minds of that cursed artifact. A memory fogger will add or subtract whatever a mind needs for this world to be a better place." Cencil admitted. "In someone else's hands when it's not completed is more dangerous than you may think."

"Was time travel getting too over your head in complexity, so you decide to create this as a solution?" Jack asked.

"I knew I didn't trust Lucius in the first place. Lucius must be leader material if he causes the most trouble."

"Where's Helba?" Jack asked.

"I'll contact her if you stop wavering that around."

"How long have you done this?" Vaughan asked.

"It's complicated."

"I'm sure it is. How long have you worked with Helba?"

"Stop while you're ahead." Cencil shook his head. "Fine. I'll arrange a meeting to meet at the

Temple of Prophecies, so she knows it's time. This wasn't meant to be anything less than a simple agreement. It would've been painless and I would have my sons back the way they were before Omega joined about..." Cencil rambled as he cut himself off contacting Helba.

"You're early with your request. Is there a reason?" Helba asked, answering almost instantly. Being straight to the point.

"Hayden is planning an attack on Omega, if they destroy each other the problem will be solved. We wouldn't worry. Start the Restart protocol."

"Hayden wanting to off Omega is great and all but you seem sure of one side's success. We still don't know if they'll team up against everyone else."

"Not going to happen. Meet me, my sons, and Lucius at the temple." Cencil explained as he ended the call. "It's done."

"I can't believe you," Jack explained.

"Lucius' been nothing but putting a bad influence on you. Some sacrifices are needed for the world to live peacefully."

"However, transferring our brains to mush is fine with the memory fogger?" Vaughan asked.

"But you'll be alive, everyone will be. Time has a way of correcting itself. I'm not a time traveler. I'm not going to play God on who lives or dies, instead let humanity restart with the artifact out of the picture. Even a fool can see this will stop the war before it becomes too much. Get Magnus down here and see if we can at least reschedule something with Hayden before he decides to attack us."

"I killed him." Kain admitted.

"You what?" Cencil said shocked.

"He was our only way to Hayden." Malyna confessed.

"I'm done with everything and anyone who works with Hayden. They'll all die for all I care." Kain confessed.

"I can't believe you." Cencil explained. "You of all people saying that is funny to me Cencil."

"Shut your trap."

"When can we go to the temple?" Lucius asked.

"We'll head our way there now."

"Bring us there then, dad," Vaughan said with annoyance.

* Unforgiven Sins *

Cencil kicked the door open with impatience. Awaiting Helba with two guards; Jousen; who was severely burned and Teigen.

"How does it feel to work with someone that tried to kill you, Teigen?" Lucius asked thinking it was funny in a sense.

"We're past that now. Whatever was in the past was in the past Lucius. Thank you for saving me though." Teigen explained.

"You may be fortunate Teigen. But I still have a little dispute with what you did to me, Lucius..." Jousen stated.

"I have the codex and I believe we can help each other out-" Helba admitted when Jack interrupted her.

"Save your breath I'm sure your plan wouldn't work without this..." Jack asked as he showed her the device. Helba's eyes widened as Jack dropped it to the floor crushing it with his boot. "I knew you were a traitor, Cencil. That's why I transferred the ownership into my name."

"You did what?" Cencil asked.

"Kill them, all of them Teigen and Jousen. They ruined our new beginning." Helba ordered.

"You are not permitted to kill Helba. Under no circumstances. She needs to transfer the ownership back to me." Cencil ordered back.

"I'm not going to do that." Teigen rebelled. "I respect Cencil more than you Helba."

"I should've killed you when I had the chance." Jousen pulled a sword out on Teigen.

"I thought you said there were no hard feelings?" Teigen asked, pulling his sword in retort.

"I lied." Jousen argued back, clashing swords.

"If no one does something right, you better do it yourself." Helba rushed out her bow shooting Vaughan in the leg.

"Vaughan..." Cencil urged out becoming red-faced charging without a weapon toward Helba. Missing each shot at him as he became closer. Disarming the bow, knocking her to the ground. Dropping her ax from her side. Cencil as he picked up an ax before she could reach it.

Cencil had second thoughts as Helba rose to her knees.

"Cencil... Please." Helba cried out.

"Go to hell. Helba Tels." Cencil said, triggering him as she begged. Hitting her with the ax into her neck. "You shouldn't have messed with my boys..." Cencil said being cut off by a breach consisting of Hayden and his men in front of them, debris flying past.

"You killed one of ours," Hayden pointed out "Drago..."

"Will do sir." Drago said as he aimed a bow.

"Wait... She hurt my son." Cencil began being met with an arrow between the eyes.

"Good, Now capture everyone here. I suspect that since they decided to skip out on our little meeting that any partnership wouldn't have been formed. They may as well not be a problem while we take out Omega." Hayden explained as his men flooded the room, matching everyone three to one as they overtook everyone to be captured. Tying a rope to their hands behind their backs.

"I told you about Helba's meeting here." Flynn confessed.

"Your reward will not be forgotten for what you've done today Flynn." Hayden tossed Flynn a gold pouch.

"I'm going to kill you, Flynn." Lucius said with glitch filled anger.

"I'd like to see that happen," Flynn confessed, kicking Lucius' face. Sending Lucius into the dark.

Memory X - Strange Allies

* The Grand Scheme *

"Wake up Lucius... Please be alright." Wariner said, patting Lucius' cheek.

"What happened?"

"Hayden threw you in here. Along with many others scattered throughout, I would imagine. Hayden wanted to keep everyone in here that may stop him from going after Omega. He's got a death wish coming."

"How'd you get here?

"He used me to get what he wanted and threw me in here. I wish I could've done something sooner." Wariner explained as Lucius pointed out a metal device on his arm.

"What's that?"

"I'm not sure...you have one as well," Wariner said as he attempted to take it off as it shocked him.

"I'll tell you exactly what that is." A man from a shadow replied outside their cell.

"Who are you?" Lucius asked.

The man chuckled wickedly. "After today, people will know my name. I'm the mind behind Hayden. How do you think he's always one step ahead?"

What you have on is the exit to the cell. Both devices power the cell to remain locked. The devices are connected to your heartbeat. I studied both of you closely and neither of you has killed in cold blood. To leave one of the devices will have to deactivate." The man said as he exited the darkness revealing Kerwyn Niles with a scar on his face.

"You want us to kill each other?" Wariner asked bewildered. Kerwyn took out a sword.

Sliding the sword under the cell door. Giving chills to both Lucius and Wariner.

"I thought you were dead." Lucius exclaimed.

"It should've popped in your head that I didn't have a funeral as Nadim had. Hayden gave me the responsibility to watch over you and the rest of our friends to spectate his prisoners. The longer you wait and try to find another way out they'll be more disciplinary actions. Which of you is born a true leader to do what is needed for others safety in the long run and which is the one to crack under pressure."

"You can't expect us to kill in cold blood like this." Wariner explained.

"One of you will, I guarantee it," Kerwyn explained as he walked around their cell turning on lights from above him as he passed by each light it revealed a black cover revealing it to a tied up Ashlyn. "Long time no see," Kerwyn welcomed as he took off a gag from Ashlyn's mouth.

"Kerwyn?" Ashlyn asked, taking deep breaths.

"It's nice you know who I am Ashlyn but unfortunately it's too late for remembering. Lucius, Wariner... you have one minute." Kerwyn said as he waited, holding Ashlyn's shoulder from behind her as he glanced at other weapons from behind him.

"One minute until what?" Ashlyn asked.

"Watch the show, Ashlyn." Kerwyn explained.

"There has to be another way out." Lucius said as he pulled on the bars feeling if they were loose.

"We don't have much time Lucius..." Wariner confessed as he gulped examining the bracelet getting shocked again as he fidgeted with it again. Lucius picked up the sword to bash against the lock in the cell as it caused him to get shocked himself. Dropping the sword in the process. "We're going to get you out, Ashlyn."

"You must have head trauma as I gained from you freaks. That time travel ruckus made me lose so much progress. Wishing soon it'll be over. You at least could be punctual in your endeavors to save your friends. You don't know pain as I do. Allow me to express it in action." Kerwyn explained as he sauntered over at the weapons picking out a katana. Touching the tip of the blade with his finger as it drew blood.

"I'm sorry Kerwyn. I didn't mean to cause you so much trouble and pain..." Ashlyn admitted beginning to sweat following Kerwyn's movement until picking up a weapon.

"Don't lie to me Ashlyn, you're better than that. I want to say this isn't personal but it is. Your friends could've helped you but they were selfish with their agendas." Kerwyn said as he shoved the sword into Ashlyn's knee far enough to get stuck onto the chair. Ashlyn groaned breathing deeply. "I learned some things while I was out of commission. Like if a patella was struck in a... particular way.

They would die in mere minutes without proper treatment. If you do survive, I'll suspect you'll never be able to walk again."

"Ashlyn..." Lucius and Wariner said at the same time as she passed out from shock.

"Don't be so surprised. I'd mark this as a fault in your book. Let's see who the next friend will be." Kerwyn said as he revealed Rosetta and Rosane. "Same rules as last time. But this time we're up the stakes with the twin wizards. It'll be a shame if these men weren't in action, fighting Omega."

"He won't stop Lucius." Wariner confessed.

"There has to be another way..." Lucius said as he looked around.

"Who are you?" Rosetta asked.

"Did you not hear, he's Kerwyn... Did you do that to the girl over there?" Rosane asked.

"Watch Lucius and Wariner decide your fate. It'll be an interesting one." Kerwyn said as he cleaned the blade with a rag.

"Kill me, Lucius. Do it. You have to." Wariner urged.

"It's a test it has to be." Lucius explained.

Kerwyn sat the blade down as he crossed his arms in curiosity.

"I won't let someone else die, Lucius. There's no way out."

"Get a hold of yourself Wariner. We'll do this together." Lucius explained as Wariner rushed at Lucius frantically trying to get the sword from the ground. Lucius reached the blade first. Rushing the sword into Wariner from his stomach to his chest.

"Don't let my death be in vain." Wariner uttered falling to the ground. Wariner's bracelet changed from red to green as the cell door opened. Lucius's bracelet fell to the ground, rushing out to chase Kerwyn. With Kerwyn out of reach.

"I still have games to play Lucius. You may want to release the brothers for this one." Kerwyn spoke as he locked the door between him and Lucius. The point at the next door for Kerwyn's next test.

"Traitor..." Jack said as he passed by a hallway. Seeing Wariner's death.

"Leave him." Kain added.

"I thought I knew Lucius," Reyner admitted as the three escaped. Only seeing Lucius' evil deed. Oblivious of other prisoners.

* Moral Compass *

"Ignore them. They don't know what happened, release us, and let's catch up with Kerwyn." Rosane explained.

"What about Ashlyn, Is she gone?" Lucius asked.

"I don't sense any life in her. I'm sorry." Rosetta confessed.

"Let's make Kerwyn pay," Lucius explained as he untied them both as he took notice they had the mage realm cuffs on as well unlocking them as Rosetta corrected himself as he rose from the chair.

"No wonder I couldn't. I do sense a faint glimmer of fighting back from the pain. Go ahead without me. I'll catch up." Rosetta explained. Rosane and

Lucius exited the room to end up in another room that you could see a courtyard in the distance of Pavel fighting Flynn.

"Where'd Kerwyn go?" Lucius asked.

"I'm afraid we're on his turf now. Kerwyn must've learned some types of magic himself from the All-Seeing Eye." Rosane explained.

"Another life for more freedom, Lucius. Kill Pavel and more friends go free. Simple instructions for grand rewards." Kerwyn explained.

"Where's his voice coming from?" Lucius asked.

"I'm not sure but Pavel could help us out." Lucius picked up a bow that was laying down on a windowsill. He propped it in the middle of the window, aiming ahead of him.

"Were you ever curious of why Hayden was in your head when he wasn't around... Welcome to Project Silverstar. You had a taste, a demo. I engineered it." Kerwyn explained.

"What's he talking about?" Rosane asked.

"Ever since I was corrupted by the All-Seeing Eye it seems that once in a while Hayden would be there. Like he was my conscience. He didn't force me to do anything mind you. Only an annoying parasite that won't stay quiet." Lucius explained.

"Just another reason to stop him." Rosane explained.

"This'll be a tough shot to make," Lucius recalled witnessing the fight.

"Are you going to let him talk to you like that Lucius?" Hayden asked spawning behind Rosane. "How about you shoot Rosane with that bow."

Hayden said as Lucius turned to Rosane with the bow drawn.

"What are you doing Lucius?" Rosane asked angrily.

"Duck." Lucius said.

Rosane reacted quickly as Lucius shot off an arrow. Hitting the wall behind Rosane. "Kerwyn did something to you. We need to get to him before it's too late. Lucius fought off his conscience. Failing to control his actions as he picked up another arrow.

"Shoot at me again." Rosane said.

"Are you sure?" Lucius asked.

"Do it before I change my mind."

Lucius was hesitant. His malice mind thought otherwise, "Give him what he wants."

Lucius shot at Rosane again as Rosane duck as he controlled the arrow's movement to be sent outside with his magic.

"If you can't think I can think for you. Who should I hit?" Rosane asked.

"Hit Flynn."

"Kerwyn isn't going to like this." Lucius thought as Hayden appeared for a moment with a glitch.

"Give me the key's Flynn... I'll spare your life if you do." Pavel said as they clashed swords.

"That won't be any fun," Flynn explained as he was hit in the shoulder with an arrow. "What did this come from?" Flynn cried out as he fell, Pavel pointed his sword at Flynn.

"The keys." Pavel commanded.

"I'll never submit." Flynn yelled out, kicking Pavel's ankle making him lose his balance. Using the time to retreat as he noticed Aelienor jumping out of a window into the outside. Flynn worked his way to Aelienor, holding his shoulder.

"You gotta help me Aelienor. I'm being hunted... Here. Take my blade and finish off Pavel."

"Alright, I will. Pavel is a threat. There's something I wanted to tell you." Aelienor confessed, raising out her hand moving toward Flynn in for a kiss. Taking Flynn's sword and shoving the arrow in Flynn's shoulder with her idle hand. "This is for using me. My brother was right about you. Where is everyone else?"

"I have no idea."

"Wrong answer." Aelienor said as she twisted the arrow as it made him fall to one knee.

"The keys he has to contain locked sections of this area, which could be where the others are." Pavel explained. Stopping in his tracks petting Aelienor shoulders.

"You don't see that every day." Pavel pointed out an arrow constantly moving in a circle to draw their attention.

"It's Lucius," Aelienor said. Looking at Flynn passing out on her. "I must've been too much for him." Aelienor pushed him aside.

"Let's go." Pavel waved on unlocking Lucius' section.

"Most disappointing. But you do surprise me. You do know that more lives must be taken to leave. Meet me in the lobby, no more games." Kerwyn summarized.

"We have to finish this..." Aelienor explained.

"In fifteen minutes." Pavel explained.

"Fifteen minutes?" Lucius asked.

"It's a countdown." Pavel admitted laughing nervously revealing he had a bracelet counting down.

"Good Lord." Aelienor said.

"It's useless to mess with it," Pavel explained. "I don't want to think about that. Let's focus on the task at hand."

"Does anyone know how to get to the lobby?" Lucius suddenly thought to go back to Wariner's body. Discovering a map in his front pocket. "Thanks, Wariner."

"He knew this place?" Rosane asked.

"It wasn't something he wanted to be part of..." Lucius said as he closed Wariner's eyes.

"Let's get this bastard," Ashlyn said as she limped over.

"Ashlyn?" Lucius asked.

"She may not be able to walk well but with what I was able to muster up she'll live," Rosetta explained.

"I'm sure Kerwyn will be more than happy with your teamwork but you still have some work to do, all the while I'm fighting someone of a high caliber." Hayden bragged.

"Shut up." Lucius yelled out swinging at Hayden.

"Is he alright?" Rosetta asked, pointing out Lucius punching in the air.

"Let's go after Kerwyn," Lucius explained as he adjusted his shirt. Lucius averted his attention as he glitched. Hayden disappeared before he was able to connect the punch.

They looked at Lucius with concern. "What?"

Not pushing the subject, Aelienor unlocked the door ahead, reaching Kerwyn.

"I'm proud of all of you for making it this far. Unfortunately, this is where your roads will meet their end." Kerwyn said standing on a chandelier as the surrounding area turned into the middle of the woods where he first encountered them. Kerwyn shot at them with a bow as he saw movement.

Dodging the projectiles at the last minute, Ashlyn pulled Lucius down avoiding the shot.

"Feel familiar?" Ashlyn asked in a joking manner. Holding her knee as she crouched.

Ashlyn noticed she was the only one with a weapon. A dagger.

"It does. Are you alright?"

"I'm alright but I'm not going to be able to move well. You'll have to bring him to me while he's caught off guard. So I'll knock him out of those trees...again." Ashlyn explained.

"I may not be able to time travel like you but I'm able to heal quicker with my condition. Hayden shot me with the artifact giving me part of the power of the healing. Nothing is better than in the future. Are you curious about your future?" Kerwyn asked. "Now you don't have to worry about it when they go after you and kill you since I gave them the idea," Kerwyn asked as he shot every time someone had the chance to peek out.

Lucius attempted to pick up one of the knives as it went through his hands like they weren't there.

"We need to run away at the same time since he can't be focused on both of us," Ashlyn said as she rose to throw the knife. Kerwyn blocked it with his bow. "You have to do better than that. Remember that your lives are at stake here."

Pavel used the time to run to a different cover as it raised Kerwyn's attention as he adjusted himself to attack Pavel.

"He's out of my view." Ashlyn said.

"Throw it anyway." Rosane exclaimed taking control of the dagger upon leaving Ashlyn's grip. Kerwyn shot the dagger out of the air.

"I sense your magic a mile away Rosane. " Kerwyn confessed. Lucius picked up Ashlyn to adjust her in a better position for a shot at Kerwyn.

Kerwyn noticed their spot as he shot at Ashlyn. Blocking the shot with a branch. Rosetta raised his hand to heal Kerwyn temporarily and redo the spell. The scar on Kerwyn's head distracted him with pain. Lucius raised Ashlyn as she threw a dagger at Kerwyn causing him to fall. Kerwyn glitched back up into a different tree.

"Where'd you go?" Rosetta asked.

"It's going to take more work than that to finish me off. Whether I die or live this day I will be remembered for my actions. Unlike you all who have no future. Filled with denial of a false sense of heroism when you're not on the side you think you truly are. You've caused many lives to be lost. A long list of them, willing to spell them out for you if you had the time to listen." Kerwyn explained as Rosane was able to pinpoint the voice to lead a health spell to his face once again.

"How about this for a butterfly effect?" Rosane asked.

Lucius picked up Ashlyn to move toward Kerwyn as Ashlyn threw a knife at him. Hitting Kerwyn in the forehead with his pummel. Causing the scenery to change back into his base as Kerwyn fell off a chandelier.

"No escape." Lucius followed Kerwyn as he crawled backward pressing a button underneath a table.

"You won congratulations. How does it feel to still be the loser?" Kerwyn asked, chuckling as he was met with a final blade thrown at his chest by Ashlyn.

As the room lights dimmed down and doors became locked. A light revealed itself on a pedestal nearing a voice recording began.

"So you've passed the test and defeated me. What you've failed to understand while I was out of focus on your 'mission'. I followed Jack's movements and it led me back to you Lucius. On this pedestal was all the lives you have affected.

The butterfly effect is real when you save a person in a timeline per se you mess up another part of the world killing more inadvertently. So showing this fact to the family members that had lost their loved ones. It was easy to create an army of people to stop you. The people who know your name around the world. I was able to know who of these people would be more successful than others. Your luck will soon run out and in history, you will be known as the bad guy, not me. Cherish this victory as it won't last long." Kerwyn summarized as the lights went back on and the doors were unlocked. Lucius picked up the list containing the names of the victims Lucius has inadvertently killed.

* Broken Hearts *

"This isn't true." Lucius browsed through the names in disbelief. "Because of your actions, I will find where you sleep Lucius Evans, and end you." Lucius read out loud the death threat from a follower of project Silverstar.

"You didn't know." Aelienor explained.

"I ruined so many lives. So many names with backstories. Thousands of promises of revenge vendettas. This is not something you makeup. And for what?" Lucius asked himself.

"What's so majorly different from all the other timelines that you think of?" Rosane asked.

"The fire of Quia but lives were saved." Lucius thought. "Who's he talking about..."

Suddenly the lobby door creaked open, gaining the party's attention to Lex. He held his hands in the air after discovering he was no longer in isolation. "Don't attack me. I'm friendly. Hayden is fighting Omega as we speak. Project Silverstar is too late to stop this far in its progression...we'll have to stop it with the All- Seeing Eye. There's no other way."

"Why should we trust you?" Aelienor asked.

"I trust him." Lucius admitted causing the room to become silent.

"Are you sure Lucius?" Pavel asked.

"I know he's not as evil as everyone else that worked with Hayden this far. He's like Wariner, he knows his mistakes and wants to fix them. I see it in him. How do we proceed?" Lucius asked.

"Appreciate it, Lucius. A Portalatrix should be somewhere in this lobby. We need to be swift in finding it." Lex explained.

"You all go I'll have to stay," Pavel confessed as he showed the device on his arm counting down.

"Perhaps there's a way to get it off..." Lex started.

"There's only a few minutes left. I'm taking this corrupt building out with me... It's been an honor working with you all. You can take my place, Lex." Pavel said as he found the Portalatrix between two books on a full bookshelf tossing it to Lucius.

"I won't let you down. Thank you for everything." Lucius said hugging Pavel.

"I knew you were different, Lucius. Go out there and save the world." Pavel admitted watching the portal summon exchanging goodbyes.

Transporting into the mage realm, Kralan, bumping into Jack, Kain, and Reyner.

"What're you doing here, turncoat?" Kain asked.

"Are you going to argue about this or will we stop Hayden and Omega?" Rosane explained.

"It seems we will have to put your verdict on a temporary pause then." Reyner summarized crossing his arms in frustration.

"Once this is over you will pay for your crimes Lucius. No matter how much your friends help you." Jack explained.

"I'll surrender when it's all done, you have my word," Lucius explained.

"Are you serious, Lucius... He saved my life." Ashlyn explained.

"He did?" Reyner asked.

"Now you're thinking..." Aelienor said as she was cut off by the sound of screeching of the roof of the building they're sent flying into the sky.

"We need to confront them now," Lucius breached the door forward, discovering Iiokio critically injured from the fight.

"They are too tough. Don't continue... it's too dangerous." Iiokio confessed breathing heavily.

"We have to make this right, where are the others?" Rosetta asked, attempting to heal Iiokio.

Iiokio stopped Rosetta by grabbing his hand. "Don't waste your time with magic, they'll notice you. It's too late to save us but there is still time to save yourselves. My comrades fell in battle. Perhaps if we had you and your brother's magic... it could've made a difference to defeat him. Follow the blood you'll eventually find the rest of us. Be careful if you decide to follow through." Iiokio said, closing his eyes.

"Is he dead?" Rosane asked.

"He's resting. To store the last of his power... I need to stay here with Ashlyn and Aelienor to do my best to heal them. I know what he said but I still have to do what I can." Rosetta explained.

Rosane passed by each of his council colleagues marking them with a flag for Rosetta to treat. Once they reach the last mage; Anne. They could see Hayden and Omega exchanging blows with different magic spells on top of a hill. One missed spell connected to Rosane as he peeked his head to the hill sending him back several feet. Twitching with agony.

"Rosane..." Lucius said, rushing toward him.

"Don't worry about me... Stop them." Rosane ordered sighing deeply as the spell wore out. Causing severe burns.

Lucius took a long breath continuing with Jack, Reyner, Lex, and Kain.

"You know Omega. I'll read everyone's minds on what they do before they do it. However, you're an exception." Hayden argued as he went to shoot Omega with the relic as Omega created a beam himself. Remaining a constant motion of energy.

Omega disabled the beam with a reflection spell temporarily disabling it. "This is where your incompetence shows. The creator of magic, Yuoki sent this gift on Solaris as a blessing, not a curse. Behind those stubbornness ideals, you have a man who is filled with cynicism. Making up a pitiful excuse that you're continuing where your father left off. It's time for you to join him." Omega yelled out rushing at Hayden parring Omega strike.

"You're wrong. My will to finish what my father started with my thoughts becoming reality, if I want you to suffer... you will." Hayden said with a yell.

Omega fell to his knees cradling his head in agony.

Lucius stealthily rushed toward Hayden behind him swinging a punch. Hayden caught and twisted Lucius's hand to make him fall to the ground.

"Today will be the day you fall, Hayden," Lucius explained.

"Ironic you say that, on the brink of failure. I could've killed you so many times Lucius. I'm almost surprised by your persistence."

Reyner and Kain rushed forward to help. Attacking Hayden from his flank. Hayden shot them with a separate beam burst as they appeared. Lucius used the distraction to kick Hayden between the legs. Causing Hayden with his mortal pain to forget about Omega. Turning his focus on Lucius.

"I'm nothing like you." Lucius retorted with an attitude.

Hayden stumbled back to his footing detecting Jack. "Let's see how you fare against your friends." Hayden used the artifact to make Jack's eyes white. A portal appeared behind Jack in the process. Followers from project Silverstar flooded in to assist.

Omega tackled Hayden causing him to drop the All-Seeing Eye before Omega could regain the advantage. Hayden made it disappear. Omega looked up realizing Hayden had it back in his possession. "You have to earn it first Omega. Funny how things work like that."

Omega constantly exchanges blows with Hayden. Omega's face reddened from bruises.

"Where's all of this magic I hear about Omega?" Hayden asked as Omega arms glowed black, eyes glared like a blinding star, summoning a shadow of pure darkness that had become Omega's ally that generated more magic at his disposal as it cured his wounds.

"You want dark matter magic, You got it." Omega said with a deep mystic voice.

"Oh no," Hayden exclaimed in awe watching Omega's transformation. Hayden shifted the shape of the All-Seeing Eye into a futuristic hoverboard taking to the sky. Shooting at him with beams of energy. Omega dodged the shots going into cover or time it well enough to destroy the beams.

"Where are you naive?" Hayden stopped shooting, losing sight of Omega from a cloud of dust. Omega jumped from the hill to buildings below Hayden.

Flying back up to give off an uppercut with golden glowing hands. Shooting beams off at Omega as the beams phased though Omega's glowing hands. "Well damn."

The war stopped for a moment watching Omega and Hayden fight. Becoming dazed until they left everyone's sight.

Jack shot at Lucius with a bow, hitting one of the followers in the process. "Where's Vaughan?" Jack asked looking down from a high position. The shot riled up the crowd causing the war to continue. "Did you kill him like Wariner... I thought you were one of us." Jack explained as he took out another arrow. Aiming as Lex knocked the bow out of Jack's hands with a rock.

"Non-Lethal blows only," Lex barked out. "They have no say in their actions. Don't let him get into your head." Lex blocked incoming attacks. Knocking one of the followers into each other. Lex used the confusion to jump over the two followers to elbow another.

Lucius elbowed his way toward Lex. Losing his view becoming overwhelmed by the followers. Lucius knew he was only growing weaker with time. Jack laughed at Lucius's expense.

"It's a shame I worked with you. You were always only a liability." Jack spoke. Looking around him to see Lex becoming overwhelmed. Lucius noticed a lever across the hill. teleported his way over using a glitch with one thought as he pulled the lever. Making the hill begin to rotate. Lex was able to escape the crowd taking on the opposition one at a time.

"You may have gotten out of their grasp Lucius..." Jack explained as Lex moved toward Jack as he climbed up to Jack as Lex pushed Jack to Lucius as he was unbalanced.

"I don't want to hurt you, Jack." Lucius warned.

Connecting a fist to Lucius' jaw to make Lucius stagger backward. Jack took out his sword with a twirl.

"Have at you then."

"The relic," Lex pointed out, covering his mouth following a pause knowing he was too late. "I shouldn't have yelled that."

Watching it soar through the sky, Hayden came crashing down onto the lever, breaking it to make the platform stop moving. Omega landed across the platform going back to his original form exhausted shoving Lucius aside. Jack rushed over shoving Lucius' head into a nearby pillar. Jack shoved his boot into Lucius' neck, choking him.

"Hayden's mine," Omega yelled out. Discovering pain from his palm. "This happened before..." Omega said under his breath realizing he was in a different reality. "If I won once, I'll win again." Omega clenched his fist. Using the last of his energy turning his hand black. Omega rushed at Hayden to punch him.

Hayden looked at the artifact fingertips away. Raising the All-Seeing Eye to his hands again with its magnetic counterpart. "Do your job All-Seeing Eye and destroy this dark matter power this instant!" Hayden ordered with veins from his forehead revealing themselves from the struggle. He rose to one knee meeting the artifact to Omega's power full force. A shred of doubt raised from Omega's face as his anger became filled with regret.

A bright light occurred, clearing out the followers of project Silverstar.

Lucius opened his eyes to reveal Hayden. In the middle of the hill battered and beaten. Laying on the ground several feet from his previous location. Raising with difficulty.

"Did I do it...is Omega gone?" Hayden asked with disbelief. Taking silence as an answer, sighing with relief. "Of course I did. My work is almost done." Hayden cunningly spoke interrupting himself with coughing blood. "Now it's your turn," Hayden yelled at Lucius raising the artifact lazily. Glowed red with a declining sound. "Wait a minute," Hayden scoffed at first thinking it was a fluke. "Why are you not working..." Hayden slapped the artifact with his hand. Discovering with a more in-depth inspection having four missing components; the four shards that give the orb inside power. Spread across the battlefield.

Lucius slapped away the All-Seeing Eye to the ground. "It's over Hayden."

"No, it's not over. Some things still need to be done. My father's work..." Hayden said as he took a few steps as he fell while his body worked against him.

"This is what you deserve Hayden. No one here to blame here but yourself." Lex said as he picked up the relic.

"I was chosen... It was my destiny." Hayden complained. Lucius turned his back to walk away. "Give me a hero's death that I deserve. Come back here... coward."

"You can't even pick up a sword. Let alone stand up. It's finished." Lucius admitted.

"Come back." Hayden ordered as he groaned with pain. Crawling toward the last one person standing behind him; Lex. "Tell Jack, I know where Vaughan is. I'll make sure to say hello to him." Hayden inevitably became weaker from all the side effects of different spells working their charms. A partial smile slowly leaving him giving his final breath.

"I'm sorry." Lex admitted letting out a tear.

** Resilient Soul's **

"He's gone. Omega is gone... but what's left." Lucius explained as he picked up the broken shards.

"Kralan's still standing. The damage he's left though will take years, even decades to repair." Iiokio explained.

"The relic can still be fixed." Lex said, meeting back with Lucius handing him the pieces.

"Do we want this to be fixed?" Lucius asked, bumping into Stephan Dermon on the way down the hill.

"It's your call." Lex stated.

"Is Hayden dead?" Stephan asked.

"Our friend Hayden we once knew died a long time ago." Lex admitted.

"I know that now. It took me a while to discover that truth."

"I know the feeling of losing someone." Lucius said as Aelienor and Ernaldus joined up with the crew.

"What happened?" Ernaldus asked.

"It needs to be repaired. We still need to get rid of this Project Silverstar business." Lex explained.

"I thought you were gone." Lucius said, hugging Ernaldus.

"Alright... Lucius, I get it. It's been a whole minute. You can get off me now. Gauvain somewhere around here."

"I'm willing to bet he took off the island without us. He missed out. I hope he's ok." Lucius explained.

"Run off?" Aelienor questioned. "he better not have."

"That coward has a beating coming to him if he leaves without us." Ernaldus rolled his eyes.

"In time Ernaldus." Lucius said reaching the mages.

"You're a hero. We saw what you did back there. We won." Rosetta explained at a loss for words.

"It's not about the victory... It's about the losses." Lucius explained looking at the injured. Is everyone ok?" Lucius asked.

"Malyna's healed the fastest thus far. It'll be best if they avoid using magic until they are well again." Rosetta explained.

"I'll keep that in mind," Lucius said kneeling to Malyna.

"Seeing you around gives me hope to do what all of us couldn't." Malyna smiled.

"Hopefully that hope can continue. The All-Seeing Eye is broken up and missing these shards. Is it salvageable?"

Malyna glanced at the pieces. "Yes. It'll be done, give me some time and I'll get it back and running again."

"Thank you," Lucius started becoming distracted from a nearby crashed meteorite. "I'll be back." Lucius worked his way toward a crashed meteorite as Rosetta followed.

"What's wrong Lucius?"

"Open this meteorite," Lucius said as Rosetta blasted a small lock to open. Discovering Hunter holding Lukin sobbing at Rehiba's corpse.

"Hunter...?"

"She's gone, my love...my everything... Lucius, please tell me the bad men are gone?" Hunter asked, sniffling, wiping away his tears.

"They are." Lucius said.

"Good." Hunter cleared his throat. "My baby boy will grow up without a mother Lucius... She was full of life, my meaning to life." Hunter said watching his boy, Lukin began to cry.

"Shh...it's going to be ok. Do you have somewhere I can stay? Everything is gone...destroyed. I don't even want to imagine my house is among all of this rubble."

"As long as you need. We'll have plenty of space." Lucius said.

"I'm sorry for your loss, Hunter. May she have everlasting peace." Rosetta said as he helped Hunter out of the meteorite. Hunter handed Lukin to Lucius. Inadvertently revealing he had an alarming gash on his arm from the crash.

"Hunter?" Rosetta asked, pointing out the injury.

"I'll do anything to protect my boy. He's all I have left." Hunter explained. Rosetta placed his hands onto Hunter's wounds becoming a scar upon Rosetta releasing. "I appreciate it." Hunter picked Lukin up from Lucius. "I suppose it's a new start for everyone. Everyone who made it."

Rosetta walked Hunter back to the group of survivors. Lucius got distracted by Jack walking down the hill.

"I'm not going to hurt you, Lucius. I apologize for all of that, Although I will have to notify Morrison about Wariner." Jack explained.

"I did say I was going to give myself up. Let me tell Morrison myself on what happened." Lucius explained.

"I'm sorry it had to be this way, after all, we had been though." Jack said he forced Lucius to put his hands out. Tying his hands together. Jack met with the others leaving Kralan.

"We have some mages living in our realm for a while since they have nothing here left," Lucius confessed.

"As long as they do their own thing and don't get in our way," Jack said heading toward the portal. Leading Lucius into the prison in Hayden's castle. Lucius' friends and other survivors didn't agree to what Jack did but Lucius explained he deserves the time.

* Lawful Duty *

A loud crash made Lucius jump. Rising out of his cot looking through the bars. An idle body laid onto the concrete below a transitional arch.

"I have plans for your son, Stephan. It has to be this way." The stranger mumbled menacingly.

"Who are you?" Lucius asked.

Peeking out of the jail cells into the hallway noticing Stephan fall. Jousen gained Lucius' attention as he waited until the coast was clear.

"Did you hear that... Something's going on here. We need to get out of here to fix whatever's going on here."

"I don't know if I need your help Jousen.

You find yourself in different prisons every time you leave one."

"There's no higher power ordering me around. I'm a good guy you got to believe me..." Jousen said as the cell next to Lucius, Drago spoke up.

"Excuse me. You weren't the only one that was screwed. If you're in the rescuing mood you gave to rescue me as well. I only wanted the All- Seeing Eye in the first place to give it back to the creator Yuoki."

"I barely believe that and I knew you pretty well." Teigen summarized to the right of Jousen.

Lucius looked around his cell to escape to investigate as once he turned his back not wanting to listen to his neighbors anymore as the cell door rattled open.

"Malyna?" Lucius asked.

"I don't care if what Jack said is justice or not. This is an unfair punishment and if he wants to put me in here for treason let him. This isn't for you to be here with all of these convicts."

"How do you get the keys?" Lucius asked.

"I summoned them, I know Rosetta doesn't want me to use magic but I find this as a needed exception." Malyna said.

"Oh," Lucius admitted. Discovering what he had asked a conjuration mage making him roll his eyes. Lucius pointed out the blood trail. "Someone killed Stephan Dermon, did you notice anyone come through?"

"I didn't go this route. I came from the back entrance, did you see who it was?"

"I didn't. They couldn't have gotten far; we need to follow the path." Lucius explained as Jack intercepted them before they were able to start following the trail.

"What did you two do?" Jack asked following the blood the opposite way back to them.

"That blood we're trying to investigate ourselves," Lucius explained.

"Go back into your cell before you do something you may regret. I have this under control. I'll let Malyna slide this once if you follow through." Jack said pointing at Malyna using his other hand to open the cell.

Malyna sighed, summoning a bench behind Jack moving the cot to soften his fall. Lucius casually moved toward Jack pushing him over the bench. Lucius closed the cell with Malyna locking the cell.

"No..." Jack said slamming the cell. "You're going to regret this..." Jack said with a growl. "Do you hear me?"

"Do you want to help us escape..." Drago asked casually to Jack flipping a gold coin. Lucius and Malyna continued the blood trail.

"I need a moment." Malyna said glitching, falling onto her hand in the middle of the hallway.

"Malyna?" Lucius asked, waving his hands.

"The magic is messing with my head. Resuming the pain I had from fighting. I gave Stephan it. I fear the worst on who has it now. It's more fragile this time around but it works as it did originally. Don't be mad."

"I'm not mad. We need to find the artifact before anything else happens." Lucius helped Malyna up onto his shoulders.

"You won't catch them by helping me." Malyna reminded. Lucius down on the ground after a few feet with a hesitation. "I just need a break. I'm a bit winded. I'll catch up."

"Just be careful Malyna." Lucius explained continuing the trail.

* Mystery Man *

Leading out of the castle into the shed. Lucius entered to be teleported into the base with Hunter checking Stephan's pulse.

"Hunter?" Lucius asked.

Hunter jumped, hearing Lucius' voice. "This wasn't me, Lucius. I found him like this. We lost another ally. What sick person would've done this Lucius?"

Lucius then noticed a pedestal with glass covering the All-Seeing Eye in its repaired state. "I'm sure we'll find out soon enough." Lucius walked toward the pedestal with close examination. Finally, deciding to open the glass.

"I don't think we should mess with that, it could've been how Stephan ended up the way he did." Hunter urged.

"We need to find out who the murderer is and there's only one way to find out." Lucius explained reaching out to the artifact. With it in his grasp, the relic disappeared.

"Did you touch it?" "No."

A new path came into view with stairs going down in the middle of the room. Following the noise occurring around them.

"I don't like this." Hunter thought out loud.

"I'm not afraid. Come on out." Lucius yelled out. Entering the room that had a faint aura within it. They worked their way down the dark steps that had torches that lit themselves as he and Hunter passed them by.

I go by many names now. Call me... The Future. The voice echoed in their mind, a voice within their conscience.

Entering a large room, the steps casually went up hearing a faint voice in their minds.

Lucius spoke from within his mind with a sudden and strong concentration.

How can you talk to us through our conscience?

I can do what I want when I want. All good and bad thoughts you and everyone else think I now know. You should know who I am.

What do you want from us, Lucius, and I would like to know what Stephan's death has to do with anything?

Power, Hunter. I sought an opportunity and I took it. Kerwyn became a hero in my eyes. I'm sure you want to meet me. Knowing who I am won't stop my progress but anyone should know who sealed their fate.

The empty room stopped moving as it began to close into itself. "This smug bastard." Lucius argued.

"There's a way out." Hunter pointing at a trapdoor in the middle of the floor. They rushed to the trapdoor, sliding down the hatch with enough time to scrape past. Hunter and Lucius landed roughly on each other in a dimly lit room seeing a man across the room holding the All- Seeing Eye.

You don't give up easily. I suppose I should've figured this after all the things you've accomplished thus far.

"Stop talking to us through our minds and speak to us," Hunter argued as he got off of Lucius as he was pummeled in the back of the head by Malyna.

"What are you doing Malyna?" Lucius asked.

"What do you want from us?" Lucius asked.

The man with the artifact came out of the shadows. "I want everyone to suffer. I want my dad to go through tribulation to end up watching his fate with his so-called 'friends'." Floros summarized.

"Floros?" Lucius questioned breathlessly. "This isn't you. This is Hayden's doing, don't follow in his footsteps in evil."

"Don't call me Floros." he snapped. Twitching for a moment. "I'm the Future. I have plans for you both." Floros aimed the All-Seeing Eye at Lucius' chest making the icon on him glow making Lucius yell in agony. "All three of us are special. We were blessed with these sigils. I could kill you but where's the fun in that if I can use you." Floros waited until Lucius fell before shooting Hunter.

"Hunter..." Lucius exclaimed watching Hunter play past him.

"Focus on me, not him," Floros ordered Lucius to look for him. Once Lucius turned back he had seen Floros' eyes change into a hypnotic trance.

"Tell me what you want me to do," Lucius said, holding his chest. Avoiding eye contact.

"That's what I want to hear," Floros said walking toward Lucius.

"I'm yours to command."

"Yes, you are..." Floros admitted with a chuckle. Lucius swung at Floros getting too close.

"What you're doing is wrong and you know it. The real Floros is out there somewhere, keep fighting." Lucius confessed.

"Floros you know is dead." Floros echoed with a sudden, deep, and outlandish voice. Shoving Lucius away with the relic.

"Why do you keep fighting? I don't understand. Right from the start, I knew what I was doing, while I was with the bandits. I allowed the bandits to give the All-Seeing Eye to Therron. They wanted coin. Everything up to now has been a test and you have failed miserably." Floros explained as Lucius grappled Floros' leg although he kicked Lucius' arm away. Rising the Eye ordering Malyna to hold Lucius down.

"Keeping the artifact away from people like you is all it takes for me to know my job is done." Lucius explained.

"Seems like a weak argument to me but what do I know. I'm not your casual bad guy, I'm the reason your story will end." Floros smirked, bashing Lucius with the All-Seeing Eye.

Memory XI - No Way Back

* One Too Many Strings *

Lucius opened his eyes. Tied up once again. Sitting on a chair on top of a tower. Along with Kain, Aelienor, Ernaldus, Reyner, Hunter, Ashlyn, and the rest of the mage council vs Floros and his followers from project Silverstar

"Wake up." Floros exclaimed slapping his father awake.

"What're you doing Floros?" Kain asked angrily.

"Simple, I'm going to kill you."

"We're going to stop you. You know this."

"Unless one of you will stop me now there's no help to come," Floros said as he sensed faint magic turning to Iiokio. "I like this guy's willingness to fight which is why he'll go first," Floros said, kicking Iiokio's chair off of the castle tower.

"Floros..." Kain yelled out.

"I'm sure Iiokio wanted to perish if he wanted to be the hero. Did you want to be the next father?" Floros asked as Aelienor released from the chair cutting loose swinging at Floros. "I'm not brainless like Flynn, Aelienor." Stepping to the side throwing Aelienor over the tower.

"Aelienor..." Ernaldus exclaimed fidgeting with the rope behind him. "Damn you."

"Quit it, Floros." Lucius yelled shaking in his chair.

"I do what I want when I want, this is my time to shine. You all had your chance to allow me to help but I'm glad Drago took me in, he was a real eye-opener." Floros summarized.

"You don't mean that. I did my damnedest to get you back." Kain argued.

"You didn't do good enough." Floros retorted, spitting in Kain's face.

"Where's my son Floros?" Hunter broke his silence as his emblem on his chest began to glow.

"You had better not lay a finger on him."

"Your only one push away from not being my problem," Floros said with annoyance taking notice of the glow. "You're too weak to cast a spell. Besides, you don't have the guts."

"I'll kill you," Hunter said grunting, making his face reddened as Floros detected magic kicking Hunter's chair to the side. Losing the scent of magic.

Lucius broke free, kicking Floros in the popliteal causing him to stumble.

"That was your last mistake." Floros asked, blocking each attack as he punched. Upon giving a kick, Floros had caught it moving Lucius off to the ledge.

"Let's see if you can fly." Floros said.

"Let him go." Ernaldus yelled out, breaking free.

"Or what?" Floros asked. Lucius used his other foot to kick Floros into Ernaldus falling off the tower with a flip. During the fall he was caught by a flagpole to the chin, the railing of the stairs to the back winding him. Landing into a bush.

Ernaldus had flown past him. Inches away from concrete before he stood still for a second to stop his momentum before landing.

"She didn't make it. I tried." Iiokio confessed to helping Lucius to his feet.

"What do you mean..." Lucius asked obliviously, cracking his back. Peeking around Iiokio. "Not Aelienor."

"You didn't try hard enough." Ernaldus said angered shoving Iiokio.

Iiokio allowed Ernaldus to shove him, taking a few steps back. "You feel the pain I understand. Now if you excuse me I'll focus my attention to try to save any others that he throws down. "

"You know nothing of my pain Iiokio... Nothing. She's all I had." Ernaldus yelled rushing at him as Lucius held him back.

"I know." Iiokio admitted as his nose bled, struggling as he generated vines. Kain landed safely with one of the vines.

Floros looked down noticing the vines. "You are weakened Iiokio. I may not know how to cast magic but I know you have a limit. You can't save everyone..." Floros then grappled Reyner to the edge before shoving him violently to the edge.

Iiokio was able to catch Reyner with another vine causing him to fall on all fours. Ernaldus broke free from Lucius kicking Iiokio into the ribs.

Causing Reyner to fall the rest of the way down, roughly a third of Lucius' fall.

"That's all you'll get today..." Floros admitted as the vines blocked his vision of Iiokio. Floros summoned project Silverstar back with a snap of his fingers. "I have other plans with your friends here. Let this be your warning to not mess with me. Make sure no one gets in or out. If they do manage away, kill them all."

"Thanks, Iiokio." Reyner said with sarcasm. Realizing Kain and Lucius subduing Ernaldus.

"Ernaldus, he isn't your enemy. Why are you like this?" Kain asked.

"We all weren't so lucky. Aelienor didn't make it." Lucius pointed out.

"I tried." Iiokio admitted as Ernaldus raised his hand in frustration.

"I'm done. I quit. Get off me."

A moment of silence ensued as Iiokio rose weakly.

Reyner spoke up. "When we get the chance the question is, should we kill Floros."

"No one will kill my son or unless they want a second grave." Kain interrupted.

"I like to see you try to stop me." Ernaldus gritted his teeth kicking a rock in anger watching the rock bounce a few times before sinking into the nearby water.

"Do you fail to see what he had done?" Reyner questioned.

"We have to remember that he still has our friends captive." Iiokio said bewildered.

"He can be fixed. I know it." Kain admitted.

"It'll take time, Kain. Time we don't have. Do you want us to wait until your narrow, stubborn-pig minded son has common sense long enough to turn himself in... I'm sure the world would rather end first." Reyner complained.

"I'm not saying that we don't do anything, you beef-witted pillock. What I'm saying is that we're rational. We'll figure something out."

"I've been cordial and more than willing to be patient with you Kain, since when did we ever solve any of our issues without violence ensuing. You're being irrational." Reyner argued.

"I'm being irrational." Kain scoffed. "I thought you were my friend Reyner. He's my son. Ever since Elena. I had to protect him."

"He doesn't need protection. Not now, Not anymore. He made a choice."

"Elena made a choice too... and it was the wrong one. I don't want him to go the same path."

"Whatever happened to Elena anyway, Kain?" Reyner asked with a scoff. "You never told me and the longer you keep it a secret the more I wonder what happened to your wife."

"All I can tell is it wasn't my fault." Kain snapped, adjusting himself changing the topic.

"Lucius, Malyna, and Hunter have the same markings on their chest as Floros does. Do we fail to remember that? They could turn on us just like my son, why should we trust them?" Kain questioned walking toward Lucius threateningly. "I'm growing on the idea of why Jack arrested Lucius in the first place. Not only simply because he killed Wariner."

"I'm sure Lucius didn't kill Wariner without reason." Iiokio intervened between the two.

"Just like Magnus had a reason to do what he did to Caroline?" Kain asked forming a fist out of frustration.

"That's not at all the same thing, Kain. You wouldn't have known about that if I didn't tell you," Lucius pointed out, "How do you know about my chest?"

"It's hard not to notice when the marking glows through your clothing when you have supernatural occurrences happen." Kain surveyed around him. "No one is killing my son and that final."

"I'm not taking this. You're not the leader here." Lucius admitted grappling Kain to the ground.

Ernaldus intervened putting Kain and Lucius into a rough headlock. One with his left bicep, one with the other.

Iiokio rose his hands before he was going to stop Ernaldus.

"Let them talk." Reyner said, crossing his arms.

"Letting them talk while they're being strangled. Yeah, sure." Iiokio admitted.

"They can still talk. I'm not going to kill them." Ernaldus admitted bargaining. "Not yet."

"Still, watch it." Iiokio replied.

"Unless you're content with his evil actions Kain. We have to take him out." Lucius explained between Ernaldus' intervals of lack of pressure to his neck.

"I don't care if you're a mage, a person who I once would call a friend or a murderer. You mess with my family, you mess with me..." Kain yelled out, powering out of Ernaldus hold. Stumbling as he shortly gained his footing by bumping into a switch. Revealing an abandoned entrance back into the castle.

Revealing Jack on the other side with other prisoners in the castle.

"Today's been a long day," Jack confessed.

"Are you all done. I can hear you behind that pathway."

"Don't get me started." Reyner snarked.

"I didn't expect you to tag along with criminals. Especially Drago." Kain added.

"It's been a while, Kain." Drago carefully worded.

"Choose your next words carefully." Jack explained.

"Explain yourself." Kain ordered.

"I didn't have much choice. What do you mean?" Jack asked annoyed as he continued. "I had to deal with what I was given. After all, Malyna and Lucius put me in prison. If it weren't for Teigen talking about a secret entrance next to the prison. We'd still be there." Jack explained.

"I told you there was a reason I didn't kill you, Teigen." Jousen joked.

"You joust." Teigen added.

"You say Lucius and Malyna put you in prison, huh?" Kain asked curiously.

"We're not corrupt." Lucius corrected. Jack raised his sword at Lucius.

"Escaping jail is a major crime. Worsening the crime itself." Jack said.

"This isn't the time for this," Lucius said.

"Blame Floros' putting us against each other." Iiokio explained.

"He's only a kid." Jack said looking beside Lucius to see Aelienor. "What happened to her?"

"Floros killed her and Stephan. Along with whoever else. Which is why Floros has to be stopped." Lucius explained.

"Is this true Kain?" Jack's face became pale confirming his suspicions.

"How about Vaughan and Pavel? I've been looking for them within all of this chaos..." Jack asked.

"Pavel left this world ensuring my escape along with others."

"This news pains me. A loyal comrade from beginning to end. Tell me this... Did my brother share the same fate?" Jack asked, clenching his fist.

"He's missing." Lucius admitted.

Jack being content with Lucius's answer. Having a sigh of relief. Yet sad about Pavel's sacrifice.

"I'm glad we're all catching up but do we trust Lucius?" Kain added.

"We'll have to find out," Jack explained walking back into the tunnel.

"We're going back?" Jousen asked.

"I'm going back to stop Floros. You have the choice of running away like cowards or you join us and your past crimes will be looked over this once."

"Always a catch." Jousen rolled his eyes. "Fine, I'm in."

"I'm tired of the prison food," Drago added. "So let's get started."

"It doesn't seem like we have much choice," Teigen said as the rest of them followed the tunnel.

"If we can't kill Floros what will we do when we catch him? Sending him to jail won't work, take me for example," Lucius said in a joking manner. "I'm just saying." Lucius exchanged a few looks.

"I have an idea," Jack said, breaking the awkward tension. Guarding the others continuing. "But you'll have to follow my lead."

"He has followers of project Silverstar out there to stop us from infiltrating him." Lucius added.

"Those followers sense power so no magic," Jack said climbing the ladder. Sliding the lid over, watching a group of followers pass Jack, he then waved to signal his friends to exit.

"I know where Floros is..." Kain whispered as Jack helped him up. "The castle would be too predictable. He would be inside the church. I have a feeling."

"How are you so sure?" Reyner asked.

"He would often go to church when the world is against him," Kain answered looking down at the ladder as Drago made a break for it.

"That son of a..." Jack yelled.

"Let him go. He's not worth it to chase him. He'll be caught again eventually." Iiokio explained covering Jack's mouth.

"He's not going anywhere, I'll get him." Teigen sliding down the ladder.

"I sense loyalty from your friends Jack." Kain remarked.

Jack rolled his eyes. "You're not leaving Jousen." Jack reminded sliding the manhole lid down.

"I would never." Jousen sarcastically remarked.

"You may know your son Kain but there are many churches around here."

"It's a few blocks away. It's the largest one around here. You can't miss it." Kain said.

* Nothing More Than A Broken Man *

"Is this it?" Jack asked.

"It is. We're going to do this my way first. I know how to talk to my son. This all can be stopped easily if everyone keeps a steady head."

"We get it," Reyner said impatiently.

"Whatever you say," Jack said.

Kain turned the marble colored knob holding the door for the group.

Lucius felt a surge of magical aura fill him as he entered the church. The church changed from the original black flooring and furnishings with a stone brick finish on the walls to the familiar colors back home. Consisting of a fair share of light khaki and cobalt. His parents await his arrival sitting in two chairs at the front of the church.

"What's going on?" Lucius asked.

Parker rose in response. "Floros Gordon told us everything..."

"You shouldn't trust Floros." Lucius added.

"Putting yourself in harm's way for others.

I'm glad you did some good while you ran away from us. Not meaning to be passive-aggressive but this is the truth, correct?" Parker asked.

Lucius nodded confused.

"Floros speaks highly of you. So what's there not to trust?"

"He's corrupted. I want you to be real but you can't be..."

"I'm not oblivious. He had to fulfill a mission. Like you do." Parker explained walking toward Lucius.

Revealing Thex from behind the curtains covered in chains.

"Don't worry he can't hurt us now son. C'mon Bella you to..." Parker and Bella rushed toward Thex as they landed a few punches. Take out some of that anger Lucius..."

"No..." Lucius yelled out with tears. "I can't. You aren't real."

"Don't be a stranger Lucius. You're always welcome to come back home." Parker said disappearing like Bella.

Remaining Thex left.

"You've bested me."

"Kill him, You've won." Floros smiled appearing behind Thex.

Lucius found himself with a dagger looking around seeing an imaginary audience.

"Fight it, Lucius," Jack said from among the crowd, being louder than the distance he saw him. Lucius shook his head to look back at Thex in the chair to see Jack instead.

Snapping into reality. Lucius let go of the dagger seeing Malyna beside him holding Jousen.

"Let him go Malyna. You're under his control." Kain explained.

"I didn't mean to do that Jack," Lucius said

with the glow on his chest became faint.

"Don't worry about it. Just maintain your distance..." Jack whispered back.

"I know," Lucius replied as he walked slowly behind Malyna that was beside him. Releasing Jousen fighting for the knife.

"Let me kill Floros... Lucius. Why are you on his side?" Malyna questioned.

"That's not Floros, although he's not much better."

"Hey..." Jousen said with a sigh.

"Floros is messing with your mind Malyna," Lucius said.

Malyna pushed Lucius aside, gaining the blade slashing Lucius' upper arm. Stabbing Jousen in the chest until the blade couldn't go deeper.

"There's one less killer in this world." Malyna summarized retracting the dagger. Once Malyna turned around, Lucius disarmed, slapping her with the handle.

Snapping Malyna into reality.

"That hurt." Malyna admitted.

"I hope it did. That was the point, are you back with us..." Lucius asked as Jousen grabbed Lucius' knee. "Jousen?"

"Lucius... Fulfill this last request of mine. Please." Jousen said, having trouble breathing.

"What's that?"

"Promise me you'll have a slow death." Jousen insisted, spitting in his face. Slumping on Lucius' lap with a faint smile. Malyna tested Jousen's pulse for a moment before pushing him aside.

"Some grand teamwork here but this is where the joke's end," Floros said as he revealed himself on the second floor of seats.

"Floros, I know you're there. You wanted to help when we admittedly denied your assistance multiple times. I'm deeply sorry. What else do you want from me." Kain explained.

"You're not sorry. I'm self-aware of your lack of empathy. I'm more intelligent than that." Floros closed his eyes to concentrate.

Reyner shot his bow and Floros caught the arrow. Seaming with rage.

"Why'd you do that?" Kain asked.

"He looked vulnerable," Reyner explained being interrupted by Floros blasting him with the All-Seeing Eye. Sending him out of the church through the window.

"You're all like Reyner. Waiting at the end of your seat to get a chance to gain power. Kain, you most of all want this power out of everyone here. How does it make you feel, knowing that I know something that you don't?" Floros asked.

"What are you talking about?" Kain asked.

"I'm talking about with all of this power I'll create a new community... No, a new world where I'm appreciated."

"I don't want power, Floros. I want you to get out of the rut you've found yourself in. I know you deep down don't mean that Floros." Kain explained.

"You degrade me like I'm some nobody. I will do such things since it's what I want. Everything is in my grasp." Floros yelled out as he became frustrated.

"You're powerful but you still can't get the one thing that you want, your father's approval." Jack snapped.

"Shut up." Floros shot at Jack several times. Jack ducked down into cover. Bothering Floros greatly.

A bright flash appeared in the church as Drago appeared behind Floros with Yuoki. The living legend himself standing with white hair and a long gray beard. Wearing a futuristic Gothic, black velvet long coat. With floral patterns along the collar.

"This is where they are at, my God." Drago confessed.

"I am not a God." Yuoki corrected.

"The creator of magic..." Floros admitted kneeling in front of Yuoki presenting the artifact.

Yuoki accepted the artifact. "Stand up Floros."

"Thank you, creator, I don't know what I would have done without you."

"Drago gained my attention to why the All-Seeing Eye needs to remain in isolation. Continue in your endeavors. I have my problems to deal with. Remember it isn't a curse, It's a blessing." Yuoki said.

"But Yuoki, I helped you get here," Drago said confused.

"You have not. You've been faithful in your ways. You will need to be punished." Yuoki said as Drago disappeared with Floros. "You attempted to destroy my creation. With the destruction of the All-Seeing Eye will be the destruction of time itself.

The end of days. This secret must remain hidden. You all must perish."

"The secret remains. You have my word." Jack explained.

"The timeline cannot have that ability to crack like it almost has done." Yuoki summarized making the church collapsed on top of them. Causing everyone inside unfathomable pain. Yuoki walked around the rubble. Looking for survivors to finish. Yuoki passed by Lucius. Lucius was able to break free of his buried arm grappling Yuoki's ankle. Creating time as he knew it to go backward for a short duration.

"Time feels familiar." Yuoki thought out loud, summoning the portal for Floros and Drago. "On second thought, keep it," Yuoki said handing the artifact to Floros before they left.

Lucius met Yuoki on the balcony with a blade to the stomach.

"Welcome to time travel Yuoki," Lucius admitted.

"This church was in shambles. I made sure of it. How can this be?" Yuoki asked as he held his stomach feeling the blood on his hands.

"You killed me but I came back in time to kill you," Lucius said intentionally.

Causing Yuoki to groan in response. "Impossible-"

Lucius moved the sword deeper.

"Where'd you bring Floros?" Lucius asked.

"I shouldn't have come out of hiding for many years for the artifact," Yuoki admitted spitting out blood. "He awaits you where he killed Stephan. We'll meet again mortal."

Yuoki disappeared into thin air pushing back Lucius with a mighty wind.

Lucius rose, raising the sword. Feeling heavier than before. The bright glow became apparent from the sword faintly going away. The sword remained with its newfound power.

"What happened?" Jack asked.

"Yuoki almost killed us from using a paradox, he called it. Leaving this sword with his imprint of magic on it." Lucius explained.

"How'd you get up there?" Iiokio asked.

"I'm not exactly sure. Perhaps from Yuoki."

"Where did he send Floros?" Kain asked.

"I do know where Floros fell back to. Beware of anything that could happen. Make sure no follower goes after us. To make this harder than it is."

"What did we miss during the time you encountered Yuoki," Ernaldus asked.

"Don't worry about me. We have Floros where we want him." Lucius explained as he worked his way back to the first floor.

"Give me that weapon," Jack ordered, receiving the weapon. Jack swung the sword with practice, being caught off guard against the wind packed inside. Reyner peaked his head back into the church in a panic. "What was that?"

Kain helped Reyner back into the church as a response. "A fighting chance."

"You bet it is," Jack explained as sheathed the sword.

"If we're going to fight Floros we'd better do this now. Project Silverstar's followers are on their way now." Ernaldus confessed overlooking the window.

Kain helped Reyner enter into the church sustaining several cuts.

"Who's all out there..." Reyner peeked his head out of the shattered window as he dodged a distant arrow. "A lot to be fair."

"We can't fight them. They outnumber us greatly." Ernaldus admitted.

"Defend the best you can. Keep their attention as good as you can. Jack, Lucius with me." Kain answered as he opened the chapel doors leading Lucius on.

Lucius put his hand on the door to hold it open as he asked. "Once this is all said and done, what should we do with the All-Seeing Eye."

"We'll figure something out," Kain explained, hesitant with an answer. Rushing to Omega's shed. Lucius spoke up. "Is everyone ready?"

"As ready as we can be. They have our friends, we need to hurry." Jack urged as he checked behind him.

The path forward became linear. "We're expected here," Lucius announced.

"I don't like this at all," Kain explained as he followed Jack. "What does Floros have planned for us?"

"Whatever it is, it isn't good." Lucius explained.

Once the trio arrived, Lucius reached the end of the path. A door laid in front of them. One of Silverstar's followers willingly opened the door for them.

"Floros has a fate sealed for you. You better enjoy the last minutes you have breathing." One of the followers joked frantically.

Seeing their captured friends who were petrified of their arrival. Seeing Anne, Rosane, Hunter, Rosetta, Fabul, and Lex sitting on the ground shaking with wide eyes watching.

Anne rushed up to Lucius, "Please, Lucius for the love of all things. Don't go after Floros. He did things to me and Rosane... Fabul... Things I would never wish on your worst enemies. Forget about stopping him... I tried, we tried. He had gotten the better of us and made us regret ever crossing him."

"What did he do?" Lucius asked.

"You need to leave... Let him do what he wants. It'll be better that way. I don't want you or anyone else for that matter to go through what he made us all go through. It's terrible."

"Anne, I'm sorry that he did whatever he did to you but this adds another reason why we need to stop him."

"How deranged is Floros...truly to do this evil," Jack explained.

"No, please don't. He won't stop." Anne argued as she went after Jack. Lucius pulled her back as she out powered Lucius with her squirming. Running into a pillar in the process.

"This is your grand opportunity, Don't waste it," Floros explained that being in the middle of the next room.

Jack, Kain, and Lucius entered the room with haste. The door closed behind them.

"This is a trap." Lucius said as he looked with the door looking for a latch.

"The only way out is through me." Floros exclaimed.

"You don't have to do this Floros. You're a fighter, you will beat this disease if you only try." Kain explained.

Floros teleported into the next room.

I will not succumb to your satisfaction. It's clear of jealousy since I wasn't in the picture for so long and now I suddenly am. Giving this up it'll be all the same again. No matter, I've wasted too much time.

A door opened to reveal Drago laying in a pool of his blood. "What'd you do to him, Floros?" Jack scoffed breathlessly. "These killings need to stop."

Don't ridicule me. Drago did that to himself. He was the first of many I've experimented with their biggest fears. Unfortunately, Drago's fears were too great as his body simply failed him. What I did with Anne and the others that you've seen was the result of my masterpieces.

"Is this your idea of a new world you were talking about...why do this to all of us if you want to start anew and play God?" Kain questioned.

My thoughts have become more advanced than others. I have adapted to the order of operations I want to be done and in what order. If I want Jack to suffer he will.

"You better not." Jack pointed at the screen. Floros grinned in response. Jack began to hold his head with anguish.

"Stay with us, Jack." Lucius said.

"... It's horrible..." Jack ordered with agony.

"Stay with us, Jack..." Lucius started as it didn't take long before Jack passed out.

Let's see what the popular Jack Arturo is so afraid of...

The land of being afraid of being alone. I mean, what can I say, he's lost so much I can't say that I'm surprised.

In Jack's mind, he passed by the people he held close and dear to his heart Vaughan, Cencil, Pavel, and his feelings for Helba.

Jack waved inside them disappearing into thin air. "Why'd you all have to go... I'd do anything to bring any of you back just for a day. Everything is not the same without any of you." Jack said out loud.

Kain and Lucius followed Jack trying to raise his attention, standing in front of him waving their hands in front of Jack as he walked past them without a second thought not noticing them.

"You could've been still alive if you didn't treat us like one of your soldiers. All I wanted to be... was your son." Jack continued as Cencil disappeared shortly after receiving an arrow between the eyes.

Lucius and Kain looked ahead of the path finding Vaughan.

"You left me to die." Vaughan admitted. "You went missing. Where did you go?" Jack asked.

"You didn't try to find me. I was in plain sight."

"What do you mean?"

"You were focused on leaving so much you left me to die next to Pavel."

"I didn't know."

"I screamed for help and no one came."

"I'm sorry." Jack said as Vaughan glitched away. way.

Jack took a few steps as Helba stood in his

"I had thought we had something until you were beside my father with these evil schemes. Were you corrupted like Hayden was or was that your true identity..." Jack summarized as Helba was cut down with an ax.

This is all up to Jack, you two are nothing more than an audience.

Jack reached the end of the path. Cencil, Vaughan, and Helba appeared once more.

"We were a family." Vaughan admitted.

"What happened to us?" Jack cried out.

"You happened." Cencil admitted.

"You ruined everything." Helba said.

"What the..." Jack said bewildered.

As Helba stood in the middle as Cencil and Vaughan changed into Kain and Lucius.

How'd you do that, quit it... This is Jack's realm.

"You forget, I have some of the relic's power in me," Lucius argued with his chest glowing gaining Jack's attention.

"Lucius... Kain..." Jack said in confusion.

"We need you, Jack. You have lost a lot, like the rest of us. We need to stay together and get through these hard times. This is another of Floros' games. I don't know how Lucius pulled it off, but he was able to get through to you." Kain summarized.

"It's crazy how surreal this feels. Why should I keep fighting if I already lost everything."

"You didn't lose everything." Kain said.

"You have us." Lucius stated.

"I want Floros to stay alive. But this isn't about me. Jack, we'll always have problems. It's the journey; the memories will remain like it was yesterday... The memories will always be with you and hence will be the reason why you will truly never be alone."

Don't listen to Kain. He knows nothing of your pain. Kain is associated with the highest of evils. If you listen to him there's no telling what he'll do to use you and throw you away once he's done with his agenda. The only way to see who you love again is by using the dagger and you know that deep down already.

"You're right Kain." Jack said after a moment of contemplation as Jack kicked the table over as Kain and Lucius escaped Jack's mind.

"Why isn't Jack awake with us?" Lucius asked.

Time slows down when in deep sleep. The power of knowing one's fears interest me since no one mind is the same. Take Rosane's fear for example, fear of a corrupt society. You could say in the face of the true evil of manipulating one's emotions. But in response to that, I say you're wrong.

"What kind of twisted things happened to you, Floros..." Lucius thought out loud.

"I get that this is a response of extreme denial of whose fault. The question is when enough is enough?"

To answer both of you. Too much has happened to me but I won't complain since I appreciate which life has taken me and it's perks. I won't change a single thing. And It's enough when I share my pain with all the others who've caused me to suffer as I have.

"You see, Floros...those you've gotten wronged by are all gone now. All of this you've been doing is fruitless. You are all high and mighty... where it seems you are afraid of commitment and betrayal." *Kain explained.*

Floros looked at the artifact as more tears escaped him. Floros grappled the artifact with a firmer grip as he spoke.

What fears do you hide deep within you Kain?

"Floros..." Kain started as he gained a similar headache as Jack. "I'm your father... Don't call me Kain."

Memory XII - Broken Shards

* Corrupted Minds *

I'm onto you, Lucius. You won't be able to mess this up so easily. Let's see what Kain has got deep in his mind. You have the fear of depending on others and failure. I don't exactly understand, so I'm going to delve deeper.

Floros entered the mind of Kain with Lucius as they underwent a flashback as Kain sat in a boat with his brother Paul fishing. "See, that wasn't so hard now was it?" Paul asked.

"I could've learned that myself. I didn't need your help." Kain insulted throwing a fish inside the bucket that he was able to catch up with Paul's aid.

"I know you could've but I'm teaching you this now for a reason. While Caroline is getting the lay of the land with Ashlyn, Floros, and Reyner. We don't know how long we're going to be on this island. I'm usually a free-spirited type of guy, you know that" Paul said as he gained Kain's full attention.

Paul cut his thumb with the hook putting bait on the line putting his thumb in his mouth for a moment. "But I'm telling you right now. I don't know if we're able to get out of this island without trouble. I know we wanted a vacation, and we chose this place but with all of these rumors of this All-Seeing Eye. There's nothing but bad vibes I'm getting from it."

"I like this serious tone you have Paul. It's different though I don't know what you're so concerned about, we're here to get away from stress. You have a loving wife and a child on the way. Did I ever tell you about Elena?"

"I don't believe you have."

"I may as well tell someone. One day getting off work I came home seeing Floros crying when he was younger and hungry. Young enough to not remember I imagine. I yelled out for Elena to come out wondering why she didn't hear him. So I picked up Floros and investigated to discover Elena hung herself in our bedroom." Kain broke down as Paul hugged him.

Elena... Mother...she killed herself?

"I'm so sorry Kain. I didn't know. Why didn't you tell me."

"I didn't have the strength to tell anyone. No matter how much it stings to admit the truth." Kain said changing the topic. "I know you're an avid fisherman and if it takes you to get your mind off things. By all means, tell me all the tips and tricks you have."

"It's a lot to take in, are you sure you are ok. I thought Elena broke it off with you. Hell, Even Reyner thought you killed her but I stuck up for you."

"I let rumors spread on what happened. I'd like to not talk about it anymore. Forget about it."

"Alright," Paul said as he adjusted himself beginning his spiel. "But you think about it fishing is a lot like life if you think deeply about it."

"I already lost you." Kain joked. "If you're trying to..."

"No. I know what you're thinking. I'm serious. Hear me out." Paul swung his line a surprising distance. "Notice how I had that flick of the wrist." Paul reminded.

"I got that from the first time you showed me."

"I'm just checking if you were paying attention. Fishing is a lot like life since you never know what type of fish you'll find. All fish have a variety of difficulties. Some are simple to catch whereas they may be hard for others. Finding what drives them to be the way they are. Life is mysterious and sometimes we don't understand why things happen." Paul felt a pull on his line making him rise. "I have a bite. I feel this one is calling your name Kain. See if you can get him." Paul handed off the pole to Kain.

"This should be simple. If it's anything like the fish you've taken thus far, it should be a breeze."

"Don't let the size fool you, Kain. You'd be surprised at how nasty some small fish are." Paul explained.

"Yeah, I'm sure. Don't be upset if I get the concept and master it faster than you may realize..." Kain dismissed as he was forcefully tugged forward. Causing Kain to use let go of the rod with one of his hands to balance himself on the boat.

"Whoa, Kain. Let me handle this one." "No, I got this," Kain ordered as he adjusted himself with a better form and firm grip of the rod.

"I don't think you understand Kain. You happened to get lucky that line didn't snap or even worse falling out of the boat. At least let me help you if you want to capture it."

297

"So what, You'll always be better than me. I'm not your baby brother anymore, I'm a grown adult. Let me have this." Kain blurted out making Paul speechless.

Before Paul was able to retort from Kain's scene, the Ferox Trout lodged out of the water over the boat. Then jumped again moments after this time around away from the boat. Causing the boat to tip sideways from the presser of Kain's fishing rod making him and Paul go overboard.

"Kain?" Lucius asked.

You're with me on this one Lucius. You can't interact with Kain as you did with Jack.

"I'll find a way," Lucius said using his mind to move the boat over to its original state to see Kain raising for air.

"Paul..." Kain asked with concern as he climbed back on the boat to get a better view while shivering. Kain repeated himself as he checked all around him as he remained with no response. After several minutes seems like an eternity, Kain saw Paul lying on the shore in the distance.

"How'd you discover that Paul?" Kain asked assuming the worst. "Paul you'd better be alright," Paul exclaimed as he picked up one of the oars that were stuck between the wooden panels for seating. Becoming halfway back to the island, noticing another man waltz by Paul who laid on the shoreline. The bandit Drago placed him up on his shoulders glancing at Kain before walking away into the woods. "This can't be happening," Kain said, roaring at a faster pace.

Kain hopped out of the makeshift boat, meeting Paul's last location. Picking up Paul's wedding ring that had dropped in the sand. "This is all my fault," Kain confessed. Figuring all was lost until he discovered footprints. A lead. Running into the woods out of Lucius' view.

Lucius rose back in the large room with now Jack and Kain lying unconscious.

I loved my uncle. I'll continue letting Kain roam free in his pain. Perhaps if he dwelt on me half as much as he did with Paul we wouldn't have been here.

"Are you satisfied yet, Floros?" Lucius asked.

Not at all, I intentionally saved the best for last. You may be able to alter their fears but I'm sure for your fear, whatever it may be...it won't be that simple.

"Give it your best shot Floros."

This newfound news about mother caught me off guard, but it won't stop my goals.

Lucius held his head in fatigue as he soon laid his cheek once more on the cool floor.

I like the tenacity to save the day, Lucius.

Fearing what the future may hold.

Does death lay with its clammy hands wanting to take you within moments or will it be another friend's loss and add it to the collection that makes you remain empty inside?

You keep going in hopes that you make that difference. At the end of the day there's no one to help but yourself.

Lucius found himself entering a room along with Hayden, Therron, and Omega.

"You're just in time for the meeting, Lucius. Here sit." Therron waved Lucius over.

"You're all dead. How can this be?" Lucius asked.

"Pinch me, if that makes you feel better." Omega with a smile signaling to sit down. Lucius listened with curiosity.

"We have some business to discuss," Hayden explained.

"I agree. I'll start." Therron said, clearing his pockets revealing a silver medallion necklace.

"Saving Jack from Draven caused Jack to go back in time and prevent Hayden from killing me with enough time for me to say my last goodbyes to my wife. I knew I'd end dying eventually. But I was able to tell her to give this necklace to my newborn when the time was right. They fled the island before my death. It's nice to know my wife was safe to come back to the island to show who I was. Son or Daughter; we agreed on the name Alex."

"A beautiful name," Hayden commented. *"I was never a family man but perhaps I should've been,"* Omega added.

"You make a difference Lucius. Don't be afraid of change." Therron summarized.

"I apologize for my wrongdoings to your family heritage. So, my turn." Hayden explained. *"Nadim's death put me on the edge. I promised myself nothing else would happen to anyone else since then. I was never more wrong in my entire life. I was always so close to victory. The haste I had was my downfall."*

"Now Lucius, you and I didn't have much face time together. During the short-lived time we did

meet, you taught me discipline. The memory of our name will change as history passes. We put our grievances aside from all that we lost. For our gifts, don't waste yours." Omega explained as they all three used magic to generate a portal to Lucius.

"What is this?" Lucius asked.

"A portal back to your timeline. Something you can't do with a Portalatrix. Now go back to attack and make Floros fall. This'll feel like you're exiting a dream. You better hurry though, You don't want to remain in this timeline, trust me it's much worse here." Therron explained.

"Thank you, everyone. I'll do my best." Lucius said leaving the timeline.

"I know you will." Hayden smiled.

Lucius weakly rose his head watching Floros saunter over to attack.

Jack rose first seeing the relic shot. Barrel rolling away. Jack slid to the wind sword. Swinging the wind sword at Floros. Causing Floros to slide back a few feet. Floros slowed himself down with the All-Seeing Eye. Shooting at the ground. Floros looked up as he shot the artifact at Jack. Jack used the wind with the sword to ricochet the shot away.

Jack bewildered at his feet. Giving him the confidence to swing more, remaining to be a stalemate at shots and swings. Some shots of the All-Seeing Eye ricocheted over Lucius' head.

Lucius crawled toward Jack with his body aching. Lucius noticed Jack's timing to use the wind on his side was poor. The relic had shot the sword out of Jack's hands. The sword slid toward Lucius. Lucius continued with determination.

Jack turned his back on Floros seeing where the sword had ended up. Floros aimed at Jack before Kain intervened ruining Floros' accuracy.

The blast hit the sword sliding further away from Lucius seconds before he was able to grapple it. Lucius retracted his hands to brace before the shot landed. Floros regained control of the artifact.

Floros blasted Kain with a burst of energy. Sending him flying across the room to land on top of Jack. Rushed toward the wind sword after regaining his posture.

Lucius ran an adrenaline, sliding with his knees to beat Floros with the sword. With all of his momentum Lucius swung. Floros generated a shield barrier once he knew he was too far as it protected him from damage making him hover away a few feet.

Jack and Kain covered Floros' flank as they bumped into each other again from the result of the wind's power.

Floros hopped down from the crashed wall focusing on Lucius. Lucius attempted to swing once more. Floros caught up with Lucius before Lucius could follow through. Twisting Lucius' wrist. Giving in to the pain, Lucius dropped the sword. Floros kicked Lucius' chest, knocking him down.

Floros got a grasp on the sword. Looking at the sword with interest in a moment before Jack grappled Floros. Attempting to grab the magnetic seal of the artifact. Floros made the All- Seeing Eye disappear and reappear into Floros' hand as Jack retracted his hands in awe.

In anger, Jack forced Floros down to one knee. Kicking the sword out of Floros' grasp as it slid to Kain.

"You have to finish it, Kain," Jack ordered grabbing Floros's hands behind him. Having trouble maintaining Floros down.

"You don't have the gull." Floros exclaimed. Kain froze looking at the sword.

Lucius reached for the sword out of Kain's hands. Kain pointed the sword at Lucius. "He's right... You'll have to kill me before you kill my son."

"Are you serious?" Jack said. Floros headbutted Jack to the chin as Jack lost his grip. Jack rose to shove Floros' head into a wall.

Lucius disarmed Kain as the sword slid into Floros' hand.

Floros swung the sword flinging Jack into a wall instead.

Lucius rushed at Floros. Before he was able to disarm Floros, he kicked his feet in a late ditch effort before falling onto his back. Luckily knocking the sword out of Floros' grasp. The sword flew past everyone as it had gotten stuck, penetrating the floor.

Jack rose first, having trouble to get the sword unstuck. Floros headbutted Jack again knocking Jack to the ground.

Lucius rushed over tiring Floros down with a series of punches. Loosening the sword enough to retrieve it. He swung the sword at Floros before he was able to fire upon Jack with another charged shot.

Launching Floros backward with the All- Seeing Eye with a stagger. Lucius saw his opportunity as he threw the sword into the artifact. Causing the room to rattle.

Causing Floros to fall backward hitting the wall behind him. The connection made the sword blow heavy wind making the shards spread out across the room. Turning the relic off.

Kain rose to check on Floros. "Floros... Are you ok?"

"He'll live despite the fact he tried to kill us... but don't let that faze you." Jack explained out of breath.

"Death isn't the answer. We stopped him and that's what matters."

"Do you want me to have a reason to kill him?" Jack asked sarcastically. "I'll make a list."

"What were you planning Jack?" Kain asked with an attitude. "Do you want him to go to jail or something?"

"You had nothing, didn't you?" Lucius said figuring out. "I have an idea then," Lucius explained looting the artifact, the four shards, and the magnetic seal. Placing the relic in the room Floros had come out of placing it on a pedestal within the room. Closing the door. Placing a lock requiring the shards as keys.

"What about Floros?" Kain asked. "Follow me." Lucius said exiting the room Floros laid unconscious.

Attaching the same requirements of the four shards to gain entry.

"You trap him here he'll die…" Kain said with anguish.

"He'll be safe here Kain. I only had a taste of the artifact and was able to survive. If I learned anything, it presents a solution to a problem as you think. He'll be stuck here, but he'll be safe. It's disabled, sure but power still rests in him to live safely. He won't be able to leave until someone brings back the shards to him."

"I won't see my son again then," Kain confessed.

"It may be better this way…" Jack said with sincerity.

Kain held the locked door with his hands punching the door with his fist. "I love you son."

"What should we do with these?" Lucius asked, holding the shards openly in his hands.

"We'll need to hide them. Even away from our friends. You should place one of the shards back into the locked door. So that if something were to happen you'd be the first respondent." Jack explained.

"Is that how this works?" Lucius asked jokingly.

"I may not know everything about Lucius. But I do know if thoughts become reality then once it's powered up again. It'll be the first thought once it's opened once more."

Kain turned and wiped his eyes. Lucius handed Jack and Kain one shard.

"Hiding these last three shards is our best bet for society but if there's an off chance someone finds them we'll need to have a plan B." Jack explained.

"What happens if Floros retrieves it again?" Kain asked.

"We will have to deal with that when the time comes. Let's just celebrate this victory." Jack summarized.

Lucius worked his way to their corrupted friends; now cured. The followers of the project Silverstar disappeared back to their correct timelines.

A brief celebration had occurred. Anne interrupted.

"You did get the artifact right?" Anne asked.

"We had to dispose of it..." Jack answered immediately.

"So we can't get Aelienor back?" Ernaldus asked, finding himself among the crowd.

"I hate to say this Ernaldus but with something that powerful, it's best in no one's hands. No more time travel." Lucius explained hurting himself to admit.

"I wish she was with us..." Ernaldus said, "Does this mean we're going home?"

"I'd like to go home Ernaldus if Jack doesn't want me in jail."

"We're past that point, Lucius. I can be your ride back." Jack explained.

"I'd appreciate that Jack, thanks," Lucius admitted.

"I'll make sure to give Gauvain a good bashing once we bump into him again." Ernaldus said as he cracked his knuckles.

"Before we depart Lucius... Did you give Morrison the unfortunate news?" Jack asked.

"I haven't seen him. The next time I see him I'll let him know." Lucius explained.

* Pros And Cons *

One by one, they all exited Omega's shed. Kain, Jack, and Lucius being the last to exit.

"I suppose I'll go out somewhere to hide this shard," Kain admitted. "I'll meet up with you all later I suppose."

"Avoid trouble," Jack said, waiting until Kain was out of the artifact's sight. "I'm not finished with Floros."

"What do you mean?" Lucius asked.

"I learned about the technology that makes this base Omega used to be as useful as it is... I disabled the ability for it to expand or decrease in size. To us, it'll stay a shed although once you enter it's a mansion of sorts. We don't want this shed to be awaiting to be entered to be one step closer to being releasing those locked doors." Jack summarized.

"What'd you do?"

"I made the shed into a rocket before I left," Jack said, revealing a remote.

"You didn't..."

"I did." Jack handing Lucius the remote.

"My honor?" Lucius asked.

"Of course."

"Will I break it like last time?"

"Not at all." Jack laughed. "I made sure of it. By the way, speaking of the time machine, it will be much more durable this time around and many new additions compared to the last version."

"Let's keep that machine for the last resort, Jack. No more adventures." Lucius reminded.

"I know." Jack added.

Lucius and Jack fell back to a safe distance.

"When you're ready."

"What will Kain think?"

"He'll get over it."

Lucius pressed the button as the rocket was sent deep into the sky and soon into space. Disappearing into the moonlight.

"Where's it going to land?"

"Based on my calculations, it shouldn't." Lucius' brow furrowed. "Let's not let Kain know about this."

"He'll find out."

"I know, but until that time comes it'll be another secret. Blame me if he gets hostile. I can take it."

"You are sending his only son to space..." "It's better than killing him."

"I have unfinished matters to attend." Lucius inquired, exploring Quia to discover that Lord Morrison was nowhere to be found. Asking around the townsfolk to no avail.

Bumping into Hunter who gave some insight. "He went on the search for answers about Wariner. I haven't seen him since Floros' little reign."

"I'd hate to leave without telling him what had happened."

"Next time I see him, I'll tell him."

"No, I want to tell him in person. Next time you find him, get a hold of me."

Hunter agreed. "I say Wariner died a hero.

I'm sure he'll think the same."

"I know," Lucius confessed, changing the subject. "Did you find Lukin?"

"I did thank goodness. He was being taken care of by some of Floros' henchmen of project Silverstar gave Lukin back. Lukin's being watched by Kain after he came back from being alone for a few hours. Claiming it's best no one knew."

"I have a feeling it's for the best. How about the sigil on your chest?"

"Malyna's been taking care of that for me. You should give her another visit before you leave to be on the safe side." Hunter sighed hugging Lucius.

"I'll be alright."

"I'm sure we'll keep in contact. Feel free to come back and visit."

"Thanks, Hunter, I will. For now, I need some time to be with my family. It seems like an eternity since I saw them last."

"I know how that feels. Again I'm sorry for your loss." Hunter reminded Jack to drop a ramp to enter Jack's ship. "What'll you do after all the celebrations?"

Lucius gave a smile. "I'll have some investments to plan." He then waved bye before setting sail off the dock.

* Roses Do Bloom *

"Is that who I think it is?" Parker asked as he raised his hand to make a shadow over his eyes to gain better vision from the brightly lit sun in the prime of summer.

"I'm sure it is. Go get everyone, it's finally happening." Gauvain said, rushing toward the dock awaiting their exit. "You're finally back..." Gauvain said happily.

"Yeah, without your help," Ernaldus said with annoyance as Gauvain frowned. Ernaldus couldn't keep a straight face. "It's good to see you again old friend. I almost forgot what you looked like." Ernaldus said bear-hugged Gauvain.

"I miss you too..." Gauvain said winded as he tapped out to be released for fresh air. Watching Lucius coming out of the ship. "Is that Lucius under all of that scruff?"

"Time flies when you're helping people out," Lucius explained.

"Where's Aelienor?" Gauvain asked.

"One of many casualties of war," Ernaldus explained dragging his head.

"I'm sorry big guy." Gauvain said as he patted Ernaldus' back.

"Why'd you leave without us?" Lucius asked.

"I couldn't deal with all of that stress. Back home has its problems but it wasn't as much of a high caliber as back on that island. Taking one of the idle ships wasn't hard but hiring a crew was. If it's any consolation I did tell everyone where you went to help, but they were...hesitant. Wanting more evidence. I can only give my word."

"You should've been a bit more patient but it's all in the past now," Lucius explained.

"I had the same spiel a thousand times over, hoping you all can forgive my actions." A momentary silence ensued. "You all want to pay your respects to Maria?" He asked himself out loud with a sudden shift of sadness. "I'll lead you to her." Gauvain summarized.

"Who's Maria?" Jack asked, lagging behind the others.

"Our best friend," Lucius said. "You go ahead and meet everyone. We'll be there shortly."

"Take all the time you need." Jack recalled. "Lead the way Gauvain." Ernaldus said with a softness in his voice.

Time passed slowly for Lucius arriving at the tombstone.

Lucius kneed on the grave as he used his thumb to unveil the grime off the tombstone as his face became bright. "There's no death date."

"How was your trip?" A sweet melody followed from the angelic voice.

Lucius looked immediately. Lucius' view matched perfectly with the sun silhouetting Maria's flowing blonde hair and face shadowing his body. He gained chills in his skin as the formation of clouds behind her, looked like she gained wispily, yet so fluffy wings.

She continued to gravitate to Lucius turning into a graceful bear hug. "I would've gone with all of you if I wasn't injured but I'm not complaining." Maria reminded, tapping on her thigh to show Lucius that she was balancing partly on a walking stick and him. From what Gauvain told me, it was quite the adventure."

"I thought you were gone." Lucius raised to his feet giving her another hug. Embracing the warmth.

"I can't believe you Gauvain... You smug naively. Not telling us about this." Ernaldus said jokingly, punching Gauvain in the shoulder.

"Yeah, it's a joyful pain." Gauvain admitted rubbing his arm.

"Let's just say I don't go out easily. Dad says it's a miracle but I think it was luck."

"It's dad now?"

"Yeah," Maria chuckled. "You caught me, but enough about me. We have people eagerly awaiting your return and what I'd imagine plenty of stories you have to tell all of us...so let's not keep them waiting." Maria explained as she led the way up the hill as the sunrise set.

Epilogue

"This can't be happening... What have I done?" Floros asked himself, waking up on the urge of crying.

You will not cry. You will be strong. We may have lost, but we always have a secondary plan. These simpletons left the All-Seeing Eye near us, I can sense the power and can feed off of it.

"Get out of my head demon. You've ruined my family." Floros yelled out storming to his feet punching a wall.

Use that strength, Floros. It'll only make you better. Contact Hudson. Stephan's Boy in the future.

"Where'd you take that poor child?"

It matters not. Make them all pay Floros. No one understands you but for me. Your father has no idea what he was doing. He was jealous of the power you had. Face it, He doesn't care. You showed weakness and that weakness could've been your downfall. Let their mistake bite them back.

"I have no choice do I?" Floros asked as tears continued to escape down his face.

Weakling... Must I repeat myself? They must pay and there's only one escape. The Future is imminent. Adapt to change boy since there's about to be plenty of it to go around. Press the hidden compartment button.

Floros cleared his face of tears following directions. Seeing a terminal that he didn't notice was there before. Hudson appeared on the other side of the transmission.

"Dad, is that you?" Hudson asked worrisomely.

"Yes, Hudson. It's me, your father. The Runtus family cannot be trusted. The loyal family has betrayed us and is too dangerous to you without my help. Our transmissions will remain sporadic and short. You need to rush yourself to safety Hudson. You will need to find the Olympic Valley and befriend the Kasion family. Then and only then will you be safe. I love you and goodbye." Floros summarized as if his voice wasn't his. A deep raspy voice. Floros impulsively ended the transmission ignoring Hudson's plea to stay on the transmission.

The message has been sent. You have done your part thus far.

"*What have you done to Hudson?*"

What needed to be done. You should be more than amped like I am, Floros. You've single- handedly created a war. Don't fret with me here and plenty of ways to survive you and I will be able to get to know each other for a long time.

Floros's mind summoned bread in front of him. Floros ate in a quick succession being relieved he wouldn't starve.

I'll take care of you, Floros. After all, I am you. No one else will be willing to do so. Now we have plenty of work to do in our new office. We'll use that transmission to make sure everything goes according to plan. If you resist this, you'll be making it much harder for yourself.

"How do you know Hudson will do so much for the future and who are these Kasions you speak of?"

You're questioning too much, my friend. Continue to follow the next directions, and we'll get along fine. Otherwise, you'll see what I'm fully capable of.

"Please, I want to see my father again."

The way I see it... You have a son now. Be better than the scum you call a father and you treat him right.

"Where's Hudson real dad, Stephan?" Floros said piecing ideas together. "You didn't."

You know what, I'm going to enjoy breaking you in a bit.

"Oh, please no..." Floros exclaimed holding his head in agony as the thoughts inside his head filled with hours of mental torture. Floros' head eventually dropped in response.

His head rose with an evil smirk with a cloud of black smoke, oozing out of his eyes. He pronounced with a dark voice. "I'm ready to get started."

www.ingramcontent.com/pod-product-compliance
Lightning Source LLC
Chambersburg PA
CBHW031335020726
47499CB00005B/1272